Rogues' Gallery

First published in Great Britain in 2005 by
Allison & Busby Limited
Bon Marche Centre
241-251 Ferndale Road
London SW9 8BJ
http://www.allisonandbusby.com

Copyright © 2005 by JOHN MALCOLM

The moral right of the author has been asserted.

A catalogue record for this book is available from
the British Library.

10 9 8 7 6 5 4 3 2 1

ISBN 0 7490 8358 1

Printed and bound in Wales by
Creative Print and Design, Ebbw Vale

It was a sharp spring day. My mind, pleasantly occupied by the prospect of antiquarian, innocuous books, was imagining the design of a stylish dust jacket. Even close to Paddington Station, literary illustration was in the offing.

A squat, narrow-eyed bruiser put an end to my euphoria. Definitely a pug-ugly he was; no mistake about that.

"Shop's closed, squire," he rasped, barring my way. His stare locked onto mine as he lowered his head slightly, like a dog ready to snap at some trousers.

At first I blinked. This was the unlikely entrance to Mr Goodston's premises on Praed Street. The place is a relic, an anachronism in that traffic-infested area, having a modest doorway and a cloudy window behind which ranks of old books, immobile for as long as I can remember, invite little interest and make no attempt at promotion. Their bindings are *subfusc*. It is not an inviting display but then the shop does not attract many visitors. It keeps a low profile. Mr Goodston, an archaically polite fat man of apparent immobility but great expertise, has a distinguished if declining mail-order list of customers, retired professionals mostly, whose interest in sporting, military and thespian subjects keeps him modestly in funds. Unfortunately, these same funds often disappear in losses sustained at the more celebrated venues dedicated to what is jocularly known as the Sport of Kings.

Mr Goodston is a racing man. Horses are his Achilles heel.

After I blinked, I could feel hackles rising on the back of my neck. "Squire" is a derisive label applied by a mockingly aggressive underclass to anyone better dressed or cleaner looking than themselves. It is not friendly.

"How strange," I said.

The bruiser's narrow eyes narrowed even further. "Oh? Strange? Why's that, then?"

My hackles remained upright. The pleonastic ending "then", indicating a patronising challenge or a condescension reserved for minors, is another dislike of mine.

"I have an appointment here," I answered. "Now."

This was true. Mr Goodston had called triumphantly to say, in his own style, that he had acquired the volume that was the object of my enquiries. In short, my esteemed order was now to hand. I responded by saying that I'd pop round just as soon as I'd seen Sue and the sprog William safely off on the train to Bath, for a visit to her mother.

"Must be some mistake, squire." The bruiser was turning abrupt. He braced himself aggressively. "He's not available now. No chance."

From inside the shop there came, over the thunder of a passing bus, the sound of a scuffle followed by a vocal squeak, which I recognised as Mr Goodston in distress. It brought a frown to my brow.

Violence was becoming inevitable.

"Kindly step aside," I said to the bruiser, keeping the preliminaries civilised but not elaborate.

He scowled back. "I don't want no trouble," he said. "No trouble at all, see? Private meeting's going on. You just toddle off, mate. Know what I mean?"

I sighed. Mr Goodston, clearly, had problems with bookies once again. He is not a good punter. Who is? Slow horses happen all the time. The bookies had a habit, when excess debts were outstanding, of turning unpleasantly illegal and sending men round to collect by force. It had happened before. An old biographical enthusiast like Mr Goodston, fat and windy, his half-moon spectacles askew, is easy to intimidate.

Or worse.

"I don't want any trouble either," I said to the bruiser. "So you just stand aside. Otherwise I'll do you such damage that you'll wish you never got up this morning. Know what I mean?

To use your own language, so that there's no mistake?"

He gaped at me then dropped a shoulder in menace, bracing himself, legs akimbo, arms forward.

"Piss off," he snapped, sticking out his elbows. "Or you'll get hurt."

I grinned at him. He was built like many of those night club bouncers up in Nottingham, or Manchester or London or anywhere. He sported a shabby suit with a striped shirt straining over a beer belly. He was short and squat rather than built for speed, with thick arms and tubby legs for the pushy shuffle of doorway work. A fine physique for throwing drunken boys out of a dance hall on Saturday night. With help from a second bouncer. But no contest for the real thing.

"Shan't ask you again." I was as abrupt as he was as I shifted my weight back onto my left heel. "Get out of the way. Now."

For a moment, as his eyes focussed on my broken nose, a flash of alarm crossed his expression. He saw that I was a couple of inches taller, leaner, fitter than he was, an ex-sportsman of some sort. Broken noses are common amongst rugby players and mine is no exception. The look of concern quickly vanished. I suppose he assumed I had no training in the sort of dirty tricks a bouncer can use. Too well dressed, squire. He shook his head and bunched his right fist, starting to move towards me.

Action was required.

I was known, in my rugby playing days, for my swift punt kick, an up-and-under designed to get the rest of the scrum alongside whilst I led them into a gratifying ruck as the ball descended. The high punt is not generally thought of as a front row man's talent, mostly coming from flankers and the girls, but I had it taped. The weight back on the left foot and the quick, stabbing upward fast kick with the right, using the power of the thigh muscles and the swing of the foot, in a good thick Church's brogue that morning, to maximum impact.

I planted it straight into his crutch.

He gave a choking squeal and keeled forward, grabbing downwards in agony, nicely presenting me with the scruff of his neck. After chopping down a solid rabbit punch to the back of his greasy shirt collar I grabbed his jacket and propelled him out of the way onto the pavement. He crumpled over like a burst sack, mouth now gaping open in a soundless scream, trying to suck in air.

Then I went through the door.

The sight that met my eyes was not encouraging. In front of me, across the shop, Mr Goodston cowered behind his desk in the grasp of a sharp-nosed, bulky codger who was shaking him by the neck. Books and magazines, good books and good magazines, were scattered all over the floor.

Mr Goodston, half blind with half-moon spectacles missing, let out a despairing squeal.

That did it.

To fight hard you need motivation. Up to then I'd been detached, taking a world-weary, oh well, bookies' men again, sort of attitude. A bit mundane, if you know what I mean, a bit civilised, we-must-all-live-together, you're only doing your job, no need for real nastiness sort of stuff. Nothing more than a friendly kick in the crutch and we'll call it quits.

The squeal ended all that.

You bastards, I suddenly thought, going all red, you lousy shit-faced cruel bullying bastards, beating up an old man and destroying his precious stock in front of him just to keep some dirty bookie's profits going, quite apart from having a go at me. Hitler and Stalin might have been proud of you two but I'm not having this.

Striding across the shop, I grabbed the sharp-nosed codger. He let out a shout of alarm as I yanked him away from Mr Goodston, upending him with all the ceremony of a dangerous tackle, swinging him off his feet with one of mine behind his knee and dropping him hard to the floor on his back. His head made the boards shake as it hit. Then I trampled him in the worst sort of foul trampling that rightly gets players sent off. I got my heel down on the fingers that had been grasping Mr Goodston so as to pin one arm fast, then set about stamping with real relish with the other whilst making sure he didn't grab me between the legs. To counter that one I dropped onto one knee with all my weight, making sure the knee went into the right place. A bubbling, choking noise ensured that it had.

Then I heaved him up, swung him round and propelled him through the door, making sure his head hit the upright smartly as it went past. A good shove made sure he fell over the bouncer on the pavement, who was just starting to sit up. They tangled over together.

I shook a fist at the pair of them, piled up awkwardly on the flags like a heap of old clothing full of random torsos and limbs.

"Shove off! If I ever see you two in the vicinity I'll push the pair of you under a passing bus. Tell your boss I'll come and do the same to him as well if he ever tries it again."

And I gesticulated at a big red double-decker thundering past en route to Notting Hill.

Then I went back inside, closing the door behind me. Mr Goodston sat gaping, unsighted behind his desk. I went over to sit in front of him. I was feeling a lot better; there's nothing more exhilarating than kicking a few villains.

"Are you all right, Mr Goodston?"

I leant over and set his glasses back in front of him from where they were lying out of range. He looked out of breath and dishevelled. There was no visible damage to his face although his complexion was mottled.

"Mr Simpson!" His voice came out from between heaves for breath. "Thank God! You have saved me again! Once again!" He paused and remounted the glasses onto the end of his nose. "My goodness. I have said it before but it bears repeating: you are a dangerous man when roused, sir. A truly dangerous man. Thank heaven you came today."

"I am pleased to be of assistance." I took a couple of deep

breaths myself; my fitness was not quite up to par. "But perhaps you should start to consider. The Turf will be your undoing. It really will, you know. I'm not one to indulge in pi-jaw but I can't keep belting these wretched bookies' men at the drop of a hat. I am frequently away on business, as you must realise. It's only because I was seeing Sue off at Paddington that I'm here today. How much do you owe?"

He peered at me perplexedly as he readjusted his tangled half-moons. He was regaining his equilibrium. "Bookies' men? Owe? I do not understand you, sir."

"You mean those weren't bookies' men?"

"Good heavens me, no. Indeed not. Why should they be?" He managed to sound quite offended. "My accounts are in credit. Sound credit, Mr Simpson I do assure you. With both Epsom 'Arry and Plumpton Pete. On Wednesday I came up trumps at Haydock Park. A palpable win, sir, on the three-thirty. Twenty quid at thirty to one. Six hundred jimmy o'goblins to the good."

"Then what the blazes –"

"I don't know! I really have no idea! That is the paradox, my dear sir. The man was spouting gibberish at me."

"What sort of gibberish?"

"He kept asking me where is it? What? I demanded. The old lady's stuff, he said."

I frowned. "Old lady's stuff?"

"Old lady's stuff were the words he used. Since I have acquired several collections from elderly ladies in the last two weeks, I was mystified. But more than that, I was angry." Mr Goodston gave me a look in which all the resilience of his splendid generation was evident. "I am not in the habit of yielding to ruffians who break into my shop and try to intimidate me as a prelude to theft. It was no business of his anyway. I told him, initially, to clear off. He got very nasty. Knocked the telephone out of my hand to prevent my calling the police. Started hurling my stock about and shouting, presumably as a means of distressing me, cowing me into submission. Then he grabbed me. I must say my recollections of his shouting are confused. He had me by the throat, hurling obscenities. I was confused as much by the motive for the attack as by the treatment; I have little of major value individually in this part of the place. It is not as though any one item is of great value and I do not keep cash here. I do not have a first edition of *Harry Potter* ready to snatch. From one widow I have just acquired an inscribed copy of Eliot's *The Waste Land* and some excellent Ian Flemings amongst other treasures – did you know, by the way, that a copy of *Live and Let Die* went for sixty thousand dollars in the Rechler sale in New York?"

"No, Mr Goodston, I did not."

"Extraordinary, don't you think?"

"I do."

"Unfortunately my widow's copy is not inscribed to Winston Churchill, I'm afraid. But vandals of that sort are surely not literary men."

"I am not sure that Ian Fleming qualifies in that regard Mr Goodston, but let us not quibble over definitions. In terms of monetary value it is another matter. You never know: thieves grab on special commission from ruthless collectors. They've just snatched a pair of early Van Goghs from the museum in Amsterdam. Carefully chosen, I believe. Is anything else you've acquired recently from – from old ladies – of particular value?"

"That's just it. While I was being attacked I tried to think which of these things they must want. What I could yield in order to satisfy them. I am still confused. I have acquired a collection of the works of Mrs Belloc Lowndes and Georgette Heyer; not exactly the stuff of smash and grab. On the other hand, I have also bought a variety of theatrical memoirs and biographies, some of them signed by quite celebrated thespians."

"Oh, God. You should have bunged him one of those. Luvvies write the worst possible memoirs."

"I entirely agree. But there is a keen market for them. It is not one likely to inspire crime, however. I also have some excellent military material from the widow of a major general who distinguished himself in the desert before succumbing to a thirst for sherry. Nothing wildly expensive there. I have a collection of copies of old magazines, the *Graphic* and the *Illustrated London News*, some of which you see scattered about on the floor, from a lady resiting herself into smaller accommodation in Ladbroke Grove. Plus a similar collection but of earlier date from an estate in Isleworth where the executor, an old friend and solicitor, contacts me when he thinks he is disposing of items of possible merit. One of the ladies was responsible for my acquisition of the book of immediate interest to you. It was amongst an agglomeration of some excellent books mixed with a dismal load of tat. That is why I couldn't respond simply to the thug's shouting. But it was a happy coincidence in more ways than I could possibly have anticipated when I apprised you of my possession."

"Evidently. My presence this afternoon is solely due to your call and to the fact that Sue decided to take William to her mother's in Bath."

"Luckily for me, my dear sir. Luckily for me indeed. See how the Fates dispose of our seemingly organised lives. How they must smile at our self-conceived supposed control." He heaved himself to his feet and poised himself cautiously. "So far we have no clue as to the reason for this appalling incident. Happily it is over. Let us ponder for a moment." He seemed satisfied with his condition and turned towards his shelves. "Allow me to present you with the volume in question while we do so."

"I'll just check those two first," I said. "They might consider a counterattack although I doubt it. But maybe I can find what it is that they're after."

They had gone. Outside, the pavement was empty. Another bus thundered past, blowing dust and grit at me as I looked up and down the road.

There was no sign of them.

I went back inside to find Mr Goodston holding a book, a very ordinary looking blue novel, which he had plucked out of the packed shelves that line his premises. He put it down on the desk in front of me with a flourish.

I stared at it, bemused. If I had known what it looked like, I probably wouldn't have bothered to call at the shop. Mr Goodston would have remained at the mercy of his attackers.

The sight was a grave disappointment.

* * *

"You seem a little crestfallen," murmured Mr Goodston, after I had sat down again and a brief interval had passed. "Had you expected something more flamboyant?"

"I suppose I had."

The book was darkish blue with black lettering. It had no dust wrapper. The title was set in bold varied type on the worn cloth: *Imperial Brown of Brixton* by Reginald Turner. Above the lettering on the front face was set a drawing of an eagle of vaguely French Imperial style with its head half inside a Napoleonic hat. The odd feather wisped down at the side and a bee buzzed above it. This emblematic motif was also printed in black. Next to the eagle two tiny initials could be made out: a W and an N. The spine confirmed the title and the publisher: Chapman and Hall. I knew that the date of publication was 1908.

Inside, after the title page, the author dedicated the book to an unspecified lady called Mabel then thanked his friend William Nicholson for designing the cover.

"This is it?" I queried. "No dust wrapper?"

"That is it," confirmed Mr Goodston gravely. "No dust wrapper."

I stared at it morosely. I might have known that in 1908 a lot of fiction did not carry a dust cover. I had hoped for a wrapper of Nicholson design that leant on his wonderful poster work or maybe a bold view, set out in clear, almost abstract strokes. There was none of that. Just another old novel like a lot of pre-1930s novels that you see lined on unloved shelves, their dusty board colours behind black print inviting no eager grasp of recognition.

The lettering and design if not flamboyant were good, though; I had to admit that.

It was a while ago that I had, after an involvement with William Nicholson investments, started a modest little collection of associated items. With school fees looming distantly ahead I avoided the expense of one of the celebrated Sir William's paintings. I had a Staffordshire jug with a redcoated and moulded Marquis Wellington on it, the subject of one of Nicholson's still lives once in the possession of Vivien Leigh. I had one of his woodcuts, a portrait of Whistler, which I rather liked. When I found out that Nicholson had designed the cover of this book of Reggie Turner's I had looked for one avidly, enrolling Mr Goodston's help.

And now here it was.

Dullsville, really.

"Reggie Turner." Mr Goodston took off his half-moons and rubbed his nose. "A wit and friend of Oscar Wilde's, not to mention Max Beerbohm. He was at the bedside in Paris when Oscar died. To be accurate, his name was an adopted one. He was one of the Levy-Lawson family but illegitimate, you know. Lord Burnham, who owned the *Daily Telegraph*, was the leading Levy. Reggie became a journalist and had a pioneer gossip column."

"I know," I said absently, staring at the book. "Stanley Weintraub thinks that Mabel was probably Aubrey Beardsley's sister. Something to do with *The Yellow Book*. Reggie Turner was not a ladies' man."

Mr Goodston was undeterred. Sitting for so long amongst so many memoirs he tends to absorb associations as if by osmosis. "His half-brother Frank Lawson, also illegitimate – there were a surprising lot of wrong sides to blankets in those straitlaced days

– inherited all the dough and bought Saltwood Castle in Kent."
He leant back the better to enjoy his dissertation. "Saltwood, as
I'm sure you also know, is subsequently famous for the family of
Bill Deedes of the *Telegraph* and then Kenneth Clark, art lord of
that ilk, and his racy diarist son Alan who, to put it mildly –"

"I know that too," I said, shortly. "Thank you, Mr Goodston.
It was not Turner I was really after. It was the Nicholson design.
Which is all right. Nothing special, though. Not like, say, a jack-
et by Michael Ayrton for Wyndham Lewis, for instance. You have
kindly done your stuff and I will purchase the book as promised.
How much do I owe you?"

He shook his big Pickwickian head as he replaced his glasses.
"My very dear Mr Simpson. You have been a steady, excellent and
if you will permit a liberty, a most enjoyable customer for a long
time. You are unique amongst my clientele; the only rugby blue
on the entire list. Things might have gone very ill for me if that
brute had pursued his inexplicable course of action. The book is
yours, sir, with my compliments and my very deepest thanks."

"Oh now look here, Mr Goodston, I can't allow that. We're
talking about your business. The very root of your existence. I
wouldn't have asked if I were not prepared to pay. Chaps in Cecil
Court say they can sometimes get up to two hundred quid for
Reggie Turner first editions."

He gaped at me for a moment then shook with subdued
laughter, making his creased waistcoat heave with an underbelly
earthquake. "Say that, do they? Turner would have enjoyed the
joke. He was an entirely unsuccessful novelist. He said that after
his death far rarer than his first editions would be his second editions. His books never ran to them. If they are rare now it is
because most have been scrapped."

I grinned. "Are they that bad?"

He pushed out his lips. "They are not all that bad. The one in
your hand reminds me, at the start, a little of Mark Twain, written when ordinary folk did not travel much. It continues with a

portrait of France having all the extravagant parody of an *'Allo 'Allo* programme. The hero is a figure like one of H G Wells's haberdashers, a kind of Kipps from a Brixton Emporium. There is a pre-Wodehousian element of plot. There is a court scene with all the melodrama of a Gallic Rumpole story. In short, it is a light comedy semi-thriller of unmemorable and derivative content despite the loyal Max Beerbohm's support. Turner was a conversational wit applauded by many such as Max, Willie Maugham and others but he was unable to translate his gift into print."

I turned the book over. "I still don't think I can accept it as a gift."

"My dear Mr Simpson! It cost me nothing! It came with the lady's other effects including some of the magazines you see strewn about here. I have had a grand week on the Turf. Please, please accept it with my compliments. Ignore the Cecil Court crowd." He frowned at me. "I must say I had rather hoped that I was the source to which –"

"Oh have no fear, Mr Goodston," I interrupted hastily. "I merely passed by in curiosity. My custom is yours, as well you know."

"Thank you." He gave me an appreciative and mollified nod. "I am happy to think that even if its decoration disappoints, the book has found a good home."

I stood up. I had a journey in front of me and it was time to get going. Outside, the two men had left no trace. The street was darkening.

"I don't think they'll come back soon," I said. "But go carefully, Mr Goodston."

"I shall, I do assure you. My door will be locked to all except known customers such as yourself."

"No idea what they wanted? Nothing obvious?"

"Nothing. But the old lady thing disturbs me. I shall think carefully which one might hold the key. Perhaps it was the Ian Fleming collection. London has become prey to sporadic violence of the kind he used for entertainment. This episode is baffling."

I frowned perplexedly at the magazines piled on the floor. "the *Graphic* and the *Illustrated London News*? Hardly the stuff of gangsterism."

"Indeed not. But often valuable source material for researchers. Libraries treasure them. Feature editors use their pictures."

"That's true," I said slowly, thinking. "That's very true. What sort of dates do they cover?"

"The two lots together?" He waved a proprietorial hand. "A random selection of the last quarter of the nineteenth century and a bit of the early twentieth. Their condition is not exactly mint. I had to take them as part of the library of books, mostly valueless, being disposed of in both cases. To find a nugget one has to clear a slagheap." He looked at me, sudden hope coming into his face. "Quite your sort of period, my dear sir, from the art review aspect. Isn't it? Contemporary comment on the RA Summer Exhibition and the West End galleries, that sort of thing? Apart from the illustrations?"

"How much would they be?"

"To you personally?"

I thought quickly. "No, for the Art Fund. It is expanding its library."

He named a reasonable figure. "I really need to get them out of the way," he said, "but there are collectors looking for them. Even though some of these are a bit tattered."

I hardly thought for a second. "Done," I said, briskly. "You've made a sale. Get them together and I'll arrange collection. I haven't time now but I'll see the Fund sends you a cheque."

"My dear Mr Simpson! I am gratified but do not think, just because of circumstances, that you are obliged to –"

"Not at all, Mr Goodston. They'll be a good investment, I'm sure."

"Quite true, quite true. In your expert hands I'm sure they will be."

I bowed back at the compliment and smiled at him.
His conceptual Fates must have smiled, too.

Chapter Two

"Ladies and gentlemen?"

The interrogative tones of the gallery's chairman cut through a murmur of conversation. The audience, after a few rustlings, settled down obediently. They were a congregation mostly of ladies of certain age punctuated by a few gentlemen of even older appearance. Seated in small rows in the large, high-windowed studio, they smiled at their chairman with the familiar anticipation of personal knowledge. In return he exuded an almost avuncular bonhomie. He was, quite clearly, at home in these surroundings.

Larry Granger has settled into a comfortable niche, my own chairman Freddy Harbledown advised me.

But it was time to concentrate.

"Distinguished guests." Larry Granger made a movement that was almost a bow in acknowledgement of these presumably eminent beings present amongst the ranks facing us. "Fellow Friends of Highton Art Gallery. It is my happy pleasure this evening to introduce our speaker, who is none other than Mr Tim Simpson of White's Art Fund. I need hardly tell you that White's Art Fund, which is a venture of White's Bank, has assembled for investment purposes one of the most celebrated collections of Modern British Art over the last few years. It is a collection that is the envy of many public galleries, not to mention ourselves. Mr Simpson is principally responsible for its acquisition. He seems to have done it almost incidentally whilst pursuing his career as a busy merchant banker. We are indeed very fortunate therefore to have him here to speak to us this evening."

He turned and inclined towards me with a slightly sycophantic grin before re-addressing his flock. I smiled back politely. Incidental was not the way I would have described the violent events surrounding the gathering-in of some items for the Art Fund but this was not the time for prevarication.

The hot seat is no place for pedantry.

"This evening he has very kindly brought with him a painting for us all to admire which, apart from being the subject of his talk, is of keenly relevant topicality." He gestured at the small painting I had placed on the big easel at the front of the room so that more or less everyone could see it, then gave his audience a significant leer so as, presumably, to whet their appetites. "Very relevant topicality. Especially to our modest throng. Without more ado, therefore, I welcome him on your behalf." He made a sweeping gesture towards me. "Mr Simpson."

There was a spattering of applause. Timmy-boy moved forward to face the expectant throng. It was time to perform.

Even if the circumstances were a bit odd.

*　*　*

It was a few weeks back when Freddy Harbledown buttonholed me in a passageway at the Bank's premises in Gracechurch Street. He asked if I could step into his office for a moment. He made it seem like a casual, fortuitous encounter which had suddenly jogged his memory rather than a formal summons to his lair. This was doubtless carefully planned so as to give a deceptive impression. Frederick, Lord Harbledown, is both thoughtful of relationships and cunning in the extreme. You would not think that a man whose hobby and apparent principal interest in life is the breeding of Old English Sheepdogs could be quite so devious.

But then he's Chairman of a merchant bank and titular head of a very devious family: the Whites.

"Tim," he said, when we'd got into his office, "I've an enormous favour to ask of you."

"Yes, Freddy?" I tried not to sound too guarded. My aristocratic chairman insists on familiar first name terms with me but is not above putting the boot in.

"It really is a favour and I'll very much owe you one, as the vernacular might express it. Do feel free to say no if you find it absolutely unacceptable. I shall quite understand."

"Thank you, Freddy." How do you refuse doing a favour to those On High?

"Have I ever mentioned Larry Granger to you?"

"No," I answered, thinking carefully, "I don't think so."

"Probably not. Not your generation. Foreign Office man, very cultured, very distant relative – I believe his mother came from Irish stock a long time back – but no shareholding or connection of that sort with us. He had a distinguished career in the FO if not a spectacular one. Too self-effacing, too discreet I think, even if an able linguist with an excellent brain. Quite a while ago, from distant outposts, mainly South America but some Arabic, he used to give us a bit of advice. Sort of consultancy, you know? A discreet FO view based on diplomatic activities."

"I see." At that moment I didn't, but so what?

"One has to be very careful about that sort of thing, naturally. The FO and the DTI have recognised channels for business enquiries. They are the conduit for information about overseas countries in the factual economic sense." He coughed modestly. "The diplomatic chaps like Larry Granger have to maintain absolute discretion about confidential political and other, er, economic decision processes."

"Absolutely."

Light dawned. The thing about working in the City is that even a thickhead can realise that the whole thing was originally based on insider knowledge. All utterly illegal nowadays, of course. But when those who ran things really were those who ran things it was entirely logical, to them, that outsiders had no right to benefit from information that they, the insiders who ran the whole show, possessed or could come to possess by belonging to the right club. Or knowing the right people. Why not? Try looking at the story of that people's hero Lloyd George and the Marconi Scandal of 1911 and you'll find what I mean. If you can be bothered.

"So Larry was very much an unofficial adviser to us. It would-n't have done for him to be seen as having a recognised role at the Bank. The FO wouldn't wear that. He was, however, available to us from time to time when certain decisions, usually overseas investment decisions by us or our clients, had to be taken."

"Very useful," I said, drily.

"Indeed it was. On one or two occasions I can recall it was quite critical. The matter had to be approached with great discretion, of course."

"Of course."

"Larry turned up trumps in the Santa Catalina Development business, for instance. Might have come a heavy cropper if it had-n't been for him."

"I see." The Santa Catalina Development project, yet another Brazilian hooley, was way before my time but I'd heard of it.

"We expressed our appreciation at the time, in the usual way."

"An *ex gratia* payment, I imagine?"

"Indeed." Freddy looked at me sharply to try and detect any element of cynicism in my demeanour but, I hope, found none. I have learnt how to keep a straight face on occasion.

An *ex gratia* payment sounds so much more respectable than a grimy commission.

"Well Larry retired with an inflation-proof pension and a nice nest-egg to a place called Highton. South Coast Sussex, on the estuary between Lewes and Newhaven. Do you know it?"

"Not really, no."

"Pretty little town, still quite medieval hilltop sort of spot, bit of a tourist trap. Stone walls, ancient church, flint and timber houses, that sort of thing. Was a port once like Lewes but beached inland by alluvial silting-up. Roman origins. Sacked by the French. I'll spare you the tourist patter. The fact is that Larry has become the Chairman of the Trustees of Highton Art Gallery. Something to keep him occupied. It's got quite a good

Camden Town collection and it does exhibitions of local artists' work. The usual thing. Economically absolutely strapped, of course, not a bean. Larry and his fellow trustees thrash about for funds but so far no dice. The arts authorities have got other fish to fry."

"Oh dear."

A suspicion was beginning to form in my mind. Surely Freddy wasn't thinking of subbing them up?

"Well they have the usual organisation of Friends to help raise funds – jumble sales, coffee mornings, outings to gardens and zoos, that sort of thing – and they organise lectures. All grist to the mill. The problem is that they can't afford much to pay the lecturers so it gets a bit amateur, if you follow me."

"Yes, I do." A horrid realisation was beginning to dawn.

"Larry is anxious to raise the standard of the lectures and to develop some outside contacts, so he's asked if we, as the Art Fund, could give them a talk. He says it'd buck his ladies up no end to have a big shot from the City come and talk to them about the same sort of art as they've got. Different perspective, investment interest, what's going on, that sort of thing, from someone on the same side. Bit of a backwater down there, I gather. No split cows, condom-infested beds, obscene videos, mock newspapers or flashing lights called Art. Just good paintings and craftwork. Quite like us, eh?"

I gave him an old-fashioned look. Investing in art for the purposes of a merchant bank is altogether different from what the with-it journals might promote by way of extreme risk in the Britart field. Even if I might like to speculate on Damien Hirst, it wasn't what the Fund was all about. The dead are so much safer than the living.

He returned my look with a bland one in which innocence and guile were neatly blended.

"Thought that'd make you sit up. Anyway, what I'm getting round to is: would you be prepared to go down there and give them a yarn? It'd be a great favour to me and I'm sure Larry would be absolutely delighted. I do feel a slight sense of obligation to him because he still drops us the occasional word. It might be useful for you to look over their collection, too. They're not allowed to sell it of course, part of a Trust and they're a registered charity, but there may be something to glean. You never know. Their funds are managed by" – he named a well-known high street bank's investment arm – "who seem competent enough. Larry's tactfully not put the fund management our way so far because of his remote family connection. Caesar's wife and all that."

"Quite so." Why did I sound even dryer than before?

"So there it is. As I say, if you don't want to –"

"Oh no, Freddy." As the late Alan Clark put it, I can be economical with the actuality. "It's no problem. No problem at all."

"You will?"

"I shall be delighted." It was an effort but I think I managed to appear cheerful.

"Good man! Oh, that's very good of you. You'll do it so well, I know you will. Your presentations are always so professional." He made it sound as though I'd burst in and made the offer spontaneously. "It's much appreciated."

"My pleasure."

"Should be no trouble. Down there for an evening talk, first Friday in the month is when they gather, stay at a good local hostelry on us, buy Larry a decent dinner with my compliments."

"OK. I'll do that."

"Er, there is one thing perhaps I'd better mention."

I raised my eyebrows in silent response. Further lies were beyond me.

He cleared his throat. "Larry Granger, you know. He's a very decent old trouper even if superficially a bit smooth. Sure you'll like him. Very keen on art. Very keen. Quite an intellectual. Elegant sort of chap. Got a few nice things of his own. A cultivated collector.

Should have quite a bit in common with you. Quite a bit. Not perhaps everything, though."

"Not everything?"

"No. Not quite." He coughed a purely artificial cough. "How can I put it tactfully these politically correct days?"

I smiled. At that time I hadn't yet got my Reggie Turner book but I'd read all about him.

"In the terms of a modern obituary, perhaps?"

"Sorry?"

"Don't tell me, Freddy, let me guess: Larry Granger, art lover, has never married?"

"My dear chap. Good old Tim. Discreet as ever. I knew you were the man for the job, really I did. I can leave it to you from now on, can I?"

* * *

"Thank you, Mr Chairman, ladies and gentlemen, for your kind welcome. It is both a great pleasure and an honour to be invited to speak to you this evening."

It's always safe to warm up with the usual routine and stick in a bit of flattery. If this sounds cynical remember that it wasn't you that got landed with having to spend a night away from home buttering up a load of blue-rinses headed by a cultured old codger with powerful credit at the Bank.

Not my idea of a riotous evening.

I wasn't going to be churlish, though. On arrival at the gallery's studio lecture space I found Larry Granger to be very much as I'd imagined him: smooth, well dressed in a sober suit, crisp silk tie and leather shoes, urbane but welcoming. It was a carefully planned appearance. He had a fine head of white hair, from the Irish trace in him perhaps, a lined but healthy narrow face with blue eyes, and a slender build. He was modestly deprecating about the gallery and its collection. He made appreciative remarks about my kind effort in coming down. We had a good look round the collection, myself making suitable noises. He offered me a cup of coffee with an apology that there was nothing stronger available, quoted a couple of Oscar Wilde's epigrams and accepted my offer of dinner after the talk with apparent pleasure. I had already checked into my hotel.

So far, so good.

I was alone. As I have already indicated, my dear wife Sue had taken the Simpson sprog William, now approaching the Terrible Twos and a bit of a handful, down to Bath. This was for an update weekend and a bit of obedience training from her mother and aunt, who own the best-behaved pair of dachshunds outside Prussia.

"You can't get up to much harm down in Highton," Sue said as I saw her off at Paddington. "It's not like Hastings or something. I've met one or two of the Highton gallery ladies visiting the Tate. Nothing after the Slade School's great years would meet with their approval. Artistically they're stuck somewhere around 1914. The place is an Eldorado to chocolate box illustrators. Quaintsville on sea. Nothing much has happened there since the Hundred Years War, when all the women were raped by the French. No further excitements since then; it's purely tourist invasions now. I can leave you without any fear of one of your imbroglios."

Little did she know.

The audience looked at me expectantly. They were pretty well dressed; a slice of elderly Middle England mostly retired to this ancient little town. One or two younger faces stood out among the ranks along with a bearded chap in exuberant clothing, introduced to me as the gallery's manager. I went into a brief description of the Fund, explaining that it had been started by my immediate boss, Jeremy White, and me, for people who wanted to invest in art without buying a Rembrandt or a Van Gogh themselves. All straightforward stuff, noting that the Fund con-

centrates mainly on British artists of the mid-19th to the mid-20th
century but includes some foreigners like Sargent and Monet
where they have London or British connections. Winslow
Homer, for example, in his Cullercoats period, and Rodin's
maquette of Gwen John.

So far, not bad.

Then I turned to the painting. If you're giving a talk, it helps
to provide the audience with something to look at other than
your own ugly mug. Slides are the obvious thing but the darkness
required by slides can induce somnolence. Many's the snore
heard by a lecturer during an evening slide lecture to senior citi-
zens. So I'd brought along a canvas which had particular reso-
nance for me.

A Back Room in Somers Town, painted by Mary Godwin.

The painting is not part of the Fund; it belongs to a member
of the White family out in Brazil, who'd repatriated it a year or
two back. It was part of the Fund's history though, and mine,
and Sue's. If it hadn't been for this particular painting the
obstreperous young William wouldn't exist. It was, in addition,
the first in a long line of art works to cause trouble, trouble of a
graphically lethal nature.

The painting has a rather poignant quality. It shows a dismal
pre-1914 bedroom interior, with a girl sitting on a bed. Not one
of Sickert's blowsy whores but a young girl in a straw boater with
a dark band round it, a blouse and dark pleated skirt with a white
apron. She sits on the edge of the mattress, staring thoughtfully
sideways at the floor. Looking down at her from a standing position, leaning against a heavy chest of drawers, is a young man
with a cigarette drooping from the corner of his mouth. His
waistcoated body is in shirtsleeves and there is an arrogant attitude in the set of his figure and the look on his narrow face. An
implication of innocence about to be or already exploited, a sense
of tragedy, is saddening. The young man is from another world
to that of the girl; one that gets its way, perhaps already has. This

is a record of something happening or about to happen that has no real joy in it.

Mary Godwin was a pupil of Sickert's, having attended the school he ran with Sylvia Gosse on the Hampstead Road. She exhibited this painting at the New English Art Club in 1914 whilst living nearby. It is deeply influenced by Sickert and his Camden Town Murder series. The concept of a dressed man and a naked woman alone in a seedy Camden Town setting is almost a monopoly of Sickert's, although you might point to Manet's *Le Dejeuner Sur L'Herbe* as an exterior forerunner of the idea.

It certainly got my audience going.

I knew that Highton had a good Sickert nude in its collection, one of the 6, Mornington Crescent ladies painted *contre jour* against the window on an iron bedstead, symbol of prostitution and its attendant social realities. I checked that before I left London. The collection Larry Granger toured me round also included Spencer Gore, Drummond, Bevan and Ginner. There were other, later, more *plein air* artists from the Newlyn School but the Camden Town lot formed a sort of core, bringing an urban, foetid contrast to Highton's wind-scrubbed coastal views.

The Friends of Highton Art Gallery knew all about Sickert. Depending on their view, he was a seedy pornographer or a magnificent depicter of social reality. To his fans he is a man who changed British painting forever. To others he is sordid. Biblical scenes and pretty gentry were anathema to Sickert. He was more Continental than English. Newspaper stories and the grim squalor of street life were his *métier*.

What he wasn't, to the indignant ladies in front of me, was Jack the Ripper.

They'd seen Patricia Cornwell's TV programme. Some of them had read her book setting out a case for him as a serial killer. They were very knowledgeable.

Cornwell states that Sickert actually committed the Camden Town Murder, which they all agreed was nonsense. Robert

Wood, who was acquitted after a trial, was almost certainly the culprit.

The evidence for the much earlier Ripper murders and subsequent letters is really tenuous as far as Sickert goes. They agreed on that, too.

But I got them going even more by musing aloud that there is something about Sickert that doesn't quite add up. All those seedy one-room studios he rented, not just in London but in Dieppe and Venice: what went on in them? That habit of dressing up almost to the point of disguise, a relict of his days in the theatre as much as a need to provide his own models: it does seem odd. Three marriages but no children. So many mistresses but supposedly only one illegitimate issue, a boy called Maurice by Madame Villain in Dieppe and that hard to prove; was he really a philanderer? Why was he so interested in the Ripper? Was it only because his Mornington Crescent landlady told him his room had been occupied by a suspiciously mad veterinary student at the time of the Ripper murders and she was convinced her lodger was the culprit? Or was there more to it? The supposedly sexually debilitating operation for a fistula when a boy, brought over from Munich after two unsuccessful attempts: was he therefore impotent or not? The ladies of Highton debated that with uninhibited vigour.

When it comes to the crunch, Middle England leaves no stone unturned. They got their teeth into all that. It became quite a boisterous gathering.

They liked the Mary Godwin, though. During the question and answer session they got out of their seats to look at it closely. They said they wouldn't mind hanging that up at home at all. They'd think twice about a Sickert nude: too raw. All very well for public galleries to depict life's horrors but "Not At Home" was their principle. However, one or two of them did think that maybe the Godwin was a bit of a gloss over the real thing, that it pulled its punches. Which is true up to a point but it has a more subtle quality, a feminine assertion of a situation which is more telling than a brutal, masculine one. Just as profound but having a bit of sensibility.

"It's all gone very well," Larry Granger murmured approvingly to me as eventually they began to file out. There'd been a formal thanks and another spatter of applause. "You did well, Tim, dear boy. Quite a chap for presentation with involvement, aren't you? I really do feel that we should be buying you dinner, not the other way round."

"Oh the Bank can take it, Larry. Freddy says it's the least we can do for you. It's with his compliments you know."

"How kind. I hope you won't think it impudent of me if I ask another guest? He's a great admirer of yours and a splendid manager for the gallery. I introduced you earlier. Dennis Cash, the chap with the beard. Would you mind?"

"I shall be delighted," I said. Once again.

Chapter Three

We went to a half-timbered bistro just round the corner from my hotel. Larry Granger said the food was palatable. He had the view, similar to mine, that restaurants in England are ridiculously expensive at whatever level of competence they operate.

We ordered steaks and I found a good bottle of claret at a half-reasonable price. Then we looked at each other.

"We're lucky here," Larry Granger smiled. "In no time at all we can get across to Dieppe for a decent meal."

The proximity of Newhaven, not far down the wandering water meadows of the Sussex Ouse, was evident from a glow in the southern sky. I seemed to recall that cross-Channel ferries didn't operate from there in the winter any longer and were quite costly in the summer, but I wasn't sure.

"Larry is a great Dieppe man," Dennis Cash grinned at me. "He nips over there regularly."

"Dieppe," pronounced Larry Granger in response to this, "is artistically one of England's most important resorts. So many British artists have lived, painted or just reclined there. And it's big. It makes St Ives or Newlyn look like the wee villages they are. I love the place and all those points along the coast. Lord Salisbury and Oscar Wilde; where else can you find such traces of our greatest foreign secretary cum Prime Minister and our keenest playwright? No wonder Sickert liked it so much. Got it from his mother, of course; she was there a long time."

"Miss Sheepshanks as she might have been," I murmured.

He gave me an approving look. "Dead right, Tim, dead right. I don't suppose you've found a splendid Sickert for your Fund yet, have you?"

"As a matter of fact, we haven't. Only some drawings."

"Quite an omission." He said it thoughtfully, with any hint of censure. It occurred to me then that as an art lover, collector and one connected with the Bank, he must have invested in the Fund.

This would give him details of its content.

"It's a fantastic collection, all the same." Dennis Cash bristled with enthusiasm from the other side of the table. He wore a wide, warm, smock-like garment embroidered with a kind of Fairisle patterning over baggy Indian trousers. Underneath this array he was of substantial build and had broad, spatulate hands capable of bending clay round a spindle or caking on paint with a palette knife. His abundant hair, down over his collar, was just starting to turn grey, as was his beard, but his brown eyes were bright.

"Thank you," I responded.

"If," he sounded envious, "we had any money, yours would be the sort of collection I'd love to put together for Highton. I'm not saying we aren't very lucky but there is so much later twentieth century stuff I'd love to add. The Harlands did very well but it's frustrating just to mark time. One should progress."

"The Harlands were the ones who left their collection to the town?"

"Indeed they were. And their house. It's the gallery now. Without the Harlands there would be no gallery here. They thought they'd left enough money to keep it going, in a Trust Fund, for ever. But I don't have to tell you how expenses have outpaced returns on capital."

"We're not going to dun you for funds," Larry Granger smiled apologetically. "I promised Freddy that. It's just that reality keeps creeping in."

"What about the Arts Council and local authorities?"

He smiled sourly. "My researches amongst the arts authorities have been both exhaustive and fruitless. They present a bafflingly Byzantine façade. Do you know that there are at county, district, borough, town and doubtless other levels, Arts Development Officers, Visual Arts Officers and Arts Advisers, Education? There are even Arts Officers, Legal and Community Services. Individually these arts officers are powerless. None of them has access to funds without the intervention of Economic Development Officers, Education Bidding Officers, Corporate Bidding Officers –" he cocked an eye at Dennis Cash, who smiled – "Education Department Bidding Officers and even a Community Development Manager. The whole bunch are subject to curtailment from those occupying the ancient and imposing office of Treasurer."

I was impressed. Here was someone who'd done his local authority rounds and got himself informed, even if only to confirm that bureaucracy loves to dabble with the arts in an elusive manner. "That's local authority stuff," I said. "What about the Arts Council?"

He smiled at my interruption. "It goes without saying that at regional level – to wit, the South East – they are supplemented by a Director of Visual and Media Arts, a Programming Adviser, a Visual Arts and Crafts Officer, a Crafts and Public Arts Officer who is, in versatile mode, also a Commissioning Officer."

"Commissioning Officer? Does he recruit soldiers?"

"It is a she. The commissions are generally for outdoor events rather than painting or sculpture. Video film creations are very favoured. Performance poetry is particularly *a la mode* just now."

"Ah."

"Some of them in turn have Assistant Officers. There is, or was, an Administrative Assistant, Visual and Media Arts but I can easily lose track of developments because the whole lot are moving from Tunbridge Wells to Brighton. There is a Planning Officer, Local Arts Development but he or she is quite separate, coming under the Resources Development bureau of the scheme. There are Information Officers both principal and assistant, along with those connected with Resources Officers and Finance Officers. I exclude for simplicity's sake a whole raft of Performing Arts Officers – Music, Drama and Dance, which presumably embraces this poetry of the performance variety – Houseman, turn in your grave – and their cohorts, who are not relevant to us."

"Christ. What do they all do? I mean, what the hell emerges from this tribe?"

Granger gave me a kindly eye. "Nothing that would help us.

They do not support galleries, public or otherwise. Although they would all dearly love to tell us what to exhibit. This should be in line with their current brief that any art in which they have a hand would be –" he paused to think before reciting – "culturally diverse, socially inclusive and mainly three-dimensional. Paintings are unpopular. They love installations, which are quite unsuitable for Highton, but one of the Directors will not fund any other form of art. They are entranced by the video camera."

"By culturally diverse," I was still trying to absorb all that had been said, "do they mean, er, what I think – ?"

"Yes they do. Nothing English, you might say, if employing tact. Despite the desires of the very English people of Highton."

"And socially inclusive?"

"Do we have facilities for the disabled, the halt, sick and lame? No, we do not. The nature of our ancient buildings makes that very difficult to achieve without enormous expense. The last time we looked at a ramp of the right incline for wheelchairs we found that it would have to start across the road in the middle of Panton's Bookshop. By law, very soon, we will have to do something about facilities for the disabled. For which we have little money. If any money were given to us, we would still have to provide half of the costs. This is known as reciprocal funding and we don't have such funding. Also, they would make the approval of our exhibition programme, and all our activities, subject to their unpainterly desires. In short, we would lose all independence and become –"

"Socially inclusive and culturally diverse?"

Larry Granger frowned. "Precisely. Any help we might get from government-controlled sources will alter what we do in line with current political policy, quite apart from requiring an administrative input we cannot afford. However, I am sanguine as to whether we would ever get any money despite the fact that the ongoing salary of any single one of these self-serving functionaries would keep our gallery safe for years to come."

"That's a bit galling, if they're not helping you."

"My impression is that the system is like a huge perpetual motion machine of the second kind, absorbing great energy to secure its continuation with out any surplus being available for external propulsion."

I grinned. "My physics master would have approved of the analogy."

"One does not have to be too technical although it is tempting."

"You really do mean that you can't get help from them?"

"Government-funded organisations dedicated to the support of the arts may, I think, be compared to a series of stately carousels on which appointed mandarins gravely ride hobbyhorses rearing obediently to the eccentric impulses of hidden cams. These cams are in turn actuated by current political, philosophical and directorial memoranda whilst the carousel continues its movement in strictly ornamental circles."

Dennis Cash and I both laughed at that, bringing a gratified smile to his face. This, I remember thinking, is a true FO *homme du monde* of the old school: urbane, sophisticated and world weary. Nothing should surprise this man. But surely the Foreign Office in his day must have had similarities to the arts situation he had just described?

There was a hint of polemic in this performance, the polemic of one frustrated by bureaucratic circumstances after doing what must have been thorough rounds of the sources he described, all in the way of charitable activity.

He made a dismissive gesture. "Let us not dwell, however, on the distressingly Byzantine nature of official arts activities." A sip of claret was taken from his glass. "I am delighted that you brought up Patricia Cornwell's strange book and TV programme. What a combination of best-selling acumen and irrational obsession hers is. Reviews by arts critics and biographers poo-hoo all her premises whereas TV reviewers mumble that there may be something in it. Such is the power of celebrity and television; scholarship and logic crumble in its glare. And the proof of her carefully orchestrated pudding is in the eating thereof: her book tops American non-fiction sales. Where is the truth?"

"Veronica would have agreed with Cornwell." Dennis Cash looked at Larry Granger with a smile. "She hated our Mornington Crescent nude and a lot more of the Camden Town paintings."

"*De mortuis nil nisi bonum*," came the reproachful answer. "Veronica was intolerant of sex in art but dedicated to the gallery. A contradiction which she totally ignored. Art, to her, was Holman Hunt and the later, religious output of Tissot. The real pursuits of society were not fit for display."

He turned to me in explanation.

"Veronica Chalmers was secretary of the Friends of Highton Art Gallery. We call them FHAG for short. In normal circumstances she would have introduced you this evening. Unfortunately she is unable to do so."

"Is she ill?"

"No, dead." He was crisp. "Last week she fell downstairs and broke her neck."

"Oh dear."

Why did a prickle of apprehension move down the back of my neck? Why was it that events connected with the Art Fund so often proved violent? Why a punch-up early in the afternoon and news of a fatality in the evening?

"She had been secretary for many years. Had known the founding Harlands well, or rather Jane Harland well. We speak of the founding Harlands but in fact George died before the foundation. The gallery is his widow Jane Harland's legacy to the town. Veronica was a rather fierce chatelaine who guarded their memory, and the gallery's progress, with rigid conservatism. I fancy she would not have approved of this evening. Not at all, even though in your painting the subjects are decorously clothed."

"She was stuck in a time warp." Cash didn't sound heated but there was strength to his statement. "Like many in Highton." He held up a mollifying hand toward his Chairman. "Don't get me wrong, Larry; much of the town needs careful preservation. But not setting in aspic the way they want to."

"Well she's gone now. We have a clear field, Dennis, to exhibit new material without her grating and prudish objections."

"Indeed. I'm pleased about that." Cash drank from his own glass. "It does seem an irony, her falling downstairs. She was always as sure-footed as a mountain goat in the gallery."

"Some of these old houses," Larry Granger said to me, "have staircases which are absolutely lethal. Steep as the Matterhorn. Veronica went down hers head first, apparently. She was a stiff old stick. Snapped on impact, the police tell me."

"I still haven't found the file." Dennis Cash looked thoughtful.

"It'll turn up, Dennis."

This mysterious aside was interrupted by the arrival of our steaks. After we'd settled once again, Larry Granger looked at me speculatively.

"How did you come to be a banker?" he demanded.

"Oh, by accident really. I was a management consultant, doing a sort of systems job on a subsidiary run by Jeremy White. It was in chaos at the time."

"Ah, the *enfant terrible* of White's, as he then was. Quite the establishment figure now, I believe."

"More accepted, I suppose, yes. Still unconventional though. Anyway he and I got on well – still do – and I left consultancy to set up the Fund and eventually become one of the Bank's inside men."

"With distinction, I'm sure. Have you always been the Art Fund manager?"

"Oh yes. It was to set up the Fund that Jeremy lured me to the Bank."

"The Art Fund administrator. A serious business, I'm sure. As ours is to us."

It wasn't said very condescendingly, but rather thoughtfully, as though something had just occurred to him. I hastened to change the subject. I wasn't in a mood to explain how far the Art

Fund was from a small public gallery like his. I didn't do rounds of local arts officers, bowl in hand.

"How did you come to join the Foreign Office?"

"A book did it. A mere book." He cut a piece of steak. "You can blame Duff Cooper for it."

"Duff Cooper? Lord Norwich?"

"The very same. I was a schoolboy, about eighteen, when a master lent me his *Talleyrand*. Until then I was all Oscar Wilde and Somerset Maugham; the most cynical boy in the school. *Talleyrand* entranced me; I went for anything of Duff Cooper's after that. He'd just been ennobled; he chose the motto *Odi et Amo – I hate and I love –* for his escutcheon. Powerful imagery, it was. There were rumours that like Talleyrand, he enjoyed the favours of a glamorous niece even though he was married to the great beauty of her time – Lady Diana."

"I've just had a banana with Lady Diana?"

"I'm Burlington Bertie from Bow! The very same. His way with her was like his career at the FO. An unbreakable relationship but lots of affairs on the side. It convinced me. The Foreign Office was the place for me. I'm afraid I never reached the heights Duff did but I've no regrets."

"How apposite, then. This evening's subject, I mean. At least the fistula part of it, anyway."

He gave me a shrewd grin. "You really do know your art background, don't you, Tim?"

"I'm afraid it has been my downfall on many occasions."

He laughed. Then he turned to Dennis Cash. "Tim and I are referring to the fact that Duff Cooper's father, Sir Alfred Cooper, was the surgeon who treated young Walter Sickert for his fistula. His great aunt, Miss Sheepshanks – Sickert's mother was the illegitimate daughter of a distinguished Cambridge astronomer-mathematician called Sheepshanks – brought him over after two failed operations in Munich. He was treated at the City Road Hospital, St Mark's. Alfred Cooper was the surgeon.

His specialities were respiratory problems, for which he was knighted after treating Edward VII, and venereal disease."

Dennis Cash smiled. "Two useful talents in foggy old Victorian London."

"Indispensable, I'm sure. When Sir Alfred's carriage stopped outside the residences of high society there would be speculative amusement as to which ailment he was treating. The carriage was jocularly referred to as Cooper's clap-trap."

Cash grinned. "I can see that I'm in the presence of two aficionados. With much in common. Are you an expert on Oscar Wilde too, Tim?"

"Not specially, no. I admire his work of course."

"Ah. Larry is a devotee. How about Somerset Maugham?"

I nodded. "An early favourite, to whom I often return. Despite his waspish reputation Maugham was a courteous man on French lines. Like some of his, to us, slightly gawky sentences. But he was very kind to young writers. Frederick Raphael gives him great credit."

"Bravo. Hear! Hear!" Granger gave me cheerful approval.

"What about Max Beerbohm?" Dennis Cash enquired.

"Um." I had to be thoughtful. "Can't say I'm wildly struck. Zuleika Dobson? A bit precious, perhaps, for me. I'm not an Oxford man."

Cash nodded. "That figures. What about his friend Reggie Turner?"

A chill struck my bones. "Who?"

"Turner. Reggie Turner, said to be a great wit. Friend of Somerset Maugham's, too. He was at Oscar Wilde's bedside when he died. Wrote terrible novels. Larry collects them. Ever heard of Reggie Turner?"

I stuck a fork into my steak. The chill deepened into a foreboding. The book was safely locked in my car. I was playing for time. Something, some inner cautious voice, irrational, illogical and inexplicable, told me to keep stumm. A sixth sense had suddenly awakened. There are times when matters are hard to believe and when it's wise to keep a bit back. A good consultant never says more than is necessary. I can't explain my sudden congealing: it's just that I hate coincidences. Absolutely detest them.

Imperial Brown of Brixton and the punch-up: why was the timing so coincidental? Why today, the very same day? It was surreal.

"No," I said, hearing myself lie for no justifiable reason except a deep inner, anticipatory dread. "No, I'm afraid I haven't."

"No reason why you should. Larry would agree, despite his enthusiasm. Not exactly mainstream, was he?"

"No." Larry Granger had gone crisp again. "He wasn't. Like many wits he was much better verbally than in writing. The flash of conversation loses impact when trudged across the page. But let us not bore our guest, Dennis. There are many more interesting subjects to pursue. Walter Sickert, for instance: we haven't even scraped the surface there. Have you read Osbert Sitwell's accounts of him, Tim?"

"I have." I took a relieved sip of claret at the chance to change the subject. The dark blue book with its bold black lettering and cocked-hat eagle was suddenly a burning image I wanted to banish from my mind.

What did those bruisers really want? And Granger, this complex, sophisticated man; why did I suddenly want to keep my Granger powder dry? I liked him; I liked his style. He reminded me of tutors I had responded to at university, of conversations I hadn't much had recently, in which an educated exchange stimulated and amused, in which cross references could be bandied and savoured like old port. Dennis seemed to be straight and relatively easy to read whereas his Chairman clearly had much depth. I liked that depth but why my sudden caution? What was the threat in the common ground?

He was waiting, head cocked slightly to one side.

I decided I might as well enjoy myself.

"Do you think," I queried, putting down my glass and facing him, "reading Osbert Sitwell, that Mrs George Swinton really was Sickert's mistress?"

Chapter Four

"Felicitations, my dear Tim." Across the hard bright shine of his polished mahogany table, Jeremy White's smile was at its most vulpine. White teeth glinted below a cascade of blond hair. "You have made a hit. A most palpable hit. Great kudos has accrued to you. Your appointment follows your outstanding performance. Clearly another scintillating presentation on your part."

"Crap."

"Not at all. Glowing is the adjective one associates with the report to Freddy Harbledown."

"Sod that."

"Appalling! Why are you reacting so badly?"

"This is a set-up, that's why. An utter bloody set-up. I can smell it."

"Such truculence! What suspicions! What an unwilling victor you are. I'm glad Freddy isn't here to witness these tantrums. He is delighted by your success."

"I might have known the sly bastard wouldn't face me in person. Where is he? Where is he hiding?"

"He is not hiding. He is in Scarborough, judging a show of Yorkshire Old English Sheepdogs."

"There is no such thing as a Yorkshire Old English Sheepdog."

"There is Yorkshire Bitter. There is Yorkshire Tea. That obstinate county is perfectly capable of creating Yorkshire Old English Sheepdogs."

"Rubbish."

It was only a week later. We were sitting in Jeremy's office at the Bank. I was seething. Jeremy was enjoying himself. Next to him Geoffrey Price, our sturdy, pinstriped, cricketing accountant, was enjoying himself too.

"Highton," he murmured, almost caressing the word, "Highton. Marvellous. Ancient. Sheltered. So appropriate as a change of venue. What a difference from the cockpit of your beloved Hastings. It'll suit you no end, Tim. Just what was needed after your many excitements and excursions. Something more soothing. A nice quiet period out of trouble, in a nice elderly environment."

"Geoffrey, I'll ram your bloody cricket bat down your bloody –"

"Tim! Really!" Jeremy intervened. "There is no need to be so petulant. It is an honour that the Bank, in particular due to its Art Fund, should be chosen for this specialised consultancy work. Larry Granger was fulsome in his praise of you. He made it clear that he can not get funds from the arts authorities for anything except advice of a professional nature. To wit, consultancy and feasibility studies of a detached, objective character. For that sort of thing acceptance by our Civil Service goes through almost on the nod. The bullshit brigade always looks after its own. All we had to do was to confirm our fees for such work and he got the OK for fifty percent of them."

"So who's paying the rest?"

"Technically, the Highton Art Gallery has to put up what I believe is called reciprocal funding. In practice, we will meet the difference. As a gesture of goodwill."

"Except that in practice we won't do anything of the sort. You've inflated the fee figure to make sure that fifty percent covers what we need, haven't you?"

"My dear Tim, we took a normal business precaution. An international consultant like yourself does not need to have the principles of transfer pricing explained to him, I'm sure."

"It's absolutely criminal. Disgraceful."

"Our image will be enhanced no end at undertaking such work for a registered charity at modest rates. A definite PR coup in terms of art sponsorship."

"God! The sheer hypocrisy!"

"The Bank, and its Art Fund manager, are manifestly suitable to examine the problems of a small provincial gallery and to make recommendations on its future survival. No one could challenge such an appointment. Especially in view of your magnificent track record in Brazil, France, the United States and all over."

"Even Lancashire," Geoffrey chipped in, with a sly grin.

"Even Lancashire! How right you are, Geoffrey. Lancashire yesterday, Sussex today; a southward move. It has a sort of historical ring."

I shook my head irritably. "What really gets me is that approval of that sort of feasibility study needs a lot of time and much form filling. In other words, Freddy Harbledown and Larry Granger had the whole thing worked out long before I went down there to give my lecture."

"Oh come come, I'm sure it was quite spontaneous." He made a dismissive gesture. "Something you probably said to Granger at dinner."

"Rats! There's more to this than meets the eye."

"My dear Tim, you must calm yourself. One day you too may benefit from the Bank's long-lasting gratitude."

"Eh?"

Jeremy leant forward. "Freddy Harbledown nearly came the most enormous cropper over the Santa Catalina project. A whopper. If it hadn't been for Larry Granger's timely advice, resignations would have been rife. Quite apart from the Bank's future being sabotaged."

"So I'm the sacrificial goat, am I? Or the roast suckling pig?"

"Such prima donnishness! A gentle stroll of a consultancy job with only a night or two away from home in the midweek while it lasts. The enduring gratitude of Freddy as well as Granger. Enormous kudos for the generous Bank. You'll eat it. A doddle to a man of your talents. Sledgehammer to crack a nut." His humorous expression changed. "You'll need to ease up from your usual scrimmage technique, mind you. Exactly as Geoffrey says, Highton is not Hastings. You must temper the wind to the shaggy old sheep. There is no acquisition in prospect for the Fund, so no violence will arise. Sweetness and light must abound. You have the stage to yourself. Everyone will hang on your words. Old ladies will dab tears from their eyes as they pass you another plate of plum cake. I cannot understand your attitude."

"Oh yes you can!"

"I agree that the gallery's present investment fund managers may feel a trifle miffed. They may consider this something of a territorial incursion. Their management is being put under a magnifying glass. We have strolled like Roland trumpeting into their camp."

"I seem to recollect that after sounding his horn Roland got the chop."

"You take me too literally. Highton is not Roncesvalles. Anyway our rivals may feel we are after the account."

"Not to mention the matter of Bill Riley," Geoffrey chipped in.

"What?"

"Really, Geoffrey." Jeremy gave him a distinctly irritated glare. "That was a matter to be raised in due course. In the fullness of time."

"Bill Riley?" A dumbfounded numbness had hit my senses. "You are not talking of the same Bill Riley I'm thinking of by any chance, are you?"

"Bill Riley has a weekend house in Highton." Jeremy was defensive. "He is, as it happens, purely coincidentally, a trustee of the art gallery. Apparently he became one about a year ago."

"Let me get this straight." I found I was gritting my teeth so that my diction was not the best. "Bill Riley of Portarlington Investments right here in the City of London is a trustee of the very same gallery that I, all unwittingly, have been shanghaied into advising on its economic future?"

"As it happens, yes. He plays golf a lot in that area as well as having extensive golf interests in Spain, I believe. But shanghaied is not appropriate."

"But me no buts! I knew there was a set-up! I just knew it! All the Bank wants is work from Portarlington, doesn't it? This so-called feasibility study bullshit, this public arts sponsorship, is just a smoke screen."

"My dear Tim, Riley's presence had no relation, no relation whatsoever, to your being asked to make an assessment for Granger. Riley is a new but conscientious trustee, as I understand it, who keeps an eye on the gallery's fund and carries out whatever other duties are incumbent on him. A quarterly meeting or so is all that is required."

"He can hardly fail to notice, can he, that Granger has inserted White's Bank into the woodwork?"

"I am sure that he will approve of our generous gesture in providing absolutely professional advice at no cost to the gallery."

I gaped at him, dumbfounded.

"Freddy did say," he went on, ignoring my stare, "that the sooner we could start, the better."

We? I nearly shouted at him. We? Who are we? Me, you mean. Muggins, as usual, ready to take the flak and carry the can when some horrendous glitch comes up while you and Freddy count sheepdogs, Yorkshire or otherwise.

"So I did promise that you'd go as soon as possible. The Art Fund needs no attention right now and your other projects will have to fit in round this."

"Let me get this quite clear. This feasibility study will cover ground already well hacked over by Granger and his trustees. Is the Bank willing to stump up to help this gallery?"

"Good heavens, no."

"So I will be mouthing the sort of platitudes you find in all such reports probably confirming what Granger has already told me."

"And searching all possible sources of funding, Tim. Bringing your expertise to bear. An objective assessment is what is required."

"Oh no it isn't! What is required is the business of Portarlington Investments via Bill Riley. That's the hidden agenda. That's why I have been shanghaied into this nonsense."

He put on a stern, challenging expression. "I don't need to tell you how things are in the City at present. It's every man to the pumps. We need business. And I do rather resent your repeated use of the word shanghaied. It has distinctly rebarbative implications."

He paused to assume a facial set, one that brooked no more adverse reactions, but he needn't have bothered.

I was speechless.

Chapter Five

"Highton." In our kitchenette in Onslow Gardens Sue actually giggled as she cracked an egg into her omelette mix. William was fast asleep in his room. "Highton. The Art Gallery. I can hardly believe it. You in Highton. Just like putting a bull into a china shop."

"Thank you. Very much."

"I wonder if they have any idea what is about to hit them."

"Hit them? Me? I am the most circumspect of men. I shall move as though treading on them there eggshells."

"Perhaps you will." She smiled wickedly. "For a change. You obviously appeal enormously to this Granger man."

"I beg your pardon?"

"Your common interests. Oscar Wilde. Somerset Maugham. And Reggie Turner. An interesting combination. He's clearly formed an opinion of you."

"I have not exposed my Reggie Turner knowledge to him."

"Oh no. I forgot about that. Keeping an intimate little secret for the right moment, were you?"

"You Jezebel. Do you want a gin and tonic or not?"

"I want a gin and tonic while one is going." She started whisking briskly. "I will have to do without my barman for a night or two each week for how long?"

"I don't know. But not long. I shall make sure of that." I shook my head irritably. "This has been an object lesson to me."

"Oh? Why?"

"It comes of being too clever by half. Showing off. Of swapping clever literary anecdotes and artistic connections with a man like Granger. I should have known better. I was a vain fool."

"You were keen to impress him. I have no doubt that it was an excellent performance. Despite yourself you enjoyed it."

"I should have been a typical dullard. A Lombard Street philistine."

"Ha! Freddy Harbledown obviously knows his man. Both

men. He's got you taped."

"Bastard."

"Is this man Riley important?"

"Very important. He is a big cheese in the City. Portarlington Investments has been a front runner for some time. The Bank would love to handle just a slice if its business."

"What a compliment to you, then. Freddy Harbledown and Jeremy have put you in there believing that you will impress."

"Rats."

"I think you're making a big fuss about nothing." She took a swig from the gin and tonic I handed her, making the ice tinkle. "It's an opportunity to succeed where it sounds as though others have failed. Anyway, it will do you good to go tactfully for a bit and see how gentle Old England has to live. It won't be easy to find a way forward for the gallery, I agree: everyone says all our local museums and galleries are in dire straits these days. All their funds have collapsed. There's a seminar coming up on provincial galleries that I'm supposed to go to."

Sue, when not dealing with the recalcitrant William and me, is a Curator at Tate Britain. Her specialisation is the Impressionists so don't ask me how that works now that they've all gone to Tate Modern. Like Larry Granger, I find myself defeated by the Byzantine workings of our arts authorities.

"I don't know why it should be thought that I have solutions others have not." I sipped my own g-and-t. "If the superb first class honours graduates of our illustrious Civil Service establishment are unable to spring a result, what chance does an old rugger hack like me stand?"

"You'll come up with something. Usually you do. You may have failings in many directions but you often get results."

"Failings? Failings? In what directions? I am your husband, remember. In your eyes I can do no wrong."

"That's not what Mummy and Aunt Hilda said. That boy, they said, meaning William, not you, is not getting the right line

from his father. He's naughty. Take it from us: he needs his father
to set boundaries as well as you, Sue dear. Which he doesn't seem
to be doing."

"Nonsense. William and I understand each other perfectly
well. We are in harmony. Considering."

"Considering what?"

"Considering that, like Cherie Blair juggling with family and
career, I have so many balls to keep in the air."

"Oh boy. Talk about role reversal."

"I might have known that those two old harpies would point
the finger at me."

"They were very fair. Fathers are important, they know that.
They love William. They just want him to behave well, that's all."

"Like the two dachshunds?"

"No! Not like the two dachshunds. If William could just be
more amenable about eating it would help. The way he hurls
food about reminds me of you at a rugby club dinner."

"They didn't serve him your mother's potato and leek mash,
did they?"

"As a matter of fact they did."

"There you are, then. That's my boy. He's got good taste, I
knew it. That mash deserves nothing better than to be bunged at
a wall."

"Tim! You can't encourage such behaviour!"

"The stuff is awful. Leeks have no place in his diet; my boy is
never going to play for a Welsh side. I'm glad that his first reactions can be trusted. It's very heartening, really it is."

"You are appalling. Utterly primitive. I really do hope William
doesn't develop too many of your characteristics." She swished at
something with a whisk. "I'm doing your omelette first. There's
some cheese for afters so I'm not putting any in this mix."

"Only *les fines herbes*?"

"Exactly. All very healthy for you."

"No leeks."

"I know better than that. You get violent over leeks. Oh, that reminds me; Mr Goodston phoned."

"Oh?"

"He said to thank you once again for his deliverance." She stopped to give me a meaning stare. "What did he mean by that?"

"Oh nothing. You know Mr Goodston; he's old, uses a dated sort of parlance full of abstruse imagery. Books do that to people."

"Hmm. Why does an implication of violence come to me?"

"I've no idea."

"Anyway, he apologised for bothering you at home but said he couldn't reach you at the Bank, you were in some meeting. He thanked you for the cheque and said when would you like to collect the magazines? He needs to clear them out."

"Ah. I've been thinking about that. I think I'll get them and bring them here. There'll never be time to look through them properly at the Bank, even though they belong to the Art Fund. I'll take some of them to Highton with me for bedtime reading."

"What are they?"

"Old copies of the *Graphic* and the *Illustrated London News*."

"Really? Good reference stuff, I suppose?"

"That's it."

"We haven't got all that much room here, Tim."

"Don't worry: it won't be for long. Once we've gone through them I'll find somewhere at the Bank."

"We?"

I smiled a winning smile. "I was thinking of you when I bought them. I shall take some with me along with Reggie Turner for evening amusement in my dull local hotel. But with me decorously away down at Highton I thought I should leave some picture books to keep you and William out of mischief during the long, leisurely day. Occupy your empty hours."

She turned, pan in hand. "Tell me something, Tim dear."

"What?"

"How would you like a hot omelette in your lap?"

Chapter Six

I parked on the double yellow line outside Mr Goodston's shop, near side wheels on the pavement. He said he'd be ready for me, and he was. A rap on the door and his bulky figure shuffled up behind it. There was the sound of bolts being shot and mortice locks being turned to the rattle of keys.

"My dear Mr Simpson. You are brave, sir, to park here. We have a rapacious strain of traffic wardens in this area, a breed with outrageous fine certificates always at the ready. Let us hope one does not appear while you are loading. I have remonstrated with them on many occasions but they sometimes sneak up unobserved to do their dirty work."

I looked up and down the pavement. There was no sign of a warden. "I take it they never appear when they might repel attackers like those of last week?"

"Of course not."

He moved inside and I followed his indication to re-arranged piles of magazines set on the floor. The shop was back to its crowded but more or less orderly self. Seeing the journals now, in the calm of the shop, my heart sank somewhat. They were of large format, bulkily stacked and doubtless heavy.

"My goodness," I said. "There's more of them than I remembered."

He waved an apologetic hand. "A rather random set of runs, I'm afraid. Incomplete, as I advised you, but these early issues are hard to find. Many families remember having the twentieth century ones, especially from the thirties onwards in the case of the *Illustrated London News* but pre-1914 is much less abundant. I was obliged to purchase them along with more attractive volumes. Books are my forte, not general magazines, although one is always looking for certain stage publications. The bound copies of these in libraries are indeed heavy, causing librarians and porters to grumble. the *Graphic* ran from about 1869 to 1932

as I recall and was noted for the engraved reproductions of contemporary artists. Which would be your interest, I suppose?"

"More or less, Mr Goodston. Tissot, Luke Fildes and others."

"Indeed. There are those on the fringes of our profession
who, I regret to say, dismember the original journals in order to
sell the engravings separately."

"The equivalent of City asset strippers, I suppose."

"How apt a parallel, my dear sir. Hateful people."

The magazines were cumbersome, being somewhere about
eighteen inches by twenty-four in size, usually with a big illustration on the front cover under the title. Almost immediately my
eye met a picture of a villainous gang of turbaned brigands
encumbered with arabesque rifles of lethal appearance. They
were clambering about among mountain rocks, taking aim with
these deadly weapons. The caption proclaimed the picture to be
one of an Afghan Sungha, or rifle pit, and I realised that I was
looking at a contemporary report of the 1880 Afghan War.

Plus ça change…

I heaved a set up from the pile and got them out to the car,
returning for another load. When I re-entered, leaving the back
door up and open, he was moving out with a smaller stack in his
arms.

"Allow me to assist."

"Take it easy, Mr Goodston. Thanks all the same, but I can
manage."

The last thing I wanted was to overload the old boy, although
I supposed he was used to moving quantities of magazines and
books about. It didn't take me too long to load up but the car
had settled noticeably down on its springs by the time I finished.
I went in to thank him and found him facing me. A small suitcase stood on the floor beside him. There was a raincoat over his
arm and a battered trilby hat in one hand.

"Going somewhere?"

"Mr Simpson, since the lamentable fracas you so ably dispersed, I have become nervous. I have had strange telephone calls enquiring about abstruse books and publications in which I do not normally deal. The callers would not give a name when I enquired and they withheld their numbers from automatic enquiry. It is as though someone is checking on my presence. The other night someone tried the front door. One caller, a strange woman's voice on the telephone, asked if I had copies of a French or Belgian magazine entitled *La Nouvelle Perspective Artistique* of pre-1914 date. Have you ever heard of it?"

"Never."

"Nor have I. She would not leave a number when I offered to enquire elsewhere and call her back. Yesterday a man I have never seen before peered into my window. I did not open up but he spoke through the letterbox, asking whether your magazines were for sale. When I told him they were sold he became persistent, asking how much more I would take for them and so on, as though conducting a Dutch auction. I had to become firm. He then asked about the Mrs Belloc Lowndes books and seemed irritated when I advised him that those, too, have been sold. He loitered on the pavement much too long for comfort. I picked up the phone and he left. My shop is suddenly a source of unusual attention."

I tried to reassure him. "Business picking up, perhaps?"

"You are too kind. I have a central core of excellent but aged collectors, yourself excluded of course, with whom I deal mainly by post. I may be set in my ways but my business has proceeded on predictable lines for years. Most of my esteemed clients are almost friends. Suddenly that has all changed. I don't like it. There are vagabonds about here but I distrust sudden coincidences. My feeling is that my recent purchases are somehow causing this unwanted interest. Your intervention has scared off immediate threats but I sense others waiting in the wings. Once they realise you are not normally in attendance they may return. So I have taken steps to discourage further interest. I have managed to dispose of most of the material I bought from the various ladies I mentioned to you. I have locked the Flemings and the Eliot away in a secure cupboard upstairs along with other precious volumes. I have knocked out a lot of items, including the Mrs Belloc Lowndes and Georgette Heyer books, at a very small profit to trade contacts."

"The Belloc Lowndes books really have gone?"

"Indeed they have."

"Was there by any chance a copy of her novel *The Lodger* amongst the collection?"

"Of course there was. It would be a sad collection of her work without it." He peered at me curiously. "Why do you ask?"

"Just that Mrs Belloc Lowndes was a close friend of Osbert Sitwell's. The novel was inspired most probably by the account of how Sickert's landlady told him that she suspected a previous lodger to have been Jack the Ripper. Hence Sickert's painting of his room as *Jack the Ripper's Bedroom*. Which transfixed Patricia Cornwell when she discovered the painting in Manchester. This arose during the post-lecture discussions in Highton after I left you last time."

"Good heavens. Do you think that the novel could be the reason for the unwelcome attention I have received? The Cornwell woman's theories have received widespread publicity and there are always cranks pursuing Ripper theories."

"I don't know. It may be a coincidence and entirely irrelevant. Once one comes across a theme it is amazing how it tends to recur, setting strong muscular hares running off all over the countryside. My mind is a bit occupied by Sickert just now."

"Beware the lure of conspiracy theories, my dear sir. Life is a random process, without much construction."

"Exactly. I must suspend judgement for the moment. The book has gone, anyway."

"Thank heavens. These magazines are now almost the last items to be dealt with. I am sorry to have pressed you for collection but they remind me of that unpleasant man with the sharp nose. I wish to clear the decks, so to speak."

I tried to ignore the maritime analogy of preparation for violent action. "Very understandable. I don't think he'll be back, though. There should be no reason now why anyone would want to bother you, is there? Apart from the Flemings and the Eliot?"

"Theoretically not. But I am uneasy. I am not particularly superstitious but there is something about the estates of the deceased that disturbs me. Sometimes it is almost as though the late owner is watching, wishing to convey a message. I have had some odd experiences in disposing of libraries from deceased estates. Books left unmoved over a long period can yield unwanted secrets. I once found an unwelcome Last Will and Testament in a volume of *Cruden's Concordance*. The family were most upset – it disinherited them in favour of the Battersea Dogs' Home – but it was my duty to report it."

"Oh dear."

"Indeed. Old books are not as inert as they seem. I am not a believer in the paranormal but a racing man like myself has his runs of fortune, good as well as bad, which can be hard to explain. It makes one a bit fey. Since the episode with *Cruden's Concordance* I have become reluctant to wiffle through pages in the way I used to. I have acquired a superstition about such checking even though common sense and commercial acumen indicate that one should."

"I'm sure that's understandable," I answered gravely. "But as I recall you said that one lot of books and magazines came from a lady in Ladbroke Grove who is not deceased; merely resiting herself to smaller premises. Surely there is no evil genie there?"

His face clouded. "She is no longer with us, Mr Simpson. That is another source of unease and even distress. I had news the day before yesterday that she was found dead before she could move to her new flat. The timing is extremely inauspicious."

Needles pricked up and down my spine. "Dead?"

"Yes. She was a charming lady with a fund of Hispanic reminiscence and I am upset. She was very old, it is true, but was very vivacious when I saw her. I know these things can happen suddenly but coming so soon after my visit, the nasty events which you terminated and now these odd, rather sinister enquiries, I am discomposed."

"Mr Goodston, I am very sorry. But presumably her death was pure coincidence? She died of natural causes?"

"I assume so. I have not heard otherwise. She fell, it seems. In extreme old age it often proves fatal."

Another chill struck my spine. An image of Larry Granger and Dennis Cash at dinner came to mind. Veronica Chalmers, late secretary and Puritanical guardian of the Highton Art Gallery, had fallen too.

I shook my head to clear it of dread premonitions and looked at his battered leather suitcase. "So where are you going?"

"I have a distant cousin, a widower, more of a friend than a cousin, down at Cheltenham. He drives a motor car. We can visit races together and pass the time agreeably. With your magazines safely away the business can stand my absence for a week or so. I am a great believer in distance as an antidote to anxiety. With most of the material gone and the premises empty for a week I believe my evil genies will disperse. You may laugh but that is how I feel. I barricaded myself in after the visit yesterday and now I am off."

"I am not laughing, Mr Goodston. We all get peace of mind in our own ways. Cheltenham? Are you going right now? Do you want a lift round to the station?"

"How kind, but it is only just down the road."

"It's no problem."

"The walk will do me good."

I went to the door. I was trying hard not to let his anxieties transfer themselves to me. Images of old ladies falling and prowlers haunting Praed Street bookshops are disturbing. "Do phone me if you have any problems, Mr Goodston."

"How kind. But I shall be fine. Some days at the races will blow my apprehensions away, I am sure of it."

"I'll call when you get back. I may even have read *Imperial Brown of Brixton* by then."

He smiled. "I do not think you will find that a burden. I wish you luck with the magazines. My pleasure at seeing them go is tempered by the rational thought that they can not have been the cause of these recent, disturbing events."

"I'm sure not."

"In any case, even if they had some bearing on the matter, they now have a formidable guardian in yourself."

"You do me great honour, Mr Goodston. But I can't believe these old magazines can attract much by way of mayhem."

"One never knows."

I smiled an agreement and stepping outside, watched him lock up. He put on his coat and hat. We bid each other goodbye.

As I got into the car I caught sight of him in the rear view mirror. Suitcase at the end of one of his short arms, raincoat flapping, hat at an angle, he was proceeding majestically towards Paddington Station like a Dickensian clerk *en route* to a legal impasse. He did not look fey at all; evil genies seemed remote from that bulky progression.

I smiled as I let in the clutch and, weighed down a little by the ponderous piles of paper in the back of the car, moved steadily away down Praed Street.

His genies came with me.

"May I introduce you to Dr Grant?"

Larry Granger, immaculate in sports coat, flannels and foulard tie, gestured towards an ample lady who had just entered the gallery. "She is not only a distinguished art history lecturer and archivist but also a fellow Trustee. Dr Grant, Mr Tim Simpson. Tim, Dr Grant."

"Binnie," the bulky lady said, taking my hand firmly. "I'm Binnie Grant. I did so enjoy your talk the other night."

It was Tuesday morning, my first working day down at Highton. We were standing in the more commercial end of the premises. After meeting Larry Granger by the reception counter where Dennis Cash presided, I had wandered round to let my eye roam over the fresh impasto of a landscape, then looked slowly at the prints, the pottery, the glinting jewellery under glass cases and the occasional textile under Cash's proprietorial gaze. The walls looked clean and the spotlights caught gleams of lustre or broken outlines of sculpture, delaying my survey. This was where today's world set out its wares in hopeful arrangements, waiting for casual visitors to be so caught in a soft web of visual appeal that they would want to carry something away with them. This part of the gallery felt cheerful and active. Through an arch lay the more passive part of the building, where the Harland's collection and subsequent additions hung silent in suspense.

"Thank you," I responded to the new arrival. "I enjoyed it, too. I'm impressed. I didn't know the gallery had an archivist."

She smiled broadly. She was draped with a paisley scarf around the neck but was otherwise soberly covered in a long pullover and woolly trousers. Beside Larry Granger's trim cut she looked soft and bear-like, with a maternal hug for a pile of manila folders under her arm. I put her somewhere around sixty years old.

"I'm not really an archivist," she answered modestly. "I'm a retired art historian. I used to lecture in Hove and London before that. I'm just trying to get some of the Harlands documentation under control. It hasn't been looked at for ages."

"Dennis has more than enough to cope with covering the exhibitions and this part of the gallery," Larry Granger explained with a gesture towards the besmocked manager, who bowed politely from behind his counter. "We don't like to call it a shop, by the way, because we do hold exhibitions here."

"I'll try not to offend, then."

"I'm sure Dennis will appreciate that. Binnie has very kindly agreed to get the historic records in order. Perhaps now would be a good time, while she is here, to go through to the gallery office. The other trustees, Frank Stevens and Kathy Marsden, will be coming in to meet you shortly. If that seems right for you?"

"Fine."

We progressed through the arch that divided the present from the past. In the calm of the rooms further into the building the paintings looked sombre, as though produced by artists with an inward turn of mind. Without spotlights the space was shadowed and inert. The passive nature of these inner chambers conveyed an air of anticipation despite the limited daylight that came from a large bay window at one end, a window with a sliding diamond-scissored grill for security. Lacking a flood of artificial bulbs or the presence of pacing, speculative visitors, the swirls of impasto and flat planes of colour on canvas, board and paper looked quiescent, producing a muted appeal quite different to the impacts intended.

Larry Granger snapped a series of switches and light flooded the walls. The paintings sprang to life, momentarily altering in the way that television images do if the contrast knob is twirled. Then they settled down. The eye caught sight of interiors, landscapes, still lives, portraits, boats, beaches, shores, streets and cliffs. A splattered abstract surprised by its random lack of subject matter. I stopped to take it all in before speaking. I had seen it briefly on my evening visit but there was a lot to absorb.

"Quite a Camden Town collection, isn't it? That's a nice little Gilman."

It was Binnie Grant who answered. "The Harlands were keen on them. Or rather George was. He met some of them over in Dieppe and the north coast of France. He prowled about North London quite a bit, too. That's why there's a section of darker scenes."

"And this is the Sickert nude."

"It is."

We were standing in front of the gallery's celebrated painting, staring at the splashed cuts of paint that made up a fat nude woman on an iron bedstead. There was a dressing mirror on a table and the window exhibited a spike, actually a church spire, in the distance.

"It is indeed," Larry Granger echoed gravely. "Mornington Crescent. The position of the church spire, demolished now, fixes it."

"Bit squalid, eh?"

"Sickert was into realism of that sort." Binnie Grant smiled. "Perhaps it's a man's painting. Not like your Mary Godwin the other night. It was George, almost certainly, who acquired this. I hope to find the details of when and where in due course."

"What about Jane Harland?"

"She liked a lighter touch. Of course she did like some of the women artists who studied under Sickert. Sylvia Gosse, Wendeela Boreel, that kind of thing. She would have liked Mary Godwin. But she preferred Newlyn in the twenties and thirties. Dod Procter and Laura Knight. Plein air techniques brought over from France. Pont Aven and its followers. We haven't got important ones like Stanhope Forbes but there are some good examples of lesser work. More spontaneous, perhaps, than the RA entries some of them submitted."

"It's a remarkable collection for – for –"

"For a backwater like Highton?" she smiled.

"I wasn't going to say that." I grinned back.

"Nevertheless, it is. Both a backwater and a remarkable collection. We don't do it justice. That's why I've made a start on the archives. They will allow us to provide students and researchers with valuable information."

"Sounds like an excellent project." I tried not to seem condescending. "I expect you'll turn up all sorts of unexpected things. You'll become a celebrity in this field, I'm sure."

Gratified, she dimpled softly. "Flattery will get you everywhere with me. But I've only just started, really. I expect to get on from the early years towards the more important period, when they started the Collection, over the next few weeks. The gallery wasn't their original objective, of course. They lost both children and their tragedy was our gain. Richard Harland died in a car crash in 1957 and this, coupled with the death of their daughter Mary in 1942, whilst serving as a nurse during the Blitz, left the grieving Harlands with a resolve to leave the Collection to the public. When George died it and the house went into the Trust."

Larry Granger gave her one of his long, blue-eyed stares. "It will be intriguing research, won't it? I mean, I realise that we have most things well catalogued but more background information will add enormous benefits. Especially if the details as to origins can be arranged so as to be accessible to scholars." He turned to me. "We'll use visual computer recording if we can get help financially. The gallery should really get publicity from that."

"Oh yes!" Binnie nodded enthusiastically. "That sort of provenance work is highly valued. It will be a long time before I can get through it all but it's fascinating material. For me, anyway. And it won't end with the correspondence and purchase data. There's a pile of supplementary documents, catalogues of exhibitions over a long period, art magazines like *The Studio* and many others. Even some French and Belgian and Dutch ones. Super raw material for scholars."

"Drawing open the myth-encrusted curtains of the past" murmured Larry Granger. "The desire of every historian at work everywhere, I'm sure." He put his expression into a curious mode. "I wonder what unsuspected tableaux your archives will reveal?"

Binnie Grant stared at him, disconcerted. I felt a strange shiver go down my back. The past, in my art collection experience, has produced many unpleasant episodes in the present. I quickly erased the incident at Mr Goodston's and images of falling widows from my mind.

"I don't know anything about tableaux. I do know about facts." Binnie Grant recovered her brisk assurance and summoned what must have been her long experience in dealing with audiences to respond to Granger, as to an unwanted heckler, with authority. She held up a manila folder from under her arm to emphasise her point. Her voice sharpened. "We shall be rewarded with the facts about our precious heritage. Don't you think?"

"Excellent." Her Chairman sounded just a touch nettled as he looked at his watch. "I'm sure Tim will be glad to cover the whole project with you in much more detail. In the meantime, shall we progress to the office? I'll get Dennis to relinquish his post at the counter and open up for us. I'm hopeless at security systems."

* * *

Further into the gallery there was a solid oak door, locked and apparently alarmed, which Dennis Cash tackled with confidence, using keys and a control panel expertly despite his artistic appearance.

"The office." He opened the door with a flourish, showing a tumble of desk, files, shelves and equipment inside. Light flooded in from another big bay window from which, despite small leaded panes, there was a fine distant view over the water meadows towards Newhaven.

My eyes took in stacked tiers of files and books, a big pedestal desk, a plan chest, an easel in one corner loaded with prints, filing cabinets, a table with photocopier, a computer and monitor on the desk, a printer over in a corner. There were papers everywhere.

It looked like chaos.

"Gosh" I said. "What a smashing view."

"Marvellous, isn't it?" Binnie Grant put her pile of manila folders down on the photocopier table. "This was George Harland's own office, well, study I expect he called it. He and Jane shared the studio upstairs but this was George's own den. It's a fine room really, square and quite high, as you can see. This bit of the house was eighteenth century. A prosperous wool merchant built it."

"It's lovely. How lucky you are to have it."

Dennis Cash looked rueful. "I don't get into it that much. That's why it's such a tip. My time is spent out there or packing things up. The Friends help a lot, but the onus is on me. You may find it odd because I live in the flat above the gallery but I'm usually too busy to tackle this room the way I should."

"It's a great office. Or would be if it were tidied. What is all this stuff?"

"Records and correspondence since things began. Documents of all sorts. Current accounts and deliveries. The other is all packing materials and cartons. It's a hell of a problem to have enough space for it all. There's a storeroom in the other part of the building but it's always full of cartons and bubble wrap."

I took a steady look round.

"What's that?"

On the walls, where there were no shelves, were one or two prints and drawings. I pointed at a pencil drawing of a street scene with a café with tables outside it, highlighted with watercolour.

Dennis Cash smiled. "Well spotted. That is rather unusual. I put it here because I like it."

"Who did it?"

"A man called Turner."

A frisson of alarm shot through me. The name was still fresh in my mind.

"Turner? No relation of..."

"Joseph Mallord William? No, I'm afraid not. This is John Doman Turner. He was a very minor Camden Town man. The unusual thing is that if you look him up in Wendy Baron's book on the Camden Town School she lists only two known drawings by him, both in private collections. One is of Montvilliers and the other, which was owned by Spencer Gore, is of St Valery-sur-Somme. I found this one in the print store, well, actually in a plan chest full of prints upstairs about a year after I came here, so Wendy Baron wasn't to know. It's St Valery-sur-Somme too. The title's pencilled on the back."

"I like it. Was he any relative of the great Turner?"

Dennis Cash chuckled. "I don't think so. He was a stockbroker's clerk who took tuition from Gore by letters because he was deaf. Wendy Baron says he was working round about 1911 to 1918 but he was still alive in the late thirties. He must have travelled round the northern French coast like they all did. Very little is known about him."

"He was a pupil of Spencer Gore's?"

"Yes."

"Maybe you could find something out about him from that angle."

"I believe Frederick Gore did something along those lines but I haven't seen it. There simply isn't time to do all that kind of curator-style work, academic research, when you're running a contemporary scene as well. To be honest, it's not my scene at all." He smiled. "Now that we have the luck to have Binnie doing it, I leave it to her."

"Well." Larry Granger had turned brisk again. "I expect you'll want to look at some figures, Tim. Our bookkeeper lady, Sylvia, only comes in on Monday and Tuesday mornings so it's a good

time to catch her while she's here. Now you've seen the layout
do make yourself at home. You can use this office as much as you
like provided you can find a surface to perch on but Sylvia's
cubby hole has a spare chair too. You'll probably be better off
there most of the time. I'll show you the way."

"Thanks. That sounds fine."

"Do ask Dennis for any facts you need, too. Binnie and I are
mere trustees. Ours is the distant view; Dennis has the detail at
his finger tips."

I turned to Dennis Cash, who looked a little apprehensive. I
guessed he had a busy morning to attend to. His broad frame
spoke a silent idea to me.

"How about my buying you a pie and a pint at lunch time?"

His face relaxed.

"That would be great," he said. "Just the ticket."

I turned to Dr Binnie Grant and smiled as I spoke. "See you
soon."

She smiled back. "I look forward to that. Oh, Dennis –" her
address made him turn towards her – "I've been through all these
folders but I can't see that any are missing."

He shook his head slowly. "Then it's a mystery."

Larry Granger hastened to explain. "The late Veronica
Chalmers had, we believe, a folder from this office with her when
she died. Unfortunately, no one knows which one it was and it
doesn't seem to be at her house. If we can't establish that one is
missing from here it will be difficult to trace." His blue eyes rested on Binnie Grant once again. "Binnie and I were allowed access
to her house. We found nothing, I'm afraid."

There was almost a challenge in the way his stare was on her
but she just shook her head slightly and smiled.

"Well," said Larry Granger. "We mustn't waste Tim's time with
our small filing problems. We must get on. If you can look a bit
more Binnie, if you have the time, an explanation may emerge."

"It may," she nodded to him, rather stiffly.

"Oh." He paused. "I almost forgot. Bill Riley is in town tonight. He asked if we would like to go over for a drink, round about seven." He looked at me. "I thought it might be an opportunity for you to meet the remaining trustee. We are fortunate that he agreed to join us last year. The other two should be upstairs in the studio by now."

"Fine," I answered. The celebrated Riley would have to be met some time. Best as soon as possible.

"Binnie?"

"Me too. Seven, then."

"Dennis?"

"I'm afraid I can't." Cash sounded genuinely regretful. "Something else booked for tonight. A blues session in Newhaven I booked to go to a long time ago."

"Pity. Another time, perhaps."

"Oh." Binnie Grant sounded regretful as she turned to Dennis Cash. "I was going to come back here again later. To use the photocopier. But don't worry. I can let myself in."

He smiled. "My loss," he responded gallantly. "I'll make you an evening coffee next time."

Larry Granger was anxious to get on. "Tim?" His manner was still brisk. "Shall we see the others before you get to it with the bookkeeping Sylvia?"

I moved away from the desk. "Lead on, Mr Chairman. Let us forget the myth-encrusted curtains of the past for the moment and see if we can assemble a crystal ball with which to glimpse the future."

His manner changed. He chuckled and turned to the others. "We've hired a clairvoyant. Exactly what we need."

* * *

The upstairs studio was the large room in which I had given my talk. It had a big skylight set into the roof at one end, above a window that gave another fine view over the Ouse meadows and Newhaven in the far distance. Standing in the middle of the now clear space were a man and a woman, both smiling slightly in an anticipatory way.

"Tim Simpson," Larry Granger was in full chairmanly mode, "allow me to introduce you to two more of my distinguished fellow trustees. Firstly Kathy Marsden, Tim Simpson."

"Hello," said the slim dark woman to whom he bowed slightly, holding out her hand to me. "This is a pleasure. Someone to help us at last."

"Kathy," said Larry Granger, still proprietorial, "is the only genuine artist amongst we trustees. Dennis paints of course, so artists do have a significant presence in the running of things, but Kathy is nominated to us by the Royal Academy, no less."

"Of which she is a distinguished member," I responded, shaking her hand. "I do of course know your work very well. And admire it. I had no idea that Highton was so fortunate."

She smiled broadly. "Don't overdo it, Tim, you'll make me blush for shame. I live in Hove. I rather think that when the RA found it was their duty to nominate someone as a trustee they looked on the map and decided that I was the nearest. So that's why I'm here."

"Surely not."

She kept her smile. "How gallant. Now I remember: you found *Kermesse*, didn't you?"

"I did." The reference was to a painting of Wyndham Lewis's which came to light after various shenanigans.

"We are honoured, then, to have so distinguished a collaborator. My humble contribution to the gallery stems from my proximity in Hove; yours has real provenance."

"Nonsense. Tim is right. We are indeed fortunate." Larry shook his head reprovingly at her. "Kathy is a great contributor to our group, Tim. As is Frank Stevens, nominated by the town council. Frank, Tim Simpson. Tim, Frank Stevens."

The man with whom I now shook hands gave me a quick smile and nodded at Larry Granger. "Larry's told us all about you. Welcome to Highton. We are all looking forward to working with you, Tim. The gallery needs help."

He was oldish, ruddy faced, with a slightly nervous expression. I found later that he had a successful ironmongery in the town and in Lewes, now mainly managed by a son with himself as senior partner.

"Frank is a connection with the founding Harlands, aren't you, Frank?" Larry Granger looked on him tolerantly, as though encouraging a shy offspring.

Stevens gave him a quick grin. "Now that Veronica's dead, you mean? Yes, remotely." He turned to me in explanation. "My father was a friend of their son, Dick. He was killed in a car crash back in 1957. My dad used to laugh about Dick's complaints that the house was full of paintings. His parents couldn't resist buying them, he said. Luckily for us."

"Luckily for us," echoed Larry Granger.

"But Veronica knew the parents. The Harlands themselves. Now that she's gone there's no one."

"None." It was another echo.

"Hope Anderson was another but she's gone, too, quite recently. Before that it was Madge Taylor. Jane Harland had quite a lot of women friends in the town. My father used to say that Jane Harland had the biggest old witches' coven in the area after George died. This studio was full of them, brewing up and chattering while she painted."

"God." Kathy Marsden was emphatic. "I couldn't bear that. No way could I paint in that sort of scene."

She looked quite fierce as she spoke. She was rather a dry, slim lady somewhere in her forties and her dark clothes made her look even thinner. Her work was not as well known to me as I pretended but I had seen it at the Summer Exhibition for a few years. Rather disturbing imagery in unfashionable Cubist-

Vorticist mode came to mind, with Hieronymus Bosch's infernos something of an influence. Animal figures with birdlike heads mixed with humans in one canvas that stuck in my memory bank; it was vaguely sexual and had the swirl of Burra's sardonic view of human downfall. Hard to reconcile with the cool control of the person now in front of me.

"Well," Larry Granger was still in the chair. "You've met us all now, Tim. Just Sylvia to follow. I know I speak for us all when I say you are absolutely free to buttonhole us on anything at any reasonable time."

"Of course," they both chimed in response.

"Um, Bill Riley has invited us all round for a drink this evening. He's in town as it happens. Can you come? It's short notice, as usual."

"Sorry." Frank Stevens shook his head. "Town Council meeting tonight."

"Ah. Pity. Kathy?"

"Sorry, Larry. I'm off back to Hove after I've left a painting with Dennis. Next time, perhaps."

"Of course." Larry Granger turned to me with an air of finality, as though the answers were exactly those he had expected. "Well. Sylvia awaits us, Tim. Unless you have anything for Frank and Kathy now?"

"Not yet, no." I smiled at them. "I'll look forward to talking to you both later."

"Excellent." He rubbed his hands crisply together as they smiled back. "In that case let us without further ado start the assembly of your crystal ball."

The pub Dennis Cash chose for the pie and pint was a quaint timbered place called The Dolphin. It was in a side alley that allowed its back windows to look over the wandering water meadows of the Sussex Ouse. We sat in a woody corner on padded benches and awaited the arrival of ploughman's lunches whilst we sipped Harvey's bitter beer, from the Lewes brewery which provides that slightly burnt flavour of bitter you get in Sussex and Kent. I wasn't complaining.

"You'll find us a bit of an odd outfit," he said, with a grin. "Trying to ride two horses, we are. One is that of a contemporary gallery and the other a museum of paintings. I expect that you'll conclude that we fall down between two stools."

"Oh, I doubt that."

"Kind of you. Wait and see. I'm afraid I'm not very good at the museum bit. I admire the Collection, of course, enormously, no one could do anything else, and I'd love to see it expanded. The Curator role has never been my forte though; dealing with the arts authorities, all those padded administrators and pontificators about Art with a capital A, gets my teeth on edge. They all know so much better yet they can't do anything and they never come up with any money." He took a sip of beer. "God, I'm beginning to sound like Larry."

I laughed. "Your chairman has resounding views on the arts establishment."

"Oh, he's absolutely right of course. And we're lucky to have someone so dedicated to help us. With any luck Larry will make the place move on a bit. Against the wishes of some of Highton's older residents maybe, especially the FHAG element, but move on we must."

"I sense that he and Binnie Grant don't altogether see eye to eye on the way forward, do I?"

He smiled carefully. "Not entirely, no. She's perhaps a little more, how shall I put it, politically correct, more open to – to being –"

"Culturally diverse and socially inclusive?"

"Precisely put. Although I tend to side with Larry on a lot of the nonsense surrounding current official policy. We had an arts advisor from Tunbridge Wells on one occasion who asked if we had considered producing the explanatory labels beside our paintings, the ones that everyone seems to read before they look at the art, in Braille. I had to lie down and have a gin and tonic while I thought about that."

I chuckled. "It was a serious suggestion?"

"What she meant was something to do with the visually impaired rather than the completely blind. But there was no offer to meet the cost of doing it. You can imagine Larry's reaction."

"I can indeed."

"All of his Foreign Office style went into a wonderfully cryptic broadside. 'Your representative advocates expenditure by the indigent for the illumination of the invisible' is just one of the sentences I remember. They haven't really liked us since. Not that it matters. They withdrew their small financial support over seven years ago. That wasn't Larry's fault."

"The figures Sylvia showed me are a bit depressing, Dennis. You seem to do a great job in the shop – forgive me, but it's easier for the moment to describe it that way – but the public role, the exhibitions, lectures, educational workshops, the maintenance, the conservation, cataloguing and so on, put you severely into loss."

"Tell me about it. The funds are steadily diminishing. With the latest Stock Market falls and low interest returns it's only a matter of time. It was always a matter of time unless someone refunded us but it was a long time. Now, the end is in sight. Maybe eight years, maybe less and we go phut."

"Your grasp of finance is admirable."

"It's not that long."

"No. But much can be done in the meantime."

"We are counting on you, Tim."

I winced. "I gather there have been several fund raising efforts in the past?"

"All came to very little. Ask for money for a Fire Brigade, or St John Ambulance, or the local lifeboat and the public stump up. An art gallery: forget it."

"But it's a cultural feature of the town. Lots of visitors come to it. Free entrance and all that. It should receive official support."

"The town council have no cash. Ask Frank Stevens, he's our local council trustee. The county have other fish to fry. Regional arts funding, as Larry told you at dinner the other night, is a multicoloured roundabout for somebody else. Street festivals and video circuses. Five thousand pounds for performance poetry and themed competitions. Painting is out of favour all right."

"Has Bill Riley come up with anything?"

"Not so far. He keeps an eye on the investments but –"

"But what?"

Dennis Cash looked round cautiously then at me. His voice dropped. "It may be wrong, I'm no finance man, but my impression has been that he's not doing all that well himself these days."

I nodded thoughtfully. No one was happy with the investment scene right then, least of all White's Bank. "It's a difficult time," I answered blandly.

"Don't take the word of an art gallery manager and painter on financial matters, though."

"You'd be surprised how connected the two worlds can be."

"In your case, perhaps. It's just a gut feeling but he's less ebullient these days. More thoughtful. It's a sore point with Kathy and Frank, I should tell you. They think there's not much point in having Bill around if he won't stump up, or at least get one of his City mob to stump up for us. I'm afraid that art is always on the scrounge, Tim."

"Tell me about it. You paint in your spare time?"

He grimaced. "I still think of myself as a painter. I took this job as a temporary measure to make ends meet. Years ago. But I paint, yes." His expression turned rueful. "When I'm not looking for missing folders. I hate admin."

"Oh, the Veronica Chalmers, missing file mystery? It seems to preoccupy Larry Granger. Which folder do you think has gone?"

"No idea. Not a clue."

I tried to bring logic to bear. "How did you know she had one? If there's nothing apparently missing?"

"I saw her go off with it." Dennis Cash spoke positively. "The day before she fell. I wondered what it was. I was busy serving at the counter and she'd spent some time in the office. The Friends use the photocopier and the PC for their mailings. It wasn't unusual for Veronica to be in there but she didn't usually take things away. I just caught sight of her as she passed the window to the street. That's what made me curious."

"So you told Larry Granger?"

"I did. When I heard about her death. I mean, I disliked her, I won't beat about the bush, but it was a shock. She seemed indestructible. But the incident was curious." He smiled apologetically. "You must think us very parochial, watching things like people carrying folders for want of anything better to do, but it was odd."

"Oh I can assure you that missing folders cause big bangs up at the Bank. Missing folders are no parochial matter."

"She was very preoccupied that morning. There'd been a meeting of the Friends the evening before – a talk on Whistler by Binnie Grant – and I thought someone had upset her. She wasn't fond of me but she usually observed the niceties, although not always. The day before she was particularly condescending before going off to lunch with an old niece of the family who'd come down to Highton for the first time in ages. Quite a coup for Veronica to rub her Harland connections in our faces. The next morning she went straight past me to the office like a terrier after a rat. That's maybe why I had an eye out for her. For what she was doing, I mean."

"You're not familiar with all the folders in there?"

"Good God no. You can see what it's like. Letters and documents going back to the twenties. Heaps of them. Various people before my time have had a go and generally made matters worse. But Binnie is methodical. She'll get it straight. It'll take time, but she'll get there. Everything annotated and ticketed and plastic foldered. I'm lost in admiration; it would destroy me but it's a kind of treasure trove to her." He hesitated, then looked full at me. "I think Binnie would prefer someone running the gallery who's more administratively inclined. More like her. There's a faction in the Friends – Veronica Chalmers was one of them – who resent the contemporary side of mine. They see things Veronica's way too. They'd like to keep the place a sort of art museum. A shrine to the Harlands. Not my way at all."

I smiled. "The museum aspect would only make sense if you had public funds or could charge entrance fees or if the archive were to prove an asset. One that could be used for income."

"Don't bet on that, Tim. Researchers in the art world come with integral tin bowl at the ready. Like artists." He paused for a moment. "We need to sell contemporary work. It's the best way to supplement income. All museums do some sort of commercial shop; look at the National Trust. Talking of researchers and Binnie though, it's a funny thing, but – since Veronica fell –"

"What?"

"Well, Binnie and Larry used to disagree about matters of principle in the role of the gallery but it was always amiable disagreement in a civilised manner. Now there's a much sharper edge to it. Larry seems quite put out about something. He looks at Binnie in a way he never did before. And he insisted on accompanying her to look for the missing folder. He's never bothered about the archive that much until now."

"Did he get on well with Veronica Chalmers?"

"Good grief, no. She was anathema to him. All that the old worst of Highton could dish up, in his opinion. 'Religion without charity and art without vision' was one of his judgements on her."

"And Binnie Grant? How did she fare with Veronica?"

"Much more sympathetic. Didn't like her opinions and disagreed on the role of the gallery, but was very patient with her. There were times when they were quite cordial with each other. Can't say that I could manage it with Veronica. She was awful. I wanted to kill her the day before she died. She rubbed my nose in her Harland superiority and wouldn't let me chat to the old niece." He smiled apologetically. "This must all seem like terribly parochial gossip to you."

"Not at all, Dennis. It's valuable background."

"Anyway, I asked Felicia Apps, who's taken over from Veronica at the Friends and who's got her keys to the gallery and so on, whether she could go through Veronica's papers and see if she could find anything. She's much more amenable than her predecessor and she did look. But she found nothing either."

"So it stays a mystery for the moment."

He nodded as our lunches arrived and we moved on to matters of contemporary arts and crafts. I was getting to like him. It seemed that behind the exuberant clothing there was a practical solidity, a man of fundament. His judgement of what to sell in the gallery certainly seemed good; he had an eye. The vision of the person in charge is what makes or breaks a place and it seemed to me that Dennis was doing his side of things pretty well.

We finished our meal and I went to the bar to pay up.

"Snap," said a quiet voice beside me.

I turned in surprise to see a long legged, oldish johnny in tweed houndstooth jacket and cavalry twill trousers smiling at me from behind a jug of Harvey's. It was a classic country outfit except that holding his soft Viyella check shirt collar together was a maroon and gold Hawks Club tie identical to my own.

"Snap is right," I said, smiling back. "Mine was for rugger."

"I know. So was mine. You're Simpson," he said, holding out a gnarled old hand as he looked at my nose. "I remember you. Tim Simpson aren't you? Front row man."

I took the hand and got a firm shake. "I am. Sorry, I don't –"

"Of course you don't. I'm Macintosh. Gilbert Macintosh."

"Heavens, I'm sorry. You were the renowned full back in – in –"

"In the year dot," he said with a grin. "I watched you play in the Varsity match but you couldn't possibly have watched me, not even from your pram. I've heard of your art fund, too. What brings you to Highton?"

"I'm helping the gallery a bit."

"Aha! Thought you might be, seeing you with Dennis Cash. They certainly need it." He let his blue eyes twinkle in a leathery face. "I'm a member of the Friends and I get the newsletters, you see. Sorry I missed your talk the other day."

"You live here?"

"I do. Retired here quite a while ago after my wife died."

"Oh, I'm sorry to hear that."

"Bit of a backwater but it suits me. Good golf area if you like links courses. She'd have hated it. Mustn't hold you up but perhaps we could share a noggin or two if you're going to be about?"

"That would be great." I was looking at a rugby legend of his time, a Cambridge blue like me but a Scottish international to boot. "I will be around on and off for a while."

"Look out for me in here." He smiled. "Old habits die hard. Time on my hands."

"I'll do that."

"I promise not to bore you too much but if I can help in any way, local knowledge, that sort of thing –"

"I'd appreciate it. Very kind."

He nodded briefly and I nodded back. I meant what I said, too.

"It's a small world," said Dennis Cash, as we left. "Gilbert's a good customer of mine. He goes to FHAG meetings despite their being mostly hen gatherings. Which is more than I will do."

I smiled abstractedly. For some inexplicable reason I was wondering whether Gilbert Macintosh had been at Binnie Grant's talk on Whistler. The last meeting Veronica Chalmers had attended.

Small world was right: Highton was suddenly becoming interesting.

Chapter Nine

Some time in mid-afternoon my mobile phone rang. I put down the sets of figures Sylvia the bookkeeper had provided with a sigh, hauled the mobile out of my pocket and pressed the necessary button.

"Tim?"

"Sue! This is a pleasant surprise. Nothing wrong, I hope? Is William OK?"

Sue doesn't usually call me during the working day nor I her unless there is an emergency of some sort.

"No, nothing like that. William is fine. It's just that I had another call from Mr Goodston."

"Oh?"

"He couldn't reach you at the Bank. He seemed upset. Well, I'm not surprised. Apparently his shop has been burgled and ransacked. He came back from a trip away to find the place in chaos."

"Oh dear. Poor old Mr Goodston. I wonder what all that could be about."

"You mean you don't know?"

"No I don't. Should I?"

Her voice became tinged with a mock patience. Always a bad sign. "He said – I use his very own words – that after the unpleasantness which occurred on your penultimate visit he felt you ought to know."

"Did he?"

"I repeat: the unpleasantness which occurred on your penultimate visit? Unpleasantness? I assume that is Mr Goodston's archaic code for some utter violence of some sort, is it?"

"Sue! It was merely a misunderstanding. Some men I thought were bookies' men were shaking Mr Goodston down. I persuaded them to desist and they left the premises. It now seems that they were thieves."

She sharpened. "You denied all this to me when he called

before and I said I had a premonition of violence. You actually said that his use of the word deliverance was merely – I quote – an example of his dated sort of parlance, full of abstruse imagery."

It's amazing what memories women have. For some things. Words in particular.

"My dear sweetheart, I did not want to disturb you with unnecessary irrelevancies. A pair of opportunists at a bookshop seemed unimportant. I merely assisted them off the premises. I'm sorry to hear that whilst he was away with his cousin at Cheltenham they seem to have returned. Or someone like them."

There was a silence whilst judgement was being arrived at. Then: "I knew you were being evasive. I just knew it. But what on earth could they want in that old shop? He doesn't keep cash there, does he?"

"No. At least, not much. But then drug addicts are after anything they can get."

"If that is who they are rather than bookies' men."

"He says he doesn't owe the bookies anything."

"Ha! That is what he says. If it is true is another matter. I have to say that somehow I can't imagine mad book collectors raiding Mr Goodston. But bookies, yes."

"You never know. He gets some quite good stuff. A set of Ian Flemings isn't small beer these days. His aren't inscribed like those in the Rechler sale in New York but mint first editions of *Casino Royale* have been going at six to eight thousand pounds at auction recently. Even slightly tatty copies of *James Bond* firsts get fifteen hundred odd."

"You mean he's got a set of *James Bond* first editions?"

"He has indeed. Acquired recently from a widow."

"He didn't say if they'd been stolen. The place is in such chaos that he was dreadfully upset."

"Poor old Mr Goodston. I'd like to throttle those two."

"But why did he specifically want you to know about this break-in?"

"Mr Goodston is old and I think he's pretty lonely. I'm one of the few people he likes to chat to. God knows I don't get there very often but it was lucky I turned up when those two were threatening him. He was very grateful. He was probably bursting to tell someone. Or maybe the police have asked for witnesses and descriptions."

Her voice softened. "Poor old man. Of course the police will go through the routines. You must help if you can, Tim."

"I will. When I get back from here."

She thought for a moment. "It couldn't be anything to do with those magazines, could it?"

I was ready for that one. "What on earth for? Trade people buy them to break up for the illustrations. I can't believe a mad librarian would go to those lengths to get them. If you need to see them you can always go to Leicester Square or the British Library's place at Colindale. They've got the lot."

"That's true."

"Have you looked through them yet?"

"The ones you left here? No. And it may be a while. You better look through yours first. I have to go in to work tomorrow, by the way. There's a complete security review after those thefts in Amsterdam. Not that we've got any Van Goghs in Tate Britain."

"Van Gogh yesterday, the odd Constable tomorrow. Or a Turner. That reminds me: what do you know about John Doman Turner?"

"The deaf Camden Town sketcher?"

"Wow, I'm impressed. Yes, the deaf Camden Town sketcher. They've got one of his down here in Highton."

"Really?" Now I had her interest. "Frederick Gore did a thing about him. Spencer Gore instructed him by post. Chalk or charcoal rather than pencil and patterns of light and shade; he thought Turner drew too much in outline. I thought there were only two known works."

"That's what Wendy Baron says, apparently. But Dennis Cash here found one in a plan chest. It seems that George Harland got it during his travels round Dieppe."

"Oh, that's interesting, Tim. Really it is. I'll have to tell Pete Carver at work tomorrow – he's mad on Camden Town painters. He'll probably come rushing down to see it. Odd that it's not much known."

"The Highton collection hasn't been much publicised or properly catalogued. There's a lady historian called Dr Binnie Grant doing an archive job right now. I have to say the Doman Turner sketch isn't an eye-stopper, though."

"But you lit on it right away."

"How true. The office it hangs in is so chaotic I had to let my eye roam around to find something positive to comment on. You've never seen such a heap of junk."

She chuckled. "I can't imagine you down in that place, sorting out the filing. But it will be good for your soul."

"Thank you. I shall come back straight away."

"That would be domestically delicious but professionally unpalatable. Jeremy would not be pleased."

"Bugger Jeremy."

"Tim! Get on with your work."

She provided an endearment or two and rang off. I sighed and looked round the cubby hole in which Sylvia, a maiden lady of precise habit, grubbed out the Highton Art Gallery accounts. It was not inspiring.

An image of the Doman Turner sketch came to me. I needed stimulus; the office might provide it.

Time for Timmy to go walkabout.

* * *

The office was empty. Dennis Cash was behind his counter, dealing with a group of visiting Belgians who had arrived unexpectedly. Larry Granger had come in to talk to a local worthy about funding and was holding forth in the studio upstairs behind a closed door which let out only murmurs of voices. The box files, piles of papers, shelves of ledgers and more box files stood in dusty silence at my arrival. I looked out of the long window at the fine view and then back inside again to wonder where, if the job were mine, I would begin to organise this mess.

On the wall was the sketch by John Doman Turner, a square in a French town with a tree and a café and shutters on long-windowed houses. No relation of Reggie Turner even if both had frequented Dieppe, Reggie with worthies like Sickert and William Nicholson quite apart from the *Yellow Book* crowd like Aubrey Beardsley and Henry Harland.

Connections were beginning to worry me. The Henry Harland who was editor of *The Yellow Book* was a bit like Reggie Turner: another forgotten novelist, an American not related to the Harlands of Highton. The name, like Turner, simply provided more confusion.

All those cross currents in Dieppe, all those artists and people from England coming, going and staying; even Larry Granger, delving over there for something, found the place magnetic. Why hadn't I yet mentioned my Reggie Turner book to him? Was it a reaction to my earlier desire to appear too knowledgeable, my childish wish to impress? Or was my new reticence due to some other instinct?

I leant forward to look closer at the Doman Turner sketch and put my hand down on the surface of the pedestal desk used by Dennis Cash and others. I almost dislodged a folder left on the edge of its surface and caught it quickly before it fell. In putting it back in position the folder opened slightly. I stopped in curiosity: there was a bit of an old magazine inside.

The illustration on the full page, when I opened the folder wide, grabbed my whole attention. The sheet was creased and rumpled, as if it had been folded up in someone's pocket. A strong smell of foreign tobacco, like that of Gauloises or Gitanes, wafted into the air as I opened up. The effect was to imbue the revealed illustration with a frowsty redolence of France, as though the previous owner had kept a pungent indulgence close to vivid imagery.

The painting faithfully reproduced on the magazine page was not exactly uplifting. It suggested a scene of despair. A man, fat and coarse, sat on a hard wooden chair, his thick moustache drooping with misery or neglect. He had removed his jacket and his stout, waistcoated torso sprouted two creased white arms encased in the stiff shirting of Edwardian times. His thick body was hunched forward. A sparsely haired head was held in both hands, looking down at feet encased in brown boots. You could almost smell the sour sweat that would tinge his armpits and suffuse an area around them with its tart fetor. He looked dejected.

It seemed as if he was disgusted with himself, at the prospect of what he was about to do, or maybe had just done; it was not clear what stage of events the scene depicted. The painter had deliberately allowed an air of mystery to imbue the composition.

My eye was soon distracted from the man.

On a bed beside him, recumbent and porcine, the swollen body of a woman was presented to the viewer. It was deliberately rebarbative. Fat flesh was lividly highlighted, breasts lolling heavily. The feet were towards the eye and one leg was drawn up, knee outwards, so that the dark pubic vee and its darker crease were startlingly thrust at the vision. Her arm was crooked under her head on the pillow, raising a puffy face surmounted by a crown of fuzzy hair. Under the bedstead on which this bloated body reposed there was a ceramic chamber pot. It was as though the artist revelled in the depiction of squalor. For an old painting it was a shocker. Only much later could scenes exhibited by, say, Stanley Spencer or Lucien Freud have been more explicit. It was not clear whether she was alive or dead.

Not far from me as I looked, silent in the passive space of the collection was the Mornington Crescent nude the Gallery already possessed, with its suggestive iron bedstead full of impressionistic folds of overripe nude flesh glinting, contre-jour, under its grimy window.

Sickert in the folder and Sickert on the wall nearby.

"It's a cross," I almost said out loud, looking up from the magazine scene to think for a moment, "between *The Camden Town Murder* and *What Shall We Do For The Rent?*"

But I kept stumm; what the hell was this pungent sheet doing here?

It was a mystery.

This magazine picture might have been painted at 6, Mornington Crescent sometime in 1908 or 1909 like most of Sickert's nudes – the one in the gallery was typical – but more likely in one of the studio-rooms he rented round the corner. The events that inspired it happened much earlier, at 29, St Paul's Road, now called Agar Grove, on the 11th of September 1907, when Emily Dimmock had her throat cut.

It was important to get these things right.

I turned the crumpled sheet over. The magazine it came from was French or maybe Belgian. The title hit me like a blow: *La Nouvelle Perspective Artistique.*

Chills went up my spine. Mr Goodston had said it quite clearly: a strange woman, on the phone, asking if he had copies of a magazine called *La Nouvelle Perspective Artistique.*

I hate coincidences.

From the style, it looked like some sort of provincial publication of around the First War period. There were so many magazines in those days, all over Europe as well as Britain; cheap reproduction of images had become tremendously popular. The page seemed to have been ripped out. Maddening. It must have been a pretty bold journal to be brave enough to publish this illustration nearly full-page in size. Its history would have to be researched.

Was that what Binnie Grant was doing? If so, why? This wasn't, obviously, part of the Highton collection. It seemed to be a hitherto unknown canvas in the Camden Town Murder series and hence an enthralling find.

The vision of Mr Goodston, hat in hand ready for departure, still persisted. Someone, a woman he had definitely said, phoned up asking if he had any copies of a magazine called *La Nouvelle Perspective Artistique*.

Of which he'd never heard.

Upstairs the studio door opened and voices rang down the stairway as Larry Granger descended, talking to an invisible man as they moved into the hallway by the front door. Instinctively I closed the folder, making sure it was back in its original position. Then I moved quietly across the room to switch the photocopier on.

"Tim?"

The voice startled me. Dennis Cash, broad and colourful, stood in the doorway looking at me. I turned to grin at him.

"Hi, Dennis. Visitors all gone?"

"Yes. Are you OK?" He seemed to glance round quickly. There was a faint implication that I was somehow out of place. "Got everything you need?"

"Just cranking up the photocopier, if it's OK with you."

"Oh." He seemed relieved at my explanation. "Of course."

In the moment that followed, Granger came into the room.

"Tim!" His voice was surprised. "What are you up to?" As he spoke I noticed that he looked quickly at the desk.

"Am I allowed to use the photocopier?"

"Of course, of course." In my imagination his voice also became tinged with relief. "I suppose Sylvia's figures need a little untangling?"

"Oh, Sylvia's a reliable lady. I just need some duplicates from the ledger. I was going to ask Dennis, but he was busy with some unexpected visitors. Didn't want to waste time. If it's OK I'll go and get the stuff I want to copy."

"Do use any of the facilities you need." He smiled graciously. "Don't feel you have to ask."

"Absolutely," echoed Dennis Cash.

"Fine, thanks."

"See you this evening at Bill Riley's."

"Look forward to that, Larry."

I smiled at him, gave Dennis another grin, and left.

When I came back from Sylvia's cubby hole, carrying some sheets of figures, both of them had gone.

So had the folder.

Chapter Ten

Bill Riley's weekend cottage was larger than most of the dinky little terraced houses in the town. It was a flint and timbered building set in its own walled garden, one requiring the attentions of a hired gardener to keep it in the spruce condition I observed as I walked up the path. Spring is a testing time for gardens and Riley's passed the tests. For a place presumably reserved for the odd weekend and holiday visit it was impressive.

My ring at the solid oak front door was answered by the man himself. A solid response to a solid door. He was thick set, almost burly, with thick hair and thick clothes for the spring chills. As I expected, he wore thick horn rimmed glasses. An expensive woollen sweater and oatmeal coloured trousers above suede shoes told me that this was off duty time; my recognition of him was due to photographs in the *Financial Times* or business pages elsewhere. In these he was always in regulation pin stripe and stiff white collar with silk tie. As head of Portarlington Investments, with public announcements to make, he had an image to maintain.

"Well, well," he said heartily, holding out a hand. "Welcome, Mr White's Bank's Art Fund. Come in."

We shook hands and I went past him into a beamed living room with an inglenook fireplace. Larry Granger was already standing in front of it, glass of sherry in hand. Beside him was Binnie Grant, with what looked liked white wine in hers. She had changed from her woolly suited outfit to something smarter in dark linen, looking slimmer and more shapely than the warm clothing had allowed.

"My wife Heather," said Riley, presenting me to a pleasant-looking middle aged woman dressed in crisp trousers. "Heather, this is Tim Simpson of White's Art Fund. Come to rescue the gallery. Isn't that right?"

I grinned as I did the necessary greetings and accepted a glass of wine.

"It's supposed to be just a feasibility study," I explained to his wife.

"But that should lead to solutions, shouldn't it? Not further words." Bill Riley was slightly aggressive. "You're here to cut down Larry's dragons, aren't you?"

"I'm afraid I left my shining white armour back in the City."

Heather Riley smiled. "You mean you do have some? Bill's never owned a suit of white armour, Tim. I think of him more as the Black Prince."

"Shards to you, too." He leered fondly at her before turning back to me. "The Black Prince, Tim, is a marital in-joke. He was infamous in France for the sacking of Limoges. I once dropped one of Heather's pieces – she collects the stuff – and have never been allowed to forget it."

"I don't have any here," she said to me. "Only pottery. Bill's like a bull in a china shop in this cottage."

So supposedly am I, I thought, in recalling my own dear wife's estimation as I looked at a Staffordshire tithe group. "It's a delightful room even without any Limoges," I said. "Your pottery suits its beamed solidity much better."

"Why thank you, kind sir."

The place was comfortably furnished without ostentation in a style one of the fashion magazines would call cosy, but expensive. My eye caught a Hockney print then a Sickert painting of Dieppe on the wall. Riley grinned as he saw me glance at it.

"Not bad for a crazed serial killer, eh?"

"The Quai Duquesne," I answered. "One of his favourites. That and the church. He was almost certainly there in 1888, or just up the coast at St Valery-en-Caux, painting away when the second and third Ripper murders took place."

He nodded briskly. "This was done later. Just about the time he came back to Camden Town in 1905. We cross over via Dieppe quite often en route to Spain in the summer so I couldn't resist it. But I agree about his being absent from London with his mother and brother at the crucial Ripper time, back in 1888."

"Ah," Larry Granger intervened with a knowing smile, "Don't be so sure. Patricia Cornwell reckons he was a genius at travel. A quick nip onto the Newhaven ferry for four hours or more. Then the train to London, rush along to Whitechapel, presumably by cab to Buck's Row – that would be on 31st August – or Hanbury Street, on 8th September – do the terrible deeds, then foot, cab, steam train and ferry back to Dieppe, even on to St.Valery, in time for breakfast. Public transport must have been much faster then or else it's absurd. Or did he stay in London unobserved the whole while, none of his family missing him at all?"

Riley chuckled. "They just omitted to mention, in correspondence, that he'd nipped back over the Channel for a quick rip of some female intestines."

"Even better," Binnie Grant's voice was amused as well, "is the double murder of Elizabeth Stride and Catherine Eddowes on 30th September. For which he must have got back to England once again, running from Berner Street to Mitre Square or vice versa before throwing down his apron in Goulston Street and writing on the wall. Then steam post haste back to finish painting a shop front in St Valery – the work is called *The October Sun* – by the 2nd October before rushing back to London yet again. On the 4th October he was genuinely recorded as having returned to execute some drawings."

"My goodness," Heather Riley looked at Binnie Grant with interest, "you are well informed, Binnie."

"Sickert was Whistler's assistant. I boned up for my talk to the Friends but I've always been fascinated by Sickert. I think Cornwell's barmy. As Tim said the other night, Sickert was strange and clandestine, but no case for his being Jack the Ripper has been proven to me."

"I agree." Larry Granger was, for this matter anyway, nodding at her. "But he was very odd."

Her eyes rested on him in rather the same way that I'd seen

him do to her in the gallery office. "Many lives," she said, steadily staring at him, "when probed retrospectively, are full of gaps, inconsistencies and puzzles."

He looked disconcerted. For a moment there was an awkward silence. Then she smiled. "I was quoting Richard Shone. His review of Cornwell's book in the *Spectator*. He was annoyed by the damage to Sickert. He called it an act of irresponsible cruelty."

"The *Spectator*?" Bill Riley boomed an interruption in something that sounded like a careful change of subject. "I never had you down for a *Spectator* reader, Binnie. Much too right-wing for you, surely?"

"Many lives," she responded, "are full of gaps, inconsistencies and puzzles."

That drew a relieved laugh from all of us except Larry Granger, who still looked a bit put out.

"I incline," he murmured, "to the view of Rebecca Daniels in the *British Art Journal*. Sickert's wish to represent urban realism was inspired by Degas, whom he knew well, and was intended to break the Royal Academy's monopoly on what was considered fit to paint. Prostitutes on iron bedsteads put up an uncomfortable mirror to society. Patricia Cornwell has entirely misjudged Sickert's beliefs and his overt thirst for publicity. Like many people – including those in this room – he was fascinated by the identity of Jack the Ripper. In this he was no different from thousands but he is disproportionately famous for the Camden Town Murders series."

"That's a reasonable *résumé*, Larry." Binnie seemed still faintly amused as she responded to him in what seemed to me a slightly condescending way, almost as archivist to amateur. "One wonders whether, if Francis Bacon had been contemporary and had produced something similar instead of screaming bishops and meaty naked gentlemen in grisly wrestling or copulative modes, some future Cornwell might not have gone for him, too."

There was still a tension between them, something indefinable that had me wondering why Larry Granger had taken the folder that might have been hers from the office that afternoon. Why was the Camden Town Murders series of such interest to him? Whose magazine sheet was it?

"My goodness." Bill Riley was wielding a bottle of white wine. "We are getting into the squalid side of art, aren't we? Or perhaps the intellectual pressure is higher than I can take. I was rather hoping to quiz Tim on his view of the gallery while we are together. What's your impression so far, Tim?"

I shut the magazine sheet out of my mind. "After only one day my impression is that I'm impressed. For such a small place it's a remarkable collection and a remarkably active gallery. I like Dennis Cash's commercial part best. Maybe that's because there are already so many museum-galleries but outside of big cities not that many that sell today's art. Whether the two things are compatible is the key question. From what I gather, the town likes the kudos but isn't prepared to pay for it. Or them?"

"It. Kudos is singular. From the Greek for glory or renown. But well said." Larry Granger had recovered his composure to indulge in a little old-fashioned didactic Classicism. "The public here is not like that of France. In France there would be outrage at the lack of funding for the gallery. My own preference is for an emphasis on the collection but that's possibly just old age speaking, or at least age's obsession with the past."

"It is, as ever, a question of the arts establishment's priorities." Bill Riley was, obviously, used to chairing meetings. "We have to assume that Highton will not come high on them. In this case there must be a limited number of options, of courses to follow. They are fairly clear. I wondered if Tim has defined them yet?"

"No. I haven't." I heard my voice go a bit short. "Not on day one. I've never been very good on instant solutions. Or immediate definitions of a problem. I like to browse a bit first and get the feel of a place."

"I understand that perfectly, even though you must have had

time to think before you actually visited us." Riley was reining in, only a little, the challenge of his question. "It is does not require much thought to clarify what alternatives are possible in a business sense does it?"

"No, indeed not. But then business has never been difficult intellectually, has it? Business is full of people whose education failed them, trying to make business an intellectual challenge. In most commercial situations the intellectual answer is easy to define. It is the practice that is difficult. It is in practice that businesses fail. Variables get out of hand. Chance plays so large a part. People fail to perform."

For a moment he looked taken aback, then he smiled. "I guess you're right."

"But this is not a business," Binnie Grant objected. "It is a public art gallery, open free of charge to anyone."

"It certainly is. And as such should be publicly funded. Or given a million by a benefactor of some sort. Otherwise it should not exist."

"Good gracious." Heather Riley looked at me with head on one side. "From Jack the Ripper to the gallery's extinction within three minutes."

"About eight years is the more likely time, given present expenditure and present trust funds. Enough time for chance and variables to play quite a large part." I smiled. "Or, as the man said in Henry VIII's favourite joke, for the horse to talk."

She laughed. "The king might die, I might die, or the horse might talk. There was only a year in that case, Tim. Then execution ensued."

"My wife," Bill Riley refilled my glass, "is an historian. Medieval England. It's why, in addition to the golf, we bought this place. Spain has much better weather for golf but Highton has the history. You've taken the right line with her, young man."

"I have three or four weeks, not a year, to make the horse talk. Whether execution will then ensue is not yet clear."

Bill Riley bared his teeth in a broad grin. "The ladies of FHAG are going to get into a rare frazzle if you use that kind of imagery my dear chap. We and they are looking for action, not endings."

"Oh, I have no intention of being contentious outside this room. Or confidential trustees' meetings."

"Good. Think of them as a gaggle of old hens and you'll find the right approach."

"Thank you!" Binnie Grant was sharp. "I'm a member of the Friends, remember?"

"My dear Binnie! You may be, but you're also a trustee. An entirely different sort of bird altogether."

Larry Granger opened his mouth to speak, formulated a silent word, and then closed it. I'm not a good lip reader but I could have sworn that the word was going to be "vulture".

"Forgive Bill." It was Heather Riley who spoke. "Bird is his chauvinist form of flattery where women are concerned."

Binnie softened. "In that case I'm flattered. I rather think I'm too advanced in years to be thought of as a bird. But the FHAG ladies are a lot more realistic than you might think. I wouldn't want Tim to get the wrong impression."

"I'm sure he'll charm them off their perches." Larry Granger smiled a bit too widely to be natural. "The great thing, as with all reports and presentations, is to gain sympathy but be trenchant. We can rely on Tim, after his recent talk, to keep the FHAG crowd on our side."

"They'll jolly well have to be." Riley was unrepentant. "They haven't much choice. Unless one of them wants to stump up the odd half million or so."

"Quarter of a million would be enough," murmured Granger.

"Or even a tenth of that." Binnie Grant seconded.

"You see," Riley turned to me with a cheerful grin, "how the scale of our respective views can be measured?"

"It gives me a sort of idea."

"Just wait until you talk to the other trustees."

"I shall of course do that. Larry has introduced me already."

He nodded approvingly. "Good. I'm sorry they couldn't come this evening. Frank Stevens is a sound fellow but Kathy Marsden is crucial. If it hadn't been for her I wouldn't be a trustee. She nailed me at one of those Art and The City evening functions sponsored by the Royal Academy – I was there as a guest – when she heard we had a weekend cottage here. In that sense she bears the responsibility for my presence. You know her painting?"

"I do."

"Not my cup of tea. But she's well thought of in art circles, I believe."

"Yes. I believe so, too." I refrained from saying that most Royal Academicians are. "It will be interesting to hear what sum of money she and Frank Stevens come up with after your estimates this evening."

His grin broadened. He gave me one of his solid, aggressive looks. "Indeed it will. I shall await your report with great interest, Tim. Very great interest indeed."

Chapter Eleven

In the quiet seclusion of my hotel room, in bed, I picked up *Imperial Brown of Brixton* by Oscar Wilde's loyal friend Reggie Turner. My section of the pile of magazines from Mr Goodston was still locked in my car. I had a quick look at one or two of them and decided that magazine illustrations, or at least one in particular, had played enough with my mind for one day. There was an agenda on the go, either with Dennis Cash or Larry Granger, that I'd stumbled on by accident, something involving Binnie Grant's research and the unfound painting of Sickert's illustrated in the French magazine. What that agenda was; why Larry Granger seemed hostile to Binnie Grant; why I was cautious about Granger and whether the folder I'd peeked into was the same folder the late, fallen Veronica Chalmers had removed I had yet to find out.

Why would Binnie Grant be photocopying in the office late in the evening? Who the hell had phoned up Mr Goodston? I hate coincidences; hate them. Binnie Grant, with her detailed Ripper knowledge, was the only obvious candidate in this chain of coincidence. She might even be in that office right now, as I retired early to bed. I sighed resignedly and tried to put the questions to one side as typical inventions of my fertile curiosity; there was nothing I could do about them just then. My consoling guess was that as my visit progressed the answers would emerge.

The wit of Reggie Turner beckoned from the page.

Now that the hurly burly of starting at the gallery had died down and the solid novel was in my hand it looked better than it had in Mr Goodston's shop. The lettering on the cover was strong and clearly the work of a professional; William Nicholson cut his design teeth on the wonderful Beggarstaff posters. His use of typefaces had a bold confidence. The cocked Napoleonic hat was, I found as the story unfolded, a clever reference to the story of events in *Mouleville*, a fictional version of Dieppe, which

Turner describes. The bee close to it was a sharp visual hint of Gallic Royalist lunacy, if you think of that sort of hat as a bonnet. Now that it was in my hands, in calm contemplation, I liked the object better.

The story starts with the eponymous Brown leaving his Wellsian Brixton Emporium in a huff with his fiancée and heading for France. There is a description of journey and travel which has the leisured pace and observation of stately days before 1914. The combination of foreign adventure using rail and steamer made anticipation more gratifying than the scrimmage of airport check-in desks allows. Brown dealt with importunate porters at the customs shed on arrival and rather slowly found his way to an hotel run by an English couple with inviting daughters. As the story proceeded I began to sense a loss of narrative drive. It was the work of someone disengaged, easy to read but lacking bite; Mr Goodston was right.

I was feeling tired. My day had been long and there were many impressions still to absorb. I wanted them to mature for a bit before sorting them out. The folder and its illustration nagged at the edges of my mind. The reading so far of *Imperial Brown* was enough.

I turned to put it on the bedside table prior to turning out the light and misjudged the unfamiliar distance. The book tumbled to the carpeted floor.

With a slight curse I heaved myself round and reached down to pick it up. My fingers engaged with only one part of the cover and the book fell open, endangering the spine. With another curse at my own clumsiness I got half out of bed and took hold of the book properly. It was then that my eye caught sight of a thin, folded piece of paper sticking out at the back.

It was a letter. It must have been compressed between the back board and the inside end page. The paper was rather fine quality and there was writing on both sides. I put the book down carefully on the bedside table and smoothed the folded sheet open. The writing was very neat, not copperplate exactly but near it, with that regular slope and tightly closed uprights and down loops of the style in which people were trained long ago.

Dear Madge,

Just a note to thank you so much for being such a sympathetic listener yesterday. Having someone whose discretion is assured and getting experienced advice is such a tonic when one feels so bottled up. I have no one else to turn to. Today George set out for Dieppe and points west along the Normandy coast once again, so I am trying to pull myself together while he is away. He assures me that the offending material is destroyed. My fears are somewhat allayed but I am ashamed to admit that I still have doubts.

You are quite right to say that time will resolve all this and that eventually it will come into perspective. Certainly I can find none of the awful things here, so it is unlikely that I will be upset by another sudden discovery.

Yet one never knows, never. There is so much good in what we have achieved and his motives are nearly always impeccable. It makes things so hard to understand. But no one can be perfect and life is life; all of us try for perfection but are bound to fail in some things.

You have been so kind. It is never easy to be the receptacle of unhappy confidences but yesterday you gave me new strength. We will meet again soon and I promise to restrain myself. Your friendship is much too valuable for me to burden it with my doleful predicaments.

Yours, Jane

I read it again carefully. There was no elucidation of who it was from or to. It wasn't an addressed writing paper, just a plain sheet. But there were brief hand written words at the top: *Ockley House.* Beneath them was a date: 18-10-38.

I stared at the letter with an electric sense of disbelief and incredulity making my veins tingle.

Above the door of the gallery, that same day, I had noticed an old, painted sign dating from the time when it had been a private residence. Before George and Jane Harland had given it to the town. The sign was faded and almost washed out by years of weather but still just discernible.

Ockley House.

Chapter Twelve

It was Dennis Cash, opening the gallery office in mid-morning after spending some time behind his counter, who found the body of Binnie Grant. She was lying inside the door, near the plan chest, face down.

Dennis apparently intended to go through the security rigmarole of opening the office door by cancelling the alarm system but found the place unlocked. His surprise at this was outstripped by the shock of finding that when he opened the door it pushed up against Binnie's foot.

He came stamping into the little cubby hole of an office of Sylvia the bookkeeper's in which I was already installed, looking like a wild steer in a panic stampede. At the impact of his entrance I looked up from a set of fairly straightforward but doleful figures, my mind still occupied by the Ockley House letter – I'd checked again and the sign was still there – and questions about *La Nouvelle Perspective Artistique* to see his white face mouthing at me in shocked anxiety through its surrounding beard.

"It's Binnie," he managed to get out. "I've found her. Dead. In the office."

"What?"

"Dead. She doesn't move. She's dead. She must be."

I jumped out from behind the desk and he turned without a word to lead the way through the gallery to the office. We practically ran together. When we got there, I saw a female shoe first, then an ankle then, as we moved carefully through the door opening, the whole body lying motionless on the floor.

She was still wearing the linen suit she had on at Riley's. Beside her were papers, strewn as though dropped by accident. Dennis Cash peered over her face, half visible beneath disarranged hair.

"It looks like head injuries," he said.

I took a quick look to see blood matting the strands at the

back of her head.

"Phone the police, Dennis, quick."

He did a sort of hop beside me. "I will. I thought I'd better tell you as soon as possible. There's no one else here but us right now. I'm not letting anyone in. Oh, God. *Awful*. She – how – she's *inside*. Place was unlocked."

"What, the whole gallery?"

"No, no, just the office. The outside door was locked as usual. Was when I got home last night."

"Was she – I mean – this morning –"

"I didn't come near the office last night, Tim. If she'd come in this morning I'd have seen her. She must have been here all night."

"Dear God." Now I was feeling shock. "She was murdered?"

"I – I – if it was an accident, I don't know how –"

"Please phone the police. Now."

He picked up a phone on the desk. I stood back, not feeling good, to take a quick look round. The photocopier wasn't switched on. The littered jumble of scattered paperwork and files I'd seen before seemed just the same until my eyes flicked automatically round the walls. Dennis's voice faded as I took in a blank space that needed a double-take to get my focus right.

The Turner, the John Doman Turner sketch, had gone.

Dennis Cash's voice cut back into my hearing. "PC Wallace says he'll be along in a minute and not to touch anything. The police station here closes at half past five and it's unmanned at night. He's alone in the station this morning. He's just come in from Denton. Where he lives. I expect the Lewes HQ will send someone."

The shock was making him stutter out these random details to me in short order as though he had to keep talking, to say something rather than nothing. His face was set in its pallor and his beard disarranged. Above the smockish garment he was wearing the effect was a bit ludicrous, like a William Morris figure chalky with outraged indignation and panic.

"Do you need any help?"

"No, no. I'd better go to the door ready for Wallace's arrival. I'll have to close the gallery completely, of course."

"Of course." My answer was automatic but I pointed at the wall. "The sketch has gone, Dennis. The Doman Turner sketch. It's not there."

There was a flash of widening eye-whites. His jaw dropped open. "What?" He stared at the space as though paralysed.

"You didn't move it somewhere?"

"Good God, no." Incredulity came on top of shock. "Oh Christ, surely someone wouldn't – I mean she must have disturbed – but how –"

His voice petered out. We stood there like a pair of prunes staring at the blank space until he suddenly pulled himself together and said, "I must check the collection."

He disappeared and I stood alone for a moment in the office, still stunned. An image of Larry Granger the night before at Bill Riley's kept coming to me. I was beginning to doubt my own vision, now.

Did he really mouth "a vulture" at the concept of Binnie Grant as a bird? And if so, what did he mean?

What had he done with the folder? Or did Dennis have it? He and Binnie Grant seemed close when they last spoke.

Dennis Cash interrupted my thoughts. His face came round the door with an expression like that of a bearded prophet apprised of an impending massacre of all the firstborn.

"What's up?"

"The Sickert." He came in and stood in front of me, clasping his hands together in an agitated wringing motion. "I've just realised it's missing. The Mornington Crescent nude, Tim. It's gone."

Chapter Thirteen

"My dear Tim." Jeremy White did a sort of agitated military two-step across the carpet of his office at the Bank. "This is appalling. Absolutely appalling. Is there nowhere – absolutely nowhere – to which you can be assigned which does not lead you almost immediately to invoke an homicidal avalanche?"

"How kind. I did not choose to go to Highton enthusiastically, as you may recall. Nor have I invoked, as you so charmingly put it, homicide, let alone an avalanche of the same. I have not stimulated, searched or otherwise rummaged in any way through the collection and personnel at the gallery, or pursued any course of action which might, in the most tangential manner, lead to murderous activity. I have merely started the objective feasibility study which it is the desire of this Bank and its client, the Highton Art Gallery, in the form of its trustees, to have carried out. In no sense of any kind can I be described as a major protagonist in the tragic drama which has ensued. And in case you had forgotten, I do not steal paintings for the Fund."

"My God you're in pompous form for a man to whom mayhem clings like glue. Don't try to pretend you're accident prone, either. I bet you were skulking in the shrubbery from the moment you got there."

"I do not skulk. There are no shrubberies. Damn it, I'd only just arrived. Hardly had time to be introduced and meet the trustees including your famous Bill Riley of Portarlington, who is quite an aggressive bugger by the way, at least where I'm concerned –"

"There you are! There you are! You've got right up the nose of our major prospect already."

"No, he's got up mine. I'll humour him but I don't do instant solutions. I'm not a spin doctor, either."

"You can say that again!"

"May I remind you that you said this assignment would be a

doddle? Easy as pie. Sledgehammer to crack a nut was the phrase you used."

"Sledgehammer? More like a piledriver by the sound of it. Gone about it like a bull in a china shop."

"*Et tu, Brute*? I have been particularly circumspect. I have carefully concealed information and material which might have offended or aroused suspicion. I –"

"Material?" His face froze in alarm. "What material? If you'd only just started how did you come by it? Offended whom? Suspicion? What suspicion? I knew it! I just knew it. You've set off a whole pack of strong muscular hares running all over the place haven't you? Murder has probably occurred due to theft and panic caused by your precipitate rummaging."

"Jeremy, the material I now wish I hadn't mentioned is of a bibliographical nature. It is purely circumstantial and coincidental. It can not have caused panic because no one knows about it."

"Ha! Knowing the way you go about things the whole of Sussex is probably well aware and stampeding for cover."

"Your confidence is touching. Almost as reassuring as the police."

"The police? Dear God, I suppose you've alienated them already, have you?"

"Not really, no."

"Not really?" he almost shrieked. "What does that mean? Your arrest is imminent, is it?"

"Oh, I wouldn't say that. The police always need a bit of time, you know. It may not happen for several days yet."

For a moment his eyes bulged and his expression reddened. Then he caught my eye. "You bastard! You've always been an absolute shit, Tim. How you love to wind me up." Then he grinned for the first time. "Tell me all about it while I send for coffee."

* * *

The interview room at Highton Police Station had been, if anything, slightly overheated. It was not very large, with one window, bare walls and a plain carpet. The chairs were covered in black vinyl and the table top was wiped clean rather than polished. Stripped for confession, you might say.

I repaired there at the request of Police Constable Wallace, a thin uniformed man with a thin straggly moustache struggling to thicken itself without much prospect of success. He asked me to assist in making a statement. When I got there he went through a long procedure of getting my rather brief version of events down while a team were crawling all over the gallery, especially the office. At the end of the form filling he was joined by a detective inspector from Lewes called Stamford. He was a rather grey individual with a morbid sense of humour.

"So," the new arrival said with a mirthless smile across the bare table, "it seems that what we have here is going on towards all the elements of the classic closed room mystery. *Murder in the Rue Morgue* and all that. Quite a challenge. What am I supposed to be looking for do you think? An orang utang?"

The Inspector's voice was not accented and his manner was not particularly aggressive. He was a medium built sort of man with a medium grey sort of suit. His hair was brown and his shirt was cream. He wore a green patterned tie.

"I'm sorry?"

"Edgar Allan Poe. *Murder in the Rue Morgue*. The first ever detective story, they say. Bit of a swizz by modern standards. Committed by an orang utang, you see."

The Inspector turned to smile at Police Constable Wallace beside him and got a gratifying grin in response.

"I'm afraid I'm not very much up on crime fiction."

The Inspector let his smile fade away. "You do surprise me, Mr Simpson. Really you do. You're a consultant investigating the affairs of the gallery, I believe?"

"I am, yes."

"I was rather hoping for a few clues from you, you see. Considering the elements of what we have here and the fact that only you and Mr Cash were in the place, I would have thought you might be an expert."

"No."

"A woman is found dead in a unlocked room inside locked premises. The unlocked room's security system is switched off. A valuable painting is missing, also a rare sketch of unknown value. There are no signs whatsoever of forcible entry. Mr Cash lives in a flat above the gallery. He is making a statement to a colleague now. You do not have a set of keys?"

"No, I certainly don't."

"So Mr Cash let you in this morning?"

"Yes."

"What time was that?"

"Nine o'clock."

"But the gallery does not open until ten-thirty."

"Not to the public, no. But I had work to do."

"Very commendable. How did Mr Cash seem when he opened up for you?"

"Perfectly normal. After a brief greeting he went into the commercial end of the place to rearrange some exhibits. I went to the bookkeeper's den. It was some time later that he went to the office and rushed back to tell me what he'd found."

"Hmm. I believe you have qualifications, apart from presumably accountancy ones, which particularly suit you to the study you are carrying out?"

"I am not an accountant. I am a director of an art investment fund, yes."

"Interested in Sickert?"

"We have drawings by Sickert. As it happens we don't have a major painting of his."

"But the Highton Art Gallery has? Or rather did have?"

"Yes."

"One of his rather, how shall I put it, rather seedy nudes in a seedy room in Camden Town?"

"Yes."

"Just at a time when this woman crime writer Cornwell claims to have solved the identity of Jack the Ripper as none other than the self-same artist? All of it out on TV then a much-promoted book? With the same seedy room depicted? So the painting is both very topical and valuable?"

"It seems so, yes."

"Quite a coup, isn't it, don't you think, for a crime fiction writer to have solved something all the world's experts, let alone the police, haven't been able to do?"

At this point the Inspector and Police Constable Wallace looked at each other and smiled broadly.

"I don't think Patricia Cornwell is right. Walter Sickert was not the Ripper."

"Ah. So you do have some knowledge of crime fiction as well as art, then. And I am told that you addressed the supporters of the gallery – the Friends – on the subject recently?"

"In a manner of speaking, yes. I might say they don't think Sickert was the Ripper, either."

"What about the dead woman? Dr Grant?"

"She was rather well informed on the Ripper dates and victims. She pooh-hooed Cornwell's assertion that he could have dashed across the Channel to commit the crimes and get back to paint work which is well documented as to dates."

"So you discussed the Sickert aspects with her?"

"I was at a gathering at Bill Riley's house at which the subject came up. Last night."

"Who else was there?"

"Bill Riley, his wife, and Larry Granger. The Chairman of the gallery."

"Ah. What time did you leave this gathering?"

"Some time after nine o'clock. I went back to my hotel and

stayed there until this morning. The porter will account for my movements."

"Perhaps he will. Dr Grant was still at Mr Riley's when you left?"

"Yes."

The Inspector sat back. "Let me run through another aspect with you Mr Simpson. Mr Cash has obligingly let us have a list of the other key holders to the gallery. You didn't ask for a key for yourself?"

"No. I've told you that."

"The office has a security system. You're familiar with that?"

"I've seen it opened."

"By Mr Cash?"

"Yes."

"Who else do you know has keys to the gallery? Who else might be able to open the office?"

"I think you'd have to ask Dennis that."

"Humour me, Mr Simpson. Who else do you know of?"

"There's Larry Granger. The Chairman of the trustees."

"Right."

"Doctor Binnie Grant, obviously, had a set. She is – was – a trustee, too. She needed to use the office."

"The dead woman. Right."

"Felicia Apps, of the Friends, has a set. They were Veronica Chalmers's."

"Ah. The Chalmers lady." The Inspector looked at Police Constable Wallace. "This is the one who recently fell and broke her neck? She was secretary of the Friends of the Gallery?"

"Yes, Inspector." Wallace nodded thoughtfully.

"I see. How unfortunate this is all becoming. Go on, Mr Simpson."

"Frank Stevens has a spare set. He's a trustee, too."

"Councillor Stevens? Of the Town Council?"

"Yes."

"Who else?"

"Perhaps one of the other trustees. A painter called Kathy Marsden from Hove."

"Would these people also knew the four-figure code to the alarm system?"

"I've no idea. Larry Granger said he was hopeless at security systems."

"He said that to you?"

"Yes."

"I wonder why."

"It was just a comment when I first arrived. Explaining why he needed Dennis to come and open up, I imagine. Is it important?"

"You have to see it my way, Mr Simpson. There is a strong smell of what we call an "inside job" about all this."

"I suppose there is."

The Inspector sat back and shuffled a file on the table top. "What might a burglar be looking for in Dr Grant's house?"

"What? What are you saying?"

The Inspector raised stagey eyebrows. "Oh, didn't you know? Someone has rifled her house. No obvious theft. But papers in her study have been severely disarranged."

"The archive? Someone's gone through the archive?"

The Inspector frowned. "Archive?"

"Binnie Grant is – was – going through the Gallery's Harland archive. Classifying it all."

"What exactly is the archive?"

"Letters and documents relating to the founders of the Gallery. The Harlands."

"Valuable, are they?"

"No, not at all as far as I know. Historical, but not valuable. Just of interest to anyone connected with the gallery, really."

"I see. Why was she going through them?"

"To get them in order. To provide a proper historical record of the gallery's founders for use by researchers and students."

"Wasn't that Dennis Cash's job?"

"No – at least – he has never had the time for it. She was an art historian. She offered to help and took it all over."

"And now she's dead. Hit over the head with a blunt instrument. Having presumably disturbed the thief or having knowledge of a lethal nature. Only the valuable, topical, sordid painting by Walter Sickert is missing and so is this sketch by a man associated with the same school of painting. And you haven't got one of either in your Fund up in London?"

"Now look here –"

The Inspector suddenly stood up. There was an air of finality about him. "I think that will do for the moment. Mr Simpson I would be obliged if you could give us any information which comes to mind which might assist us with our enquiries."

"Of course."

"Any detail at all which may be relevant. I am obliged to advise you that it is an offence to withhold any fact which might be material to this matter."

"I understand. I expect I shall have to suspend my feasibility study for the time being?"

"The Gallery is a Crime Scene, Mr Simpson. We have closed it. It will remain closed until forensics and the scene of crime officer and his assistants have finished with it."

"I see."

He went to the door at nodded at PC Wallace. "Mr Simpson is free to go. For the moment."

* * *

"Damned cheek," said Jeremy indignantly. "Implying that the Fund might steal a Sickert."

"What about me? Free to go 'for the moment'?"

"Well naturally you and this Cash chap must be the prime suspects."

"I beg your pardon?"

"You were both in the place with the body. No one else was. If her time of death was in the morning it could have been either of you. Or both."

"I like that!"

"Just theorising. Getting into the mind of the Force, as it were. They have to think along those lines. But this chap Cash must have first claim for their attention. After all, he had keys and knew the office security system. What's more he lives above the place."

"His flat is upstairs and on another level. You get to it by a separate door in the entrance. A set of stairs goes virtually straight up from that door. People with keys could come and go through the entrance hall without him knowing anything about it."

"He'll have to convince the rozzers of that."

"For Heaven's sake! What motive could he have?"

"Theft? He doesn't earn that much, does he?"

"No. What curator does? Sue's one at the Tate and they aren't on lavish pay. But how does he sell a hot Sickert? And a unique sketch by Doman Turner?"

"He punts it to one of these mad collectors presumably, like those Van Goghs from Amsterdam."

"You think he knows a mad rich collector? Say Bill Riley for example?"

"Tim! Riley is a potential client! I do hope Freddy Harbledown doesn't get to hear of your mounting antipathy to him."

"Dennis Cash says he thinks Riley is showing signs of monetary delapidation. Have you had Geoffrey check Portarlington out?"

He bridled. "Portarlington has a magnificent portfolio. Since when has an art gallery manager under suspicion of murder been an authority on investment management?"

"That's pure contentiousness. Since when has a golfing port-folio manager been an authority on art?"

"Tim! You're being deliberately difficult."

"I'm upset. I'm upset because of what's happened and I'm upset because I don't see Dennis Cash as an incompetent thiev-ing murderer. The whole thing is bizarre."

"Are you not upset about this woman Grant? Did you not like her?"

"Binnie Grant? She was pleasant enough. I think there was a tough side to her, though. She and Larry Granger were at odds about something."

"Granger is our client. I'm glad that at least you haven't taken a dislike to him as well. Don't go chasing after some theory that he's responsible in some way; we need him on our side."

"Oh, I get on with Granger all right." I decided to keep my reservations to myself. "We're quite the art-loving chums."

"Thank heaven for that. But try to take the longer view, will you? It's Riley we're after. The Highton assignment is small beer. A sprat to catch a mackerel. I don't have to tell you how things are in the City right now do I? I mean I don't have to –"

"No, Jeremy," I interrupted. "You don't."

Nor, I nearly added, do you have to make it quite so plain that business is more important than murder.

Chapter Fourteen

"My dear Mr Simpson." Through a front door cautiously cracked ajar Mr Goodston essayed a smile of welcome. "My very dear sir. Do come in. It is both a pleasure and a relief to find that it is you."

He opened wide and I followed him into the bookshop. Everything looked unremarkable and undisturbed, though slightly less dusty than usual.

"I have taken the opportunity," he said as we sat either side of his scarred oak desk, "to have a little clear-up following the disgraceful upheaval of my break-in. It is an ill wind, as they say, that blows no good. During the tidying-up – the place was in chaos – I found one or two items about which I had forgotten. Very saleable volumes they are, too. It is surprising how one puts items to one side in a busy moment and then they slip from the memory."

"It happens to us all, Mr Goodston."

"It may, it may. Rather more often as age advances, my very dear young sir."

"So did you lose much of value?"

He shook his head. "Indeed not."

"The Ian Flemings?"

"Are safe and sound."

"TS Eliot?"

"In his place."

"So what, then?"

"Nothing. That is the extraordinary thing, as I have informed the police. I can not find anything obviously gone."

"Nothing?"

"Nothing. The police say this is not unusual. It may be that I shall find something missing after a few days, when I come to look for a particular item." He smiled gently. "I rather think they find my shop such a jumble that I could lose almost anything in it and that missing items might not reveal their departure for a long time."

"That is not so, Mr Goodston, at least not in general. It has always struck me how well apprised you are of an item's where-abouts."

His dated circumlocution is infectious.

"You are too kind, my dear sir. I try to keep tabs on things as best as an old memory can. In my youth I was something of a demon at the game of Pelmanism, a great memory training and ideal for an antique or antiquarian book dealer. But I am not as sharp as I was."

"You still can't think what they were after?"

"Indeed not. Even what cash was on the premises I stuffed into my pocket as I left for my holiday. So there was none for anyone to plunder. It is strange. My desk here was ransacked but there was nothing of value in it. I have to say that once I ascer-tained all this, the local police's interest declined sharply. They do not even seem to be interested in descriptions of my intrud-ers. With nothing evidently gone, it is apparently difficult to bring charges and they are very busy chasing terrorists, bursting into mosques, that sort of thing. Doubtless much more exciting than my humble books."

"Inexplicable, then."

"All may yet be revealed. So far however, it is a disturbing mystery."

Perplexed, I frowned. Behind his desk he peered at me curi-ously. Any minute now he was going to ask me the real purpose of my visit.

"Mr Goodston, it is I know considered somewhat imperti-nent to enquire into a dealer's sources. I would not raise the mat-ter if it were not relevant to an important matter with which I am presently concerned. But if it is not too much to ask, can you tell me from whom you obtained *Imperial Brown of Brixton*? You see, I have found a letter folded inside the back cover which could perhaps be returned to its owner."

He took off his glasses, rubbed his nose for a moment and thought before replying.

"I appreciate your principles Mr Simpson. They are most correctly stated. Your reluctance to enquire is most circumspect of you. But in this case do not concern yourself with my concealment of sources. The book came from the lady resiting herself to smaller premises in Ladbroke Grove. She was called Mrs Anderson. Mrs HB Anderson to give her full name."

"Was? You mean she's –"

"Dead? Indeed I regret to have to advise you that yes, she has passed on. She was the lady who sustained a fall shortly after I took delivery of most of her library. She never made her move. It was all very tragic. She and her husband had returned here after a long retirement in Spain. Not long after they came back he became ill and died. After quite a long interval of widowhood she decided to move to smaller premises but alas events overtook her."

"Some of my magazines came from her?"

"Indeed they did. Her late husband had intended to acquire missing issues from the chronological sequence but never got round to it. The Ian Flemings were his also. Commercially I have no qualms of conscience about her, I have to say. I gave her a very fair price."

"I'm sure you did, Mr Goodston. Was there any family, do you know?"

"Indeed not. Had there been any, the books would have gone to them. She was quite specific about it. The couple had no children."

"So my letter has no possible returnees."

"It would seem not."

"Oh dear." I sat back. "In that case you have answered my query. The letter is not important in a bibliographical or even ephemeral sense but it was on my mind."

"How admirable. Many people would not bother. You have an advanced sense of duty, my dear sir."

"Ah. Well." I was feeling hypocritical now but I didn't want Mr Goodston to be the recipient of knowledge that might endanger him. "I have tried."

"I am sorry I can not assist further."

"Maybe you can. You said that someone phoned up asking whether you might have come across a magazine, French or Belgian, entitled *La Nouvelle Perspective Artistique*."

"I did. A woman did make such a call."

"No idea who? No address to recall? No number to contact?"

"None. And when in trepidation I dialled 1471 it advised me that the number had been withheld."

"And you've never come across the magazine?"

"No. Do I sense that you now have?"

"A page from one. With a Sickert Camden Town Murder series painting illustrated on it. Torn from the magazine."

"Good heavens! Scandalous! Barbaric. People are such vandals. Why do they do such things?"

"Now that's a good question. Presumably for a clandestine purpose. For reasons of shame, perhaps. Or maybe because the painting is an undiscovered one."

"Have you got this illustration?"

"No I haven't. It vanished pronto. I believe that one of two people has got it."

"Then you must show enormous circumspection my dear sir. One who desecrates a magazine for clandestine purposes must be approached with great caution."

"Very true." I got up. "I must go. It's a pity we don't know who called you about it. If there's ever another call –"

"I shall contact you at once."

"Thanks."

"Kind of you to drop by. Let us hope that life can return to normal now."

"Indeed." A thought struck me. "You say they ransacked this desk? With your account books in it?"

"They certainly did. Everything was in a terrible jumble. The drawers were still open and my ledgers tossed about."

"I see."

"Do you find some significance in that?"

"Er, no. Not really. Just curious, I suppose. I must be off. Thank you, Mr Goodston."

"Take care, my dear sir, please take care. I am still in your debt for my deliverance. I know that you sometimes tread a perilous path. I hope not at this time?"

"Not right now, Mr Goodston. Not right now."

I smiled at him and left. I was thinking hard. Whoever ransacked through those account books would know that White's Art Fund had made a purchase by cheque from Mr Goodston, almost immediately after the punch-up with the two thugs. They also knew that the magazines had gone.

Was that what they really were after?

Chapter Fifteen

"My goodness." Sue smiled wickedly. "Talk about a bull in a china shop. Smashed crockery and missing folders everywhere."

"Thank you."

She was sitting on the big settee in front of the fireplace, over which Clarkson Stanfield's marine painting of hulks and an Indiaman on the Medway congealed its watery scene in oil forever. I was in an armchair to one side.

"I did think that you'd be safe for a few days down in Highton. I really did. I should have known better, shouldn't I? It's not just the environment that does it. I used to blame Hastings before but now I realise I was wrong. It's you. You are a magnet to mayhem. You only have to arrive in a place for pandemonium to break out. I really feel quite sorry for those old biddies down there. They thought they were getting a nice sympathetic banker and art investment boffin to look at their gallery. Whereas in fact they got a combination of Mars and Dionysius."

"War and bibulous disorder? That's a bit over the top, Sue."

"I bet Jeremy's had a few stronger things to say."

"He did go on a bit. I had to bring him up short. You know how he gets sometimes."

"Surprising, isn't it? I can't think why. He sends you down to a sleepy picturesque backwater to do a simple survey of a small gallery and try to win the sympathy and respect of a golfing financier. What happens? In no time at all, on the way there in fact, you're pounding the guts out of two bouncers, widows are hurtling to their deaths, folders are stolen, bookshops are being broken into and a lady art historian has been bludgeoned to death inside the office of a locked gallery, the only persons present being you and its curator. While her house is being ransacked."

She paused to take breath and I managed to get a word in edgeways.

"I like the way you manage to interconnect all this –"

"It is interconnected! You are the interconnection!"

" – when there is, as yet, no such connection."

"Except you."

"That's purely coincidental."

"No, it isn't. I know you too well for you to get away with that one."

"What do you mean, 'get away with'? Stop talking as though I were involved in some sort of clandestine subterfuge."

"Ha! That's a good one. Knowing what I do about you, if I were that police inspector – Stamford? – I'd arrest you right now. Peace would break out immediately."

"Charming. My own wife. Supportive as ever. I am your husband, remember? In your eyes I can do no wrong."

"God! With your back history it's amazing you've still got a wife."

"Prejudice and disaffection ill become you. Don't push yer luck, doll. You enjoy solving these little problems as much as I do."

"Maybe I do. Or did. But there's William to think of now. You're a father, remember?"

"Really? I had no idea. When did this happen?"

"Tim!"

"I thought the noisy little bugger I was pushing down Onslow Gardens the other day was someone else's."

"Very funny. I agree I have liked being involved because if I weren't God knows what you'd get up to. And I can't stop you. I know that. The only stricture I have to make is that anything that does happen doesn't involve William."

"Ah. With that I am in absolute concordance."

"You promise?" Her voice had changed timbre to one I recognised as having real warning notes in it.

"I promise."

"Don't break it, Tim. I'm telling you: if William is in any way threatened or in danger I'll find it hard to forgive you."

"Rest assured. I am trying to foresee all eventualities. Which leads me to a question: have you had time to look through those magazines – the *Graphic* and the *Illustrated London News* – yet?"

"I've had a very quick whiffle through but not really, no."

"Pity. Doesn't matter, though. I'm taking them away with me tomorrow. I have a vague worry that they may be connected with Mr Goodston's break-in and I don't want their bad karma, or whatever the right New Age nonsense word is, to cast its aura here."

"My goodness, we are getting superstitious in old age. But if you do think they carry a threat then yes, get them away from William."

"The people who broke into the bookshop know that White's Art Fund made a purchase. They probably know that the magazines are involved. I hope they think they are at the Bank. I certainly don't want them thinking they're here."

Her face went serious. "In that case, take them quickly. I shall be extra vigilant about locking the place up and keeping William carefully watched if I'm not here myself."

"Good. How did the security meeting go at work, by the way?"

"The usual thing. It's not as though we've got any Van Goghs or Monets at Millbank, though. They're the popular targets right now, it seems. The break-in at Amsterdam was a bit odd: they took two early paintings and not perhaps the more valuable ones from his later work at Arles or even Paris."

"Maybe their client already has some of those."

She smiled. "It'd be a hell of a collection if he had."

"It might be a she."

She tossed her head. "Never. Men will be responsible."

She looked terrific; she always does when she gets emphatic and passionate about things.

I moved towards her.

"How about my getting in a curry and we have a snuggle on the sofa afterwards?"

"How vulgar! You've got a nerve. Certainly not!"

"Prejudice and disaffection," I said, getting up and closing in on her regardless, "ill become you, my dear."

Chapter Sixteen

Kathy Marsden's flat in Hove was in a big old Victorian house at the back end of one of the long avenues leading to the sea. It overlooked a park and might have been in somewhere like Clapham for all the presence of the seaside you could detect. Traffic buzzed along a rather busy road parallel to the promenade a quarter of a mile away.

She opened the door almost as soon as I rang the bell and smiled quickly.

"You've come down from London pretty smartly."

"Needs must when the devil drives."

Her face went back to being serious. She led the way into a large room with an easel and all the trappings of painting activity, brushes and pots and clutter on tables and shelves around its sparse walls. Big canvases were stacked along one side. The impression was one of frugal working conditions carried out in cold light from a big window at one end.

"It's awful," she said, turning back to face me once we were in the room. "Binnie, I mean. I really liked her. She was a marvellous break for the gallery. She was doing an enormous amount. No one bothered with all those archives before. It made me feel really guilty."

"She'll be greatly missed. It's a terrible event."

"Why? Why? What danger could Binnie have been? Why kill her? Just to steal the Sickert and the Doman Turner?"

"No one knows. The Sickert is pretty valuable. The police aren't saying much."

"I hope to God they find the culprits soon. I hate the idea that art can destroy in that way. The commercial aspect of it, I mean."

She looked very sincere. Her face was creased with concern. I nodded in what I hoped was a sympathetic style whilst reflecting that I, as the representative of commercial interests, was probably a major villain in her mind.

"It will give the gallery the kind of publicity it really doesn't need," she went on, "just at a time when something might be done. From your work, I mean."

"Well. Let's hope the publicity won't be too lurid. Although the police are very interested in me and Dennis right now."

"Oh, that's ridiculous! Dennis couldn't possibly be involved. And you – well – I can't imagine that they'd suspect you. It's absurd."

"Thank you, Kathy."

"Are you going to go on with your work?"

"Oh yes, as soon as I can. I'll go back now and see how things are shaping up. Larry Granger will want to know my intentions."

Her face softened. "Thank heavens. We need to get things on an even keel as soon as we can. Larry has been a marvellous chairman and given so much time to the place. He loves Highton and the art gallery is his special thing. He's done a lot in his way to help Binnie, too. With the Harland material, I mean. Not that he needs much urging to go over to Dieppe and all that sort of thing."

I smiled. "Larry told me he finds Dieppe an important English art venue."

She smiled back. "Indeed he does. All those artists like Sickert and those were always around there. He thinks the place is wonderful."

"We had a discussion about that my first night in Highton. Sickert and his family knew Dieppe well."

"The toothless brother, the one-eyed brother, the brainless brother and the paralytic old mother? They certainly did."

I blinked. "I beg your pardon?"

"I'm quoting Wyndham Lewis. He went over there to attend a mistress's discreet accouchement with one of his several illegitimate children. Which is why he hated Dieppe. The vitriolic remarks about Walter's family in a letter to Sturge Moore were despite Sickert's hospitality and kindness to him."

"Sounds like Wyndham Lewis." I glanced round the studio, taking in work in progress. I had been wrong to think about a Burra influence in her painting. She was Cubist-Vorticist all right: an image of the *Reading of Ovid* portraits owned by Osbert Sitwell came to mind. Wyndham Lewis and his beaky, toothy Tyro paintings were more relevant to her sharp, bird-headed figures than Burra's soldiers at Rye. Odd that she should know all about Sickert and his family, his Ripper alibi in the sense we had discussed the evening at Riley's, and their sojourns in Dieppe. Although no, it wasn't odd; anyone with any knowledge of modern English art history would know all about that.

"Speaking of Wyndham Lewis –"

Her voice broke into my thoughts.

"Yes?"

"Could I see *Kermesse* some time?"

She was referring to the large Cubist painting once advertised vengefully for public sale at a derisory price by a man lampooned by Lewis. It was lost for many years until, almost by accident, I acquired it for the Fund.

"Of course. I would be happy to arrange a private view for you."

She smiled almost skittishly, face lighting up. "That would be really great. In London? A private view?"

"In London. A private view. It's big, but let me know when you are coming up and I'll make sure the Fund store brings it out for you."

"I really look forward to that." Her manner seemed quite flirtatious. Then, suddenly, changing: "What was it that you particularly wanted to ask me?"

I hurried to adjust. "It was about Bill Riley, really."

"Oh?"

"I don't want to tread on any toes, you see. I gather that you were the one who persuaded him to become a trustee?"

"I suppose I did. I met him at an evening reception at Lloyd's that the RA set up. Art and the City, that sort of thing. No one bought mine. Somehow he mentioned he was off to Highton that evening. I followed it up. Well, to be fair, Larry and I followed it up. Nabbed him in his house – he calls it a cottage – a few weeks later. Why do you ask?"

"I just wanted to get my mind clear about his role. He hasn't offered any sponsorship has he? Funding, I mean?"

Her expression was rueful. "I'm afraid not. Frank Stevens and I were rather hoping he'd put up some cash. He's a conscientious trustee but he hasn't offered us any money so far."

"Just wanted to make sure I'd got it right."

She looked at me oddly. "I'm sure Larry would tell you all this."

"I'm sure he would. But I like to hear everything from the horse's mouth, if you'll forgive the expression."

"Like the police, you mean?"

I winced. "I didn't mean it that way. Just wanted to be sure everyone gets their version correctly over to me."

"Very punctilious." She was cool now. "I approve. I'm afraid I have no solutions to offer you on the gallery's monetary situation though. I'm a painter and no good at money. I'm glad you're on the case for that reason."

I smiled and glanced round at the sparse surroundings that seemed to confirm her statement despite the prices I seemed to remember her paintings fetched. She didn't let anything go cheap.

"Thanks. I'll do my best. Well: I have to get back to Highton."

"Good luck, then. I won't let you forget about *Kermesse*."

"It will be a pleasure."

She let me out rather briskly and I stood on her doorstep, uncertain as the door closed. It had been a strange conversation. I could understand that she wasn't good at organisational finance. I could understand that even though her paintings were expensive her gallery would take half the proceeds and maybe didn't sell very many. I believed in her concern about Binnie Grant. It was the shaft of knowledge about Sickert and Dieppe that was unsettling me. Over everything that had happened at Highton those seedy scenes seemed to brood: the painting, the magazine, the squalid images, the theft and murder.

You could come to believe in Mr Goodston's superstitions about the deceased if you weren't careful.

Walter Sickert? Jack the Ripper?

I shook myself like a ruffled dog and strode back to my car.

It was time to face up to Highton.

Chapter Seventeen

"Well, well." Gilbert Macintosh put down a jug of Harvey's bitter and gave me a long amused stare. "Quite a carry-on, isn't it? No sooner do you get here than one of the trustees comes to a sticky end. Behind locked doors at that. Poor old Dennis Cash has been released on police bail but the town is in an uproar. Half of them say he did it and half of them say he didn't."

I looked own at my ploughman's lunch of cheese, crusty bread and pickle before replying. I hadn't been near the gallery yet. I had flinched again and popped into The Dolphin for lunch before tackling what needed to be done. Gilbert Macintosh buttonholed me as soon as I entered the pub and asked me with elaborate courtesy if he might join me. Now we were sitting at the same table.

"It does look bad," I agreed. "But I don't believe Dennis is their man. He seemed genuinely upset to me."

"Well, you are the chief witness of the time." Macintosh glanced quickly round the Saloon Bar. He seemed to be enjoying being seen with me in public. "Mind you, I have to tell you that a certain degree of suspicion is directed towards you by certain elements in the place."

"On what grounds?"

"You were there. You are an outsider. Why not you?"

"And my motive?"

"Theft, of course. The same as the Dennis Cash accusers attribute to him."

"It's absurd. How would I flog a painting so easily identifiable?"

"You wouldn't. Not for a long time. Although you might more rapidly to a villainous foreigner. Your Art Fund might conceal it within its multifarious collection. Your Fund doesn't exhibit its stock, does it? At least only occasionally and selectively. Your Art Fund apparently lacks an important Sickert. The sketch by Doman Turner is apparently quite a rarity. Some collections would give their eye teeth for the two missing items, wouldn't they?"

"True."

"There you are, then. Who knows what skulduggery you City men may get up to?" He grinned happily. "Dealing as you do with Johnny Foreigner so easily. One of the members of the Friends has vouchsafed that the painting is almost certainly in Texas or Minnesota by now. Others suggest Saudi Arabia. Not to mention Milan."

"Vivid imaginations, your Highton residents have got."

"Highly coloured."

"How do they think I got in?"

"You were let in by Dennis. Innocently on his part if you're a Simpson contender, not if you're a collusion fan."

"Oh, there's a collusion theory as well, is there?"

"Of course."

"But surely Binnie had been dead long before I got to the gallery that morning?"

"Ah. That may be a snag. The police are playing the game close to their chests on that one. No one knows exactly when the dastardly deed happened except them. At least, I assume they know. Perhaps that knowledge is vital to identifying the murderer."

"Heavens, the gossip must be hot."

"Molten. Haven't known anything like it since the local traffic warden ran off with the chiropractor. Both ladies, of course. Both married, too."

His grin became even more cheerful. I had to grin back at him. He sat there four square, corduroyed and tweed jacketed, skin healthily pink and figure lean. Shrewd blue eyes with clear whites focussed on me. I thought that if all rugger men could look like him on retirement I had nothing to fear for the future. But then he was a back, one of the girls, not a front row forward like me.

"Glad to break the monotony," I said.

"My dear chap. Any change from the trivial but depressing national and local news is welcome. Anything actually happening here is marvellous. Police given you a grilling, have they?"

"A man from Lewes called Stamford did me over, yes. Said I was free to go for the moment."

"Ah. Keeping his options open, eh? Thumb screws and rack to follow later?"

"Without doubt."

I put a knob of cheese on a cob of bread and chewed thought-fully. Something he'd said before had come to mind.

"You said you went to Binnie Grant's talk on Whistler?"

"I did, yes. Quite good it was."

"Veronica Chalmers was there?"

"She was."

"Did you speak to her?"

"Indeed not. Not my cup of tea at all. Too many of her sort in the Kirk when I was a boy."

"Did anybody else?"

"Surely." He spun round, glanced about and made a noise of triumph. "Let me get her for you, seeing as she's just come in."

He got up, went across the room and brought back a slightly flustered lady of certain age clad in a big navy blue coat.

"Felicia Apps," he announced. "The new secretary of the Friends of Highton Art Gallery. Tim, Felicia. Felicia, Tim."

I got up, shook hands and arranged a chair while he went off to get her a gin and orange. She gave me a rather cautious smile.

"I did enjoy your talk," she said. "But isn't it awful? First Veronica and now Binnie."

"Indeed it is. At least Veronica was an accident."

She shook her head firmly. "Never. Veronica would never have fallen down stairs. She was as nimble as a cricket."

I stared at her in consternation. "So – ?"

"Pushed. No question of it. She was pushed."

Gilbert Macintosh came back with her gin and orange as I sat in dumbfounded silence. She took a good swig from this some-what dated drink and nodded again in confirmation.

"I know Veronica better than most. She was not everyone's cup of tea. My late husband, who was in the Navy, said she should have been keel hauled. But you could get along if you knew how. She meant well. The galley was her whole life. She'd known the Harlands, you see. She had a desperate thing about preserving their heritage. Jane Harland was a model to her."

"Why would anyone want to kill her? Veronica, I mean."

"She knew something."

"What?"

"I – I don't know. At least, I'm not sure. It was that night. The night of Binnie's talk. Oh dear, I'm not sure I should be telling about this but since Binnie – well –"

"Don't worry." Gilbert Macintosh's voice was soothing. "Tim and I are the souls of discretion."

"Veronica had been lording it, you see. That day. The day of the talk. The Harland's niece came down after years away and went round the gallery after talking to Dennis Cash. Veronica soon cut that short. She didn't approve of Dennis and his new ideas. She was pretty condescending to him and very quickly took Hope off to lunch. Showing us all her position close to the family."

"Hope?"

"Yes, Hope. Hope Anderson. Mrs Hope Anderson was a niece of Jane's. She used to live in Spain but they came back to England. Her husband died there. Ladbroke Grove. Good heavens, Tim, you've spilt your beer."

"An accident. Clumsy me." I mopped up with a handkerchief. "Sorry. Please continue."

"Well, Hope went back to London after lunch and Veronica came to Binnie's talk looking like thunder. Something was defi-nitely wrong. She looked right through me. After the talk I saw her talking to Binnie very earnestly, looking really serious. Binnie looked serious too. Then the next day Dennis saw her take that folder."

"Do you know what was in it?"

She shook her head. "No idea. Some of those folders haven't been looked at for years. Too many of them, aren't there? Anyway she went home with it. That afternoon she had her fall. Someone pushed her. I know someone did. The folder has never come to light."

"But why? What could there be in it that was worth killing for?"

"I've no idea about that either. Most of the folders are full of dull old documents. Some have prints and sketches in them, though. Things done by the Harlands. They were quite good artists you know."

"Have another of those?" Pointing at her empty glass, Gilbert Macintosh was quick on hospitality. "I'll top up Tim for his lost ale at the same time."

"Oh, Gilbert, I shouldn't but what with everything –"

"Good girl."

He took our glasses to the bar and we sat silent for a moment while my mind seethed. Mr Goodston's Mrs HB Anderson of Ladbroke Grove had to be the same Hope Anderson Felicia was talking about. Had to be. The letter to Madge I found inside *Imperial Brown of Brixton*: there was a Madge someone had said was a friend of Jane Harland's. Madge Taylor, that was it; the town councillor Frank Stevens mentioned her. Dead now, though; no explanation of the letter in my hands would come from her.

"It's not as though we could check with Hope Anderson," Felicia Apps broke my train of thought. "She died only a couple of days or so after the meeting and Veronica's fall."

"Really?"

"I don't want to sound macabre but there does seem to be a strange pattern to it all, doesn't there?"

"I think one has to be careful not to let these things assume a conspiratorial aspect. So many things go in threes, after all."

"That's true. Well, disasters anyway."

"Here we are." Gilbert Macintosh returned with full hands and distributed glasses in triumph. "You were saying, Felicia?"

"I was saying that I shouldn't have another and talk like this. But I've kept it bottled up. I have to tell someone."

"Tell someone what?"

"About Binnie and Veronica. Thick like that at the meeting. And then the day Veronica was pushed. All right, fell. I mustn't say pushed, must I? It'll go round town like a shot."

"One has to be prudent," murmured Gilbert Macintosh.

"Indeed one has. And everyone says there was no one at Veronica's when she fell. But I saw her, you see. I was going that way and even though the light was fading I'm sure I saw someone come out. Of her house. Just about then."

"In that case," Gilbert Macintosh was at his most Caledonian. "It is your bounden duty to report it."

"Oh heavens, Gilbert, I don't dare. Not a chance. I have to live here you know. So do you but get away golfing and so on. My life wouldn't have been worth living if I'd told someone at the time. Still wouldn't be."

"Great Scott." Now he was really hooked and so was I. "Who on earth did you see?"

"I couldn't be certain. I really couldn't. The light was going. That's why I haven't said anything. And now I can't, ever."

"Why not?"

"*De mortuis nil nisi bonum*, Gilbert. It was an absolute rule of my husband's. And he was right. About that, anyway."

"You mean it was – it was –"

"Binnie Grant, yes."

Chapter Eighteen

The police and their teams had gone. Dennis Cash was out some-where. The gallery shop had bravely opened and a middle aged lady, one of the Friends, recognised me and made no demur as I went upstairs.

I stood in the big studio room in which I had given my talk and, after a glance at the fine landscape outside, took a careful look round me. On the walls was a selection from the gallery's permanent collection. Strong swathes of colour on an Ivon Hitchens abstract landscape boldly met my eye. George Harland must have been an advanced buyer of paintings. Hitchens might have been a favourite of the late Queen Mother's but back in the thirties he was for the more progressive intellectuals.

I moved across to the opposite wall, where one of George Harland's own paintings was hung. It depicted a scene outside a country house, on a lawn tennis court, some time in the nineteen-twenties. Everyone said that George and Jane Harland were com-petent, traditional painters so there were no stylistic surprises, but the scene was well composed. The players of mixed doubles, in dated tennis costumes, were set apart against the green fore-ground, with the white line of the net and tramlines of the court markings anchoring the composition. Beyond them, under some trees, a group of blazered men with white trousers sat amongst some women round a table, presumably set with tea things. It was a sunlit scene of middle class enjoyment, something dated and leisured yet once identifiable with a large section of the popula-tion. A social record, some museum wallah would pompously declaim, as though always having to talk down to an imaginary, uneducated audience unversed in any history of their own.

Like Larry Granger and Dennis Cash I have a resistance to the condescending educational aspects of official art curatorship; it's something Sue has never exhibited in any form despite her reser-vations about my mercenary involvement in art.

Beyond the trees, vaguely impressionistic with suggestion rather than definition, was the silhouette of the house to which the tennis court belonged. It was behind a hedge and rose bower but its outlines, early nineteenth century by the look of the windows and shape of the roof, rose above lawns that led to a summer house and fields beyond.

"Tranquil, isn't it?"

The voice behind me was quiet but it gave me a shock. Frank Stevens stood quite close with a slight smile on his face. The town councillor must have come in softly whilst my thoughts were elsewhere. I shook myself mentally and smiled back.

"Yes it is."

He stood beside me to get nearer the painting. "It's the house they had before they moved here. In Kent somewhere – Tonbridge, it was. Their children were born there, I think. At least, that's what Dick – Richard Harland – told my father. George and Jane met at a tennis party, so the game had significance for them. A vanished age, I suppose."

"Oh, I don't know. There are still quite a lot of houses with tennis courts. By no means all of them in Surrey or Kent."

"Maybe. But society is very different now. Not so many people play tennis that way. Of course there are no tennis courts in Highton: you have to go to Newhaven or Lewes. I'm afraid it's a world I've never known. We were too busy working in the shop on Saturdays to get to tennis matches."

He said this without any rancour, as though the ironmongery business into which he had been born was a perfectly acceptable way of life. To have been busy, to have expanded into other branches elsewhere had perhaps been, to him, so absorbing that leisure pursuits were a mere curiosity, something that other people did. His ruddy face had lost the nervous expression I had noticed at our first meeting. He seemed more relaxed, despite the events that had shaken the town.

"It's very different painting from the kind of thing they collected," I said, seeking to probe a little. "In a way I would have expected their taste to have been a little more conventional."

"Ah. I've always thought that Jane was quite conventional. She liked those Newlyn ladies and the softer, feminine touch. George was different."

"Oh?"

"Yes. The Camden Town school." He paused for a moment, keeping his eyes on the tennis match frozen in time before him. His face had gone serious. "I think there was a dark side to George. I think George wanted to be a very different painter from the one who created this very competent tennis match. There was another side to painting which enthralled him but it would have involved an end to his conventional life. He was no Gauguin, prepared to abandon wife, family, everything, the man in Somerset Maugham's *Moon and Sixpence*. He recognised his limitations and fulfilled his desires differently. Art is supposed to be all about appearance and reality, isn't it?"

"It is one theme," I answered cautiously. "Shakespeare was rather keen on it, too."

"Well. Here you have a sunlit summer party. Everything looks hunky dory. Yet they left this idyllic tennis place and moved to Highton so as to be nearer the Continent. Tennis was dropped. Art took precedence."

"They both painted. This studio was theirs. Jane was as keen as George, wasn't she?"

"Yes she was. And Dieppe was very much a place for English painters. At first they went over together. But soon George was going alone."

"The children, perhaps, increasingly kept her here?"

"The Harlands were quite well-to-do. When they first travelled together a nanny looked after the kids. Dick said he liked her."

"So why did Jane stop going?"

"I've often wondered. There was a dark side to George; he

made friends with Sickert when he had a studio in Brighton – Kemp Town – and Jane certainly disapproved. She thought Sickert was sordid. She didn't like the Mornington Crescent nude at all. I rather think she might have sided with this Cornwell woman."

"The Ripper? It's a bit far-fetched."

He smiled again. "I was wondering what might come out of Binnie's researches. Larry Granger had deep reservations, you know."

"Something about 'drawing aside the myth-encrusted curtains of the past' perhaps?"

"His very words. What unexpected tableaux might emerge. The files had been left undisturbed for so long. I think Larry had thoughts along the lines of letting sleeping dogs lie. But we have duties as trustees, I suppose. Nowadays there is pressure to catalogue everything, as though TV's *Time Team* is absolutely necessary, must set the agenda for digging everywhere. It's to do with an obsession with the past caused by fear of the future, I think."

"I agree that there's too much past and too little future in our thinking."

"Dennis is much the same. He and Binnie disagreed about that but it was purely a professional disagreement. I'm very distressed by the suspicion that has fallen on him. I think it's very brave of him to stay and face the town rather than cutting off somewhere."

"It is. But Dennis strikes me as a man of considerable bottom, to use a dated description. Of fundament, I mean." A thought struck me. "Dennis mentioned her but you may know more: have you heard of a lady called Madge Taylor?"

"Madge? Of course. I knew her. She's been dead for, what, eight or nine years. She was a friend of Jane Harland's, although a bit younger than her. And a lot older than me. She used to come to coffee mornings here."

"Did she know George?"

"She knew him but they weren't close."

"And Mrs Anderson? Hope Anderson? Did she know her?"

"Oh yes, long ago. The niece of Jane Harland's. Hope left when she married and her husband went round the world. He was in the diplomatic service, you know. Retired to Spain. When he died, Hope came back to London. Sad about her accident."

"She came to Highton quite recently."

"Yes. Veronica Chalmers rather monopolised her. But she had been a friend of Madge Taylor's too. They kept in touch. It rather irked Veronica; she wanted to be the queen bee as far as Harland associations were concerned. I'm afraid that Veronica wasn't popular. She had complete access to the gallery and wanted it to be something that was in conflict with Dennis's view of the way forward. Binnie dealt with her much better."

"But she never bothered about all those old documents until her last day? From what I've heard of her, she seems entirely the type to want to delve in other people's affairs. Read their diaries, cluck in disapproval. Yet she left the office undisturbed and ceded ground to Binnie Grant on it."

"Ironic, isn't it? She wanted everything preserved in aspic." He thought for a moment. "Perhaps subconsciously she feared what might come up."

"I understand that Jane Harland did indicate some sort of problem to Madge Taylor."

"Did she? I didn't know that. You're really getting into Highton's history, aren't you?"

"I'm just trying to make sure I don't miss anything."

"I'm glad. Kathy Marsden and I have been worried about this place for a long time. We hoped that when Bill Riley came in last year things would look up. Financially, I mean. It doesn't seem to have happened so far. He comes to meetings OK and takes an interest but that's it up to now. Binnie has been very preoccupied with her archives; she wasn't into funding. Kathy is an artist and

I'm struggling with helping my son in the business; times are tough right now. Larry has worked really hard for the place, he really has, but he's got nowhere with the arts authorities. I've watched him getting more and more frustrated. We told him it needed an outside view. So you see Kathy and I are really pleased to see you here."

"I'll do my best."

"You've obviously not missed very much up to now. I hope this terrible business of Binnie's death won't set us back too far. You need to get on with your project. You should come and go as you wish. Have you been awarded the key to the gallery already?"

"No. Do all the trustees have one?"

He looked at me calmly. "Oh yes, all we trustees have a key. And Dennis of course. And the secretary of the Friends. Which was Veronica; she could go into the place at any time, and did."

"What did Larry Granger think about that?"

"I think you'll have to ask him, won't you?"

Chapter Nineteen

The house was impeccably neat. The windows were crisply painted in white and the front door of solid oak was smoothly matt
varnished so as to provide a suitably old yet smartly presented
appearance. I rang the bell just once, briskly.

It was as almost as though I was expected.

"Come in, Tim." Larry Granger, in jacket, cavalry twill
trousers, shirt and tie, was as smartly turned out as his house. He
appeared not the slightest perturbed at my sudden call. "This is
indeed a pleasant surprise. How very glad I am that you have
come back to see us. The times are not propitious but we must all
try to get on with life. We must not let the troops of Midian deter
us. Do please come in."

I stepped across the threshold into a well-furnished room
equipped with the large fireplace apparently essential to all better
Highton houses. He closed the front door and stood aside to let
me move onto the carpet in front of the inglenook. I caught sight
of a small Spencer Gore painting of a French market scene on the
wall behind him. It gave me a moment to defer my real interest.

"Nice," I said. "Forgive me for commenting, but it's a Spencer
Gore, isn't it?"

"Well spotted. I do rather like it. It's one he painted while
staying at Neuville, Dieppe. In Walter Sickert's house. He took a
good deal from Sickert but his touch was lighter."

"There's a Spencer Gore in the studio at the gallery. A small
Camden Town scene."

"Indeed there is. George Harland bought it from the artist's
family I believe."

"Oh? I was just saying to Frank Stevens how different the taste
is between George's own painting and what he collected. That tennis scene is so unlike the social realism of the works he bought."

"My dear Tim. Tennis brought him his wife Jane. Maybe it
brought him to his collecting taste, too."

"How's that?"

His voice took on the indulgent tone of the expert. "Spencer Gore's father was the first champion at Wimbledon. In 1877, at the first Wimbledon championship ever held. Gore painted sport – cricket amongst other things – but he painted tennis, too, perhaps in memory of his father. So Harland had an example to follow."

"Of course! *Tennis in Mornington Crescent Gardens*. Before the Carreras factory was built. It's a famous painting of Gore's. I'd completely forgotten."

"So you see George was not so far away from his idealised realists of Camden Town. The leafy scene of Spencer Gore's, with two or three people playing and two sitting on a bench watching may have inspired his own very atmospheric painting. The one of George's you have been looking at in the studio is rather bourgeois and conventional, however."

"One was stolen recently wasn't it? Of Spencer Gore's, I mean. A year or two ago. It's never been recovered."

"Was one stolen? I didn't know that. There are several versions of *Tennis in Mornington Crescent Gardens*, I believe. The Art Gallery in Auckland has one and there have been others at auction. Wendy Baron recorded them. But George must have seen one at an early stage. Gore painted various versions in 1909 and 1910. Perhaps George saw one in the twenties and that's what started him off."

"So he progressed, if that is the word, from tennis in Camden Town to naked ladies in Camden Town."

He smiled. "A not illogical sequence since tennis normally induces disrobing after the match."

"Not quite the same thing as Sickert's iron bedstead studies."

"Ah. You refer to our sad loss. In addition to Binnie Grant, I mean." Despite the lightness of touch he had displayed so far an undercurrent of real despair seemed now to seep into his voice. "I do not know what I have done to be present at such a terrible time for the gallery. The arts authorities will do nothing for us and now we have a murder and a theft to contend with. We will never get anything; they have even more excuse to ignore us."

"Was the painting insured?"

"Oh yes. But I believe that the funds may, under our trust deed, only be used for replacement. I doubt if the money will run to another Sickert. We must make do the best we can and face the future resolutely."

"Spoken like a true chairman."

"A true chairman?" His spirits seemed to recover at the word. "According to C Northcote Parkinson," he fixed me with an authoritative eye in which there was a returning glint of humour, "of Parkinson's Law, the ideal committee, or cabinet council, appears, to comitologists, historians, and even those who appoint cabinets, to consist of five people. Exactly like the Highton Art Gallery. With that number the plant is viable, allowing two members to be absent or away sick at any time. Five members are easy to collect and can act with competence, secrecy and speed. Of these original members four may well be versed, respectively, in finance, foreign policy, defence and law." He smiled, timing himself carefully. "The fifth, who has failed to master any of these subjects, usually becomes chairman, or prime minister as the case may be. Would you like coffee or tea or a drink?"

I grinned at him. "You are too self-effacing, Mr Chairman. I am sure you have mastered everything necessary."

"You are too kind."

Wondering which two trustees might be away at any time now that one was permanently gone, I said "Tell me: using Parkinson's description, into which category of committee expert would Frank Stevens fall?"

"Defence, perhaps? He is a local council expert of long standing. Without him to defend us against the local trade we might have been mulcted for rates."

"Riley would be finance. Katy Marsden might be foreign policy since she is the outside artist anointed by the Royal Academy.

You lack a lawyer; Binnie Grant was not legal."

"She was not far from it. Oh dear, how awful everything has become. Things are really terrible. Do have something?"

"Tea would be fine, thank you."

"Come through to the kitchen; I have no domestic staff here today."

I followed him across the room, past a sketch by Augustus John, through a door to a passage and then into a rather modern-looking, light and airy kitchen.

"China or Indian?"

"Indian, thank you."

He picked up a kettle. "I will have China. But I understand the prejudice against its perfumed aroma. I'm afraid I acquired my taste for it in the Far East."

"My wife likes Earl Grey."

"In that case she is a civilised woman. Although one has to be careful; there are some very mongrel Earl Grey blends about these days."

"Did you serve for long in the Far East?"

"Long enough. But I liked it. There was such a contrast between it and my days in South America. The Far East was mystical whereas life in South America was applied hedonism. The delicate as against the gross." He gave me an appraising look. "Freddy Harbledown told me you went to school in Buenos Aires?"

I ignored the inference. "I did. Still have a soft spot for Argentina."

"Me too. The affair of the Falklands was ridiculous. But what will happen to such a naturally rich country ruined by greed?"

"I wish I knew."

I wondered, as I spoke, if elaborate courtesies, cutting inferences and circumnavigation preceded all Foreign Office conversations. The terrible event at the gallery so prominent in my mind had only been a fraction of our conversation so far.

"Binnie," he said abruptly, as though he had read my

thoughts. "This is not about gallery finance. You've come to talk to me about her murder, haven't you?"

He poured out tea as he spoke, producing a mingled fragrance of a delicate China and the stronger pungency of my Indian.

"I have."

"Milk? Sugar? No here: help yourself."

"Thanks. Why? Why was she killed?"

He gave me a reproachful look. "*Et tu, Brute?* You haven't been sworn in as a deputy by the lugubrious Detective Inspector Stamford, by any chance?"

"Indeed not. I'm sorry; I didn't mean to sound interrogative even if, grammatically, I was. Curiosity got the better of me."

He sighed, stirred his tea, which he took without milk but a dash of sugar, and gave me a more receptive glance. "May I take it that we are speaking in complete confidence? I mean really complete confidence?"

"Of course."

"I have not voiced my suspicions to the Inspector. I have answered his questions truthfully, of course. I returned here from Bill Riley's that evening and did not leave until morning. I have therefore only myself as an alibi, if one is needed. Which means that I have no alibi at all."

"I'm sure one is not needed. It is only because I went back to my hotel that I have one; I was seen by the porter. Bill Riley, I assume, was at home with his wife. I'm sure yours will be vouchsafed somehow."

"That is kind. As I say, I have been honest but I am not obliged to voice my theories to the Inspector. Pure conjecture is not evidence."

"Indeed not."

He stirred his cup with a slim silver spoon. "In my view Binnie's death is something to do with the death of Veronica Chalmers."

"Really? How?"

He gave me an unwavering stare. "I believe that Binnie Grant murdered Veronica Chalmers."

"*What?*" I almost choked on my tea.

"Murdered her." He was emphatic. "By pushing her downstairs."

"But – but – why?"

"For her obsession: the archive."

"The archive? What was worth killing for in that?"

"The evening before she died, Veronica, who was one of my least favourite people, attended a lecture by Binnie Grant. She had spent most of the day with Mrs Hope Anderson, a late niece of the Harlands, lording her possession of this distinguished visitor around the town after a visit to the gallery and then lunch. But when she arrived for the lecture she was clearly very disturbed. Something her visitor had told her had upset her visibly."

"What?"

"Bear with me a moment, Tim. You have to remember that her life, for as long as it mattered, had been dedicated to the memory of the Harlands. To her they were sacrosanct. She revered the gallery and its cultural influence on an otherwise arid small town which, however historic, is slowly being spoiled by day trippers, a steady increase in souvenir shops, and what she thought of as the malign influence of the Town Council. She thought the Council to be composed of the most mendacious, cheapjack tradesmen, people with no concern for the standards the older residents wanted to maintain. She and Frank Stevens disagreed fundamentally. The Council is dallying with Frenchmen these days, begging for European money." He made an odd circular gesture vaguely towards the Newhaven direction with a silver teaspoon. "Everyone knows it is a mistake. The French will make sure they get precious little. They always do. Highton is on the slide."

I blinked over my tea. Somehow Veronica's entrenched view had been superseded by Larry Granger's; the changeover was quite seamless.

"The good quality shops are being replaced, steadily but

remorselessly with bric-a-brac and ice cream parlours catering for the worst sort of visitor." His tone rose slightly, like a schoolmaster addressing a class that threatens to lose interest. "Charabancs of blue-rinsed pensioners from the worst ends of southern towns troop gawking through the streets, looking bored. French schoolchildren come to deprecate a lesser culture. Even Northerners arrive, filling the church. Most are people with only the money for a cup of tea and a mass-produced sausage roll. Motor bikers. Young people from the estates around Newhaven, raucous and drunk, yes drunk, on foul sweet drinks of high alcohol content sold to them in pubs by unprincipled landlords. Brawling, some of them, in the street. The police seem to do nothing. This was not the image of Highton, medieval, beautiful Highton, quiet and respectable, suitable for better retired people that Veronica treasured. It is a terrible decline."

"Is it that bad?"

He ignored me. "But for Veronica there was still the gallery. For her the gallery stood like a beacon on the corner of Dolphin Street and Pearson's Lane, a lighthouse of culture and art despite attempts to inject what she thought of as lower-grade, contemporary images into it. The protection of the Friends, and their representations to the Trustees, acted as a brake on such attempts. Then along came Hope Anderson with some appalling news, long hidden from sight. At the meeting where Binnie gave her lecture Veronica was still shocked by the information she had been given over lunch. She confided in Binnie and said she knew where something damaging to the gallery's reputation could be found. In the office."

"So that was the folder Dennis saw her take?"

"That was the folder. When she got to the sitting room on the first floor of her tiny cottage in Church Street, she sat horrified, holding it tight shut in both hands. To her it was awful. It was disgusting. Everything she most hated and despised was depicted in the foul images the folder contained. There were others, less degrading, less shocking, no matter how sophisticated – degenerate would be a more accurate description – the attitude of the viewer might be. But to her the worst were truly awful. If only dear Hope hadn't mentioned, offhand, the circumstance that had led her, Veronica, memory suddenly alerted, to come back and, after a search of the office, find this appalling evidence. Now she intended to take action. There was a precedent: Lady Clementine Churchill had destroyed the foul portrait of Winston by Graham Sutherland. She was going to destroy these images by Sickert and George Harland."

"And she did?"

"It was ironic. Sickert, when in Dieppe, humorously drew a portrait image of Clementine Hozier on her hockey stick. She was a young girl in exile then and Sickert befriended her as might an uncle. To invoke her as a precedent for destroying his work was more significant than one can imagine: Clementine bound tape over the image because it embarrassed her and the stick was broken in play."

"So did Veronica destroy them?"

"Wait, wait! She needed sanction. She sent for Binnie Grant. Binnie was a trustee; she was a mature woman; she was friendly to the Friends. Thank God, her visitor came fairly quickly. Veronica had to have someone in whom to confide. It was too much to bear this dreadful blow alone. Constitutional issues were involved. The trustees as a body could not be relied upon. Dennis Cash would almost certainly want to display these awful images. It needed someone ready to act vigorously. Someone with whom she could feel an affinity."

"Binnie Grant? That's really ironic; Binnie was dedicated to the preservation of the archive. It was the life work of her retirement. To her any destruction of historical reality would be absolute anathema. Documents were precious."

"You put your finger right on the nub, my boy. Veronica had decided that she must take action in this matter. Parts of the past, to her, were better not to have happened. She would keep Hope, the casual and unknowing generator of this terrible knowledge, out of it. Hope was very old; it would do her no good to hear what had been revealed. She, Veronica, had been guardian of the gallery's reputation for so long. No one else had her understanding and experience of the place. She would take all responsibility for the discovery and the action. However, she did need a kind of sanction, an approval that would not emerge into the daylight of vicarious public curiosity. Modern life had no respect at all."

"And so she asked Binnie Grant to sanction the destruction of a folder of, presumably, drawings by Sickert and George Harland that were, how shall I put it, pretty ripe? Possibly even fuel for Patricia Cornwell's theories?"

"We can only guess. She was dead before we could know. The folder has disappeared. I'm sure Binnie Grant was outraged by the idea of the destruction. Maybe there was a struggle; maybe Binnie Grant knew that she dare not leave the folder with Veronica because its contents were sure to be destroyed. I think she killed Veronica to preserve the folder."

"God Almighty. Wait a minute. How do you know all this?"

"I don't. But fifteen minutes before Binnie was due to arrive, Veronica phoned me. She respected me as Chairman. It was a kind of insurance policy. She told me that she had found awful evidence about George Harland's acquisition. This was absolutely in confidence. She and I had our differences of course, always had had, but we were both committed to the gallery. This was the first time she had come across this appalling evidence. It came from a chance remark from Hope, who should remain in ignorance. Her memory had led to this unexpected discovery from Veronica's own deduction and detection. She hesitated to take the decision alone; that was the reason for this discreet meeting with Binnie. There was no doubt in her mind, however. Action was needed. Once her visitor had taken a thorough look, there could be no other course. Her mind was set on it but she was advising me, too."

"Binnie didn't know that Veronica had phoned you?"

"No she didn't. I think that Veronica said this was all in confidence. You see, after Veronica was found dead I waited for Binnie to tell me what had happened. To admit to her visit and show me the folder. I didn't want to start a town scandal. I kept absolutely stumm. I think Binnie was disconcerted by Dennis's witnessing of the taking of a folder but she went all through the charade of looking for it without owning up. I waited and waited for her to come clean by herself but she never did. And without the folder or a witness, I had no evidence. I didn't record the phone call. But I'm convinced Binnie Grant didn't know it had been made. She was relying on secrecy."

"You didn't tackle her about it?"

"I hinted. I gave her every opportunity to explain. I couldn't tackle her head on; she'd have denied everything. She was a warm, maternal figure here. I would have incurred deep dislike in the town. It caused tension between us."

I thought quickly of Felicia Apps and her same belief. "This was dire knowledge you had."

"The only real knowledge I had was of the existence of the folder and of the meeting. Nothing else. My presumption of what happened would be dismissed as pure speculation."

"It must have been a dreadful burden to carry."

"It is a relief to tell you about it. I know I can rely on your discretion."

I licked my lips, which had gone dry despite the tea. "How would she have explained? About the folder, I mean?"

"Easily. She only had to pretend, after a suitable interval, that it was one she had come across during her archival researches."

"But why would anyone kill Binnie, then?"

"Maybe she confided in someone."

"What would they hope to gain?"

"Either the preservation of the gallery's reputation, especially that of the Harlands if they were of Veronica's inclination or –"

"Or what?"

"Or more likely, if the images were what they might be, some enormous value in supporting the claims of Patricia Cornwell. Or tremendous publicity for the gallery of a scandalous nature."

"Dear God."

"It is a serious enough thought to invoke the Almighty, I agree."

"They'd be a bit pushed to explain how they came by the material."

"Not so difficult, Tim. We have no record of what those images are. We have not seen them so we could not in all honesty say they came from here. Almost any story as to their origin might be concocted. Alternatively, they could still be 'discovered' in the office."

"That would implicate a trustee or Dennis."

"I agree. An outside person is the only thing my mind will accept. And a concocted story."

"If a story were to be concocted at all. They might by now be in the collection of some mad Croesus who keeps them hidden for his own gratification. Like the Van Goghs that have gone from Amsterdam."

"Van Goghs?"

"Two Van Goghs were stolen recently from the museum in Amsterdam. Early ones. It seems unimaginable that they could be sold on the open market so they must have been stolen to order at the behest of a rich maniac."

"I see. In your Art Fund dealings you must come across some strange aberrations."

Yes, I nearly answered, and one of the strange aberrations I could mention is a cultured old codger who might have a folder containing a French or Belgian magazine print of an unusual version of *The Camden Town Murder* by Sickert. Which he hasn't mentioned so far despite complaining of Binnie's reticence to him over another folder containing God knows what images of a squalid nature. They certainly weren't in the folder I looked at in the office, with its Camden Town bedroom tableau. Is that painting somewhere he knows about?

Or – or – did Dennis Cash leave it in the office and then remove it? Was I maligning Larry Granger? Dennis could have equally taken it while I was getting ledgers to copy from Sylvia's cubbyhole. I might be on the wrong track.

"Tim?" My silence was disconcerting him.

"Me? Well – oh, hell!"

I swore because at that moment my mobile phone rang, peeping its mad insistent cadence through the air of the kitchen.

"Damn! I'm sorry about this."

"My sympathies. It is for this sort of reason that I refuse to have a mobile. But doubtless to you it is essential. By all means answer it."

I pulled the thing out of my pocket, cursing that it was probably the Bank but it wasn't. It was Inspector Stamford of the Sussex Police.

"Mr Simpson? I gather you are in Highton?"

"Yes I am."

"Would you be so kind as to come in to the station? There are one or two things I would like to discuss with you. They would be better covered in private."

"When?"

"As soon as possible."

"You mean now?"

"I mean as soon as possible. I am conducting a murder enquiry and time is of the essence."

"In other words, now."

"If you wouldn't mind, Mr Simpson. I am sure you would not want to be the cause of any delay?"

"I'll be right along."

"Good."

My eyes met Larry Granger's. "That sounded rather like Inspector Stamford," he murmured.

"It was. I'm afraid I have been summoned to the station. Now."

"How irritating; but we can finish our talk later. My best wishes, Tim. And I'm sure I don't have to remind you: absolute confidence?"

"Oh, stumm," I answered. "Absolutely stumm."

Chapter Twenty

"I'm glad you've dropped in." Inspector Stamford smiled signif-icantly at his own courtesy, as though it pleased him to pretend that I had just been passing by. "Very kind of you, sir."

It was the first time that he'd called me sir. I wondered whether this was genuine or an audible concession to the record-ing tape that PC Wallace had carefully switched on. The inter-view room was just as sparsely furnished as ever and was if any-thing still a bit overheated. The table was not quite as clean as it had been and the smallness of the room made Stamford and Wallace seem closer to me than I remembered. They were in shirtsleeves; I wasn't.

"My pleasure."

"We've been doing a little checking, you see. And it came as a bit of a surprise to find that you didn't tell us that you are already known to us. In the purely general sense that is, rather than to the Sussex Police in particular. You seem to have held that back. Modesty, I suppose?"

He and PC Wallace smiled smugly at each other, making Wallace's straggly moustache bristle weakly. I sighed. There is, in the computer records of the Metropolitan Police, and therefore presumably in the country in general, a little flag that comes up whenever the name Simpson, Tim, is punched into the system. It says, "refer to Chief Inspector Roberts, Scotland Yard" and this was presumably what Stamford was referring to.

"You have been talking to Nobby Roberts, I suppose."

"Detective Chief Inspector Roberts, at Scotland Yard, was kind enough to answer our enquiry, yes." Stamford produced what was meant to be a significant expression, including a smile that turned his mouth down, rather than up, at the corners. "Quite forthcoming, he was, on the subject of your good self. Very forthcoming in fact. His reactions were specific and thor-oughgoing, if I may put it that way."

"That sounds like Nobby. I don't suppose he was pleased at the interruption to whatever his vital investigations are just now. He used to be on the Art Fraud Squad but he's after much bigger game these days."

"He is rather occupied with terrorist activities at the moment, I believe. Occupied enough to express impatience that you have become embroiled in what he referred to as 'another of Tim's bloody imbroglios' if my memory serves me right."

"That sounds like Nobby."

"Known the DCI long, have you?"

"We were at college together. Played rugger on the same side."

"And since then you and he have collaborated, if that is the right word, in several cases he mentioned." Stamford managed somehow to shuffle a single sheet of paper with inky notes on it. "Cases which have a certain similarity to this one?"

"Oh, I wouldn't say that."

He raised his eyebrows. "How would you describe them, then?"

"Well, er, I suppose they involved art crime in some form or another."

"Including murder?"

"Including murder, yes."

"Similar to this one, then. And during those cases, according to DCI Roberts, you distinguished yourself by withholding information from the police until it suited you, for your own ends, to reveal it."

"The ungrateful bugger! Is that what he said? After all the help I gave him to solve the cases and further his career?"

Stamford leant forward. "He said, specifically, that I should make sure that you told me everything, absolutely everything, that you know because you have a very bad habit of being less than forthcoming until – I quote – *you have satisfied your own devious, mercenary and company-political priorities*."

"The lousy bastard. That's not true."

"He also advised me, from his extensive experience, to demand that you come clean in every sense from the very beginning. As it happens his advice confirms my own suspicion that there is a great deal more you know which you have not told us about this matter."

"I like that! I have answered everything you asked me."

"It is your duty, in addition to answering our questions, to impart any information you may have which may be of assistance to us in this matter. This is a very serious murder enquiry connected with the theft of a painting about which you are something of an expert. Any ramifications which are relevant to this case should be put into our cognisance. We should not have to extract information by tedious questioning. A responsible citizen proffers it voluntarily."

He looked at Wallace for support and got a gratifying, to him, series of affirmative nods.

"Heavens. I only just got here for one day or so before the whole thing happened. I'm not nearly as familiar with Highton as almost any of its residents and particularly PC Wallace here, who is your local man."

"Nevertheless, when at our last meeting I asked you for a few clues –"

"With some sarcasm at the time –"

" – I had not realised quite how prescient I was being. In terms of your propensity, according to DCI Roberts, for possessing clues but not imparting them."

He sat back and raised his eyebrows at me. The expression was unmistakable. Timmy was supposed to cough up. An image of Larry Granger, sipping Earl Grey tea, came to me. So did his reminder that my confidence had been exhorted. I had no qualms about keeping quiet about what he'd said; it was up to Larry to reveal his speculations, not me.

"You have my assurance, Inspector, that if I am in receipt of any concrete facts relating to this tragedy I will pass them on to you without delay."

"That is an encouraging start. It may not be enough, however. Concrete facts have a habit of revealing themselves anyway. It is background innuendo and connections which are more difficult to dig out."

"I'm not in the business of relaying servant's hall gossip. PC Wallace will get much more of that than I can."

Stamford glanced at his colleague. "PC Wallace lives in Denton, not Highton. He has certain sources of course, and we shall make best use of those. But when it comes to art theft, and in particular international art fraud, you are something of an authority are you not?"

"As director of an art investment fund it is my business to ensure that we are not bamboozled, yes. But you have art crime experts in the police force, particularly in the Met., who are infinitely better informed than I am."

"We are in contact with them. But DCI Roberts says that in any case in which you may appear – however unintentionally and however far out on the fringes, as it were – it behoves the investigating officer to keep a beady eye on you."

"What a bastard. That's the last time I buy him a breakfast. Or a lunch."

"I am not happy about your referring to a highly respected senior police officer in abusive terms."

"That's between Nobby and me. Tell me: when did Binnie Grant die? I mean when was she attacked?"

"That is confidential to our enquiries."

Oh, I thought, is it? Well, I'll help you when you help me.

"Why can't you tell me?"

"I am asking the questions, not you. And I am going to ask you now, specifically and carefully, an important question." He set his face into a stern mode. "Think before you answer because this interview is being recorded as evidence."

"Fire away."

"Have you any information, directly or indirectly relevant to this case, which you have not yet imparted to us?"

"No."

He scowled at the promptness of the answer. "You'd better not have. You'll regret it if you hold back on us. I shall be watching you like a hawk from now on, do you hear me?"

"I hear you. I might point out, for the benefit of your tape, that I am in Highton merely as a consultant to the art gallery and not as some sort of private detective or expert witness. I am not involved in any investment here. It is not my business to retail gossip or speculation about the crime in any sense. I have imparted the facts known to me."

"What gossip? What speculation?"

"You must be well aware that the town is buzzing with gossip. I suggest, in a purely helpful vein, that if you want to hear it you should go to the locals, not me."

"Which locals?"

"You could start with the Friends of Highton Art Gallery. They'll give you earfuls of scandal and innuendo. Are you going to charge Dennis Cash?"

"I said I am asking the questions, not you. We are proceeding with our enquiries and Dennis Cash has been released on police bail. That has been publicly announced and that is the case."

"I see. May I go, now?"

"You may. But I've told you –"

"I heard. For the benefit of the tape, I heard."

* * *

I came out of the police station in a bad temper. Stamford had interrupted my revealing talk with Larry Granger merely to act like an officious dog whose tree has been peed on. Or might be peed on by interference from a "highly respected senior police officer" at Scotland Yard, as he had described Nobby. Not quite how I would have described my old friend at that moment but one has to allow for a certain looseness of expression from ex-wing-threequarters busy with terrorists. I'd tackle Nobby in my own way about that, some other time.

The interruption was very irritating. At his house, Granger had become revealing, but not revealing enough; I needed to know about the magazine sheet with the Sickert illustration on it. Who did take that folder? Where was the painting? There were probably perfectly good reasons why Larry Granger was behaving the way he was but I needed to know them. I had to be careful; he was *persona grata* with Freddy Harbledown and that made it necessary for me to keep him on side. Yet there was an obsessive aspect to him; he'd dealt me a couple of polemics now and it bothered me. Old people get bees in their bonnets but Granger's minor rants sat ill on a man of what had seemed, initially, such urbane, worldly detachment. The gallery's wellbeing was clearly getting under his skin. On the other hand life in a small place like Highton must lend itself to local bees buzzing in local bonnets. An image of the cover of Imperial Brown came with that thought, its black bee hovering beside the Napoleonic hat. My mental meanderings were becoming vivid; perhaps Highton had that effect.

The magazine sheet was disturbing. Magazines, right now, were disturbing. I still had too many in the car.

I'd divided them up into piles. Those I'd looked through were back in my office at the Bank, those I hadn't were still separated: Hope Anderson's in one large lot and Mr Goodston's friendly solicitor's – the Isleworth detachment – in a lesser one. I'd left Hope Anderson's in the back of the Volvo after carrying the solicitor's, which were less bulky to go with my overnight case, to my hotel room. I decided that the Anderson magazines would be safer if I locked them up at the hotel too, ready for perusal in the evening.

I had other priorities, though. I needed to speak to Dennis

Cash. I strode up the hill from the police station and arrived at the gallery slightly out of breath. Highton was without doubt a hilltop settlement but the exercise did me good; I was calming down after my interchanges with Stamford.

The shop area was presided over by Felicia Apps, who smiled at me a trifle nervously and said that Dennis had come back in and was upstairs in his flat. The passive area through the arch, leading to the office, was unlighted and unvisited; presumably there was still a gap where the Sickert nude had hung. I didn't like to think too much about the office and what had lain behind the door.

The entrance to Dennis's flat was in the lobby, providing a quite separate access to the upstairs area not taken by the big studio. I pressed the bell at the doorway three times before I heard heavy footsteps coming down.

The door opened and his broad figure stood at the bottom of a carpeted flight of stairs going up behind him. He was wearing a long ravelled sweater over canvas trousers. He looked pretty washed out.

"Tim. I wasn't expecting you."

He sounded as though he might have been expecting yet more visits from Stamford and Wallace, or worse.

"Hi. Can I come in?"

He hesitated for a moment before answering, his eyes watchful.

"I've just been given a lecturing by Detective Inspector Stamford," I explained. "I need to talk to you."

He relaxed a little. "Of course."

We went up the carpeted stairs to a small landing then through to a modest sitting room with a view out over the town. The place was sparsely furnished but there were bits of artwork and pottery everywhere, quite apart from some striking and rather tormented sketches and paintings of a figurative kind. Dark skies lowered over dark figures highlighted by chalky backgrounds. There was a smell of fresh paint.

"These yours?"

"Yes."

"Striking stuff. Do you exhibit?"

He smiled slightly. "Not much. I paint when I'm fraught. Which is now."

"I'm not surprised. 'Out on police bail' is the phrase Stamford used. I don't think he'd like the idea of my being here but that's a load of rubbish."

"Not done to be seen with the guilty party, eh?"

"Come on, Dennis; I'm considered by some in the town to be as guilty as you. In fact some, including Stamford, might think I've come to see you so that we can concoct alibis."

He grinned for the first time. "An outsider like you would be bound to attract suspicion. Especially with your Fund as recipient of the theft."

"We've always accumulated paintings that way."

"Ha! So have I, apparently. At least that's what Stamford thinks. As though there were some precedent."

"You and I did it together. We killed Binnie Grant because she caught us stealing a painting and a sketch we knew we could never sell."

"Logical, isn't it, Tim?"

"How's Larry Granger taking it? Has he talked to you at all?"

"Oh, Larry's being a good, loyal Chairman. Quite supportive. The whole thing has upset him terribly of course, despite his reservations about Binnie. Well, it's not exactly calmed me. I still get nightmares about opening that door. The resistance behind it." He shivered a little. "Poor Binnie."

"Any idea when she was killed?"

He shook his head. "The police aren't saying. I got back well after midnight – I was at a blues session in a pub in Newhaven as I think you know – but I didn't go to the office. I just let myself in the front door and then came up here. In the morning I opened up to let you in and then went into the contemporary gallery. It wasn't until – what? – about half past ten that I went to the office and found her. If you ask me it happened the night before, though." He shivered again. "She was lying there all the time. If she'd come in the morning I would have been bound to see her."

"So she left Bill Riley's soirée and came here."

"She might have gone home first."

"True. But she had keys and she knew how to open the office?"

"Of course. Not like Larry who's hopeless with systems."

That made me think. Whoever had killed Binnie Grant had left her in the office, with systems still open even if the door was closed, but had been able to lock up when he left. Assuming it was a he. Blows to the head usually suggest a he. The sequence would fit Granger.

"Multiple head injuries," Dennis said, as though reading my thoughts. "Wallace told me that much."

"Weapon?"

"Not found. It seems unlikely to be Larry – I bet you're thinking about the office not being alarmed – because I don't see him as a blow-to-the-head man, do you?"

I was slightly taken aback by his frankness and let my gaze move off his face towards a small painting on the wall in which a strange figure with a naked female body but Cubist equine head was being pursued by a galloping angular bull of rampant character. It disturbed my train of thought.

"Tim?"

I turned back to meet his eye. "No I don't, but you never know. Even fragile people driven to distraction can lose control. You remember we talked about something going more wrong than usual between Binnie Grant and Larry Granger? Something you couldn't put your finger on?"

"I have thought and thought about it. I still can't believe in Larry as a killer, though."

"No more than I can believe in you."

"Thanks, Tim. You are probably unique in Highton right now. But my physique and opportunity all point my way. Not only that but Wallace picked up gossip from someone in the Friends. He and Stamford have been harping on at me about how Binnie might have liked to have me replaced with a more curatorial-archivist type of manager. Which would have mollified Veronica Chalmers, too."

"Someone more like Binnie herself, you mean?"

"I hadn't thought of that."

"Even Larry Granger admitted to a preference for the museum-collection side rather than the modern sales, despite differences with Binnie Grant."

"That hasn't made him restrain me in any way up to now, Tim."

"The police are scratching for motive, mixing ambition with common theft. They're confused. There's no sign of the Sickert –"

"They searched in here, in my flat, I can tell you."

" – and they haven't yet got forensic evidence of her killer. Nor a weapon."

"Stamford keeps hinting at some line they've got." He made a rueful grimace. "My prints are all over everything, as might be expected. So are everyone else's though. The inference is that I've been at some kind of art theft game for years, using my expertise and art training. The laugh is that I've little time for archivism or art history. The Binnie replacement motive is at a hundred and eighty degrees to my acting as a scout for some mad art collector. Even if you were my cohort in crime and I was scouting for your Fund, it's Larry Granger who got you down here, not me."

"I wonder why."

He blinked in surprise. "Surely we know that?"

"Dennis, I've now had a couple of rants from Larry. One about arts funding and one about the deterioration of Highton. He was at odds with Binnie Grant over something. Is he all right?"

"You suspect Larry?"

"I just worry a little, that's all. Behind that urbane exterior he's tense."

"Look, everyone in Highton is pissed off about the way the town's gone down in tone. And the arts funding thing is an absolute scandal. I can't say what the beef was between him and Binnie but he's always been OK with me. I'm sure he's very upset about her death. You'll have to talk to him about these things."

I held up a mollifying hand. Clearly, Dennis had his loyalties. "Sorry, Dennis. Just thinking out loud. I'm paid to consider the unthinkable. No nasturtiums being unnecessarily cast or anything. I have to ask you one more question, though."

"Fire away."

"The day before Binnie died I was in the office. You remember that you had some unexpected Belgian visitors, then you and Larry came in and I asked if I could use the photocopier."

"Of course."

"Before you came in I opened a folder on the desk by mistake. There was a sheet torn out of a magazine in it. An illustration from an old magazine called *La Nouvelle Perspective Artistique*. Belgian or French. Was it yours?"

He frowned. "Doesn't ring any bells with me, Tim. Much more likely to be one of Binnie's. What was the illustration?"

"A Sickert of the Camden Town Murder series. One I've never seen before."

His eyes went round. "Really? What sort of date? I mean, how old was the magazine?"

"Somewhere round the First World War, I'd guess. You really do mean that you never saw it?"

He shook his head emphatically, making his beard crinkle. "No I didn't. I'd certainly remember a thing like that. What sort of scene was it?"

"A cross between *L'Affaire de Camden Town* and *What Shall we Do For The Rent*? Really an eye-stopper."

His eyes widened. "Christ. It must have been Binnie's. But was it there the next day? When she was – when I found her, I mean?"

"No it wasn't." I hesitated for a moment. Should I tell him that it had gone five minutes after my photocopier excuse, when I returned from Sylvia's cubby hole?

He decided for me. "Then her murderer must have taken it."

I shook my head, perplexed. "You never saw it?"

"No Tim, I didn't."

"Sorry to press it." I had gone as far as I dared. "I'll get on my way. Thanks for levelling with me."

"I understand, Tim, and it's OK. Are you staying here tonight? I won't be going out but if you want to come round –"

"No thanks. I've got some work to do. See you soon."

I took another quick look at his paintings and retraced my steps downstairs. Dennis was best left for a bit. Besides, I had magazines back on my mind. Why didn't Larry Granger – and what on earth was Binnie doing…

Then there was another more immediate thing that had just started bothering me. That Vorticist painting of the naked female horse-lady, a sort of reverse land-mermaid being pursued by a bull, put me in mind of only one artist of a kind of Wyndham Lewis mode: Kathy Marsden.

How did the manager of the gallery come to own a painting by its Royal Academy trustee? Her stuff, when it sold, was wildly expensive. And extremely sensual. I recalled that some of her work made Sickert's sordid nudes look very static; there was a mobility about her geometric mythological figures that left no doubt as to the intentions and outcome on either side. Her work explored the dark regions of erotic imagination without flinching. Sickert, moving on, would have approved – an idea suddenly hit me –

Could it be Kathy who phoned Mr Goodston about *La*

Nouvelle Perspective Artistique, not Binnie? On Dennis's behalf? He had been as near to the folder in the office as anyone. And owned one of Kathy's paintings.

Or was it one of his own canvases, a kind of copy inspired by her work?

Or was I getting just too suspicious?

*   *   *

Dusk was starting to fall. The car was parked down on the flat land of the estuary, in the municipal area provided by the town council for use after stumping up three quid for every 12 hours. Cheaper than London but doubtless a minor gold mine to Highton Town Council.

It was as I descended the cobbled hill towards the flat zone that I heard the car alarm go off. I started to run.

In the distance I saw the side lights flashing and the back door high up, opened as it turned out by a quick jemmying of the lock. A man had his whole body stooped inside and he emerged with a bulky pile of paper in his arms.

The magazines. Hope Anderson's magazines.

"Oy!" I bellowed, accelerating down the ridiculous ankle-turning cobbles, deliberately set up high to give a false "ye olde medieval" surface capable of knocking the soles off your shoes.

He was running away towards a white van parked alongside the main road. As I stumbled and damn near mowed down an old dear carrying a shopping bag up the hill, he threw the pile into the side door of the van and slammed it shut. I hit the flat running like a demon, legs pumping like pistons as he scurried round the van and jumped in the other side. It screeched off at once down the road towards Lewes and the main coastal highway.

By the time I got to the pullulating, hooting, flashing Volvo the van was well away into the distance. I tried to slam down the back door and jump in to give pursuit but the jemmied lock wouldn't shut and the door yawned open. There was no way I could drive fast after the van with that door flapping in the air behind me. By the time I'd tried to close it and searched for something to tie it down with the van was long gone.

The enemy had scored.

I recognised the thief, though. It was the thick-necked, sharp-nosed codger who'd been shaking Mr Goodston in his shop.

Chapter Twenty-One

In the calm safety of my hotel room, I sat down at a small table equipped with a lamp and sipped a cup of tea. One of the better things about British hotels is the tea and coffee kit cleanly set up in the room. I hate having to go down to a coffee shop and sit like a spare part over a single cup.

I was back in a bad temper. The Volvo would have to go into a local garage for a door repair. I would have dutifully reported the break-in to the police station but by the time I got there it was closed. Five-thirty was knocking-off time for PC Wallace; home to wife and high tea in Denton, presumably. Muttering to myself, I returned to the hotel. By now it was getting dark.

My irritation spilled over into phoning Nobby Roberts. His direct line to the Yard is on my mobile but I can recall it from memory. Since he'd messed me up with Stamford I thought it was only fair he should know that things were taking a more complicated turn than a mere murder in the course of robbery. He answered the phone himself. My old friend was still at work, even if PC Wallace wasn't. Catching the sharp tone in my voice, he adopted a bantering attitude when I spoke to him.

"Nobby, you bastard. It's me: Tim."

"Why am I not surprised? Where are you?"

"In Highton. Pissed off."

"Serve you right. I hear you're at your old habits again," he answered.

"Oh, is that what you think? I've just been read the Riot Act by a local Sussex plodder called Stamford, mainly because you gave him an entirely misleading account of my past history."

"I merely conveyed the facts."

"You creep. You ungrateful creep. You fellows in the backs are all the same. We throw the ball to you from a terrible scrum and you claim all the credit when you prance across the line."

"You have a conveniently short memory."

"My memory is excellent. But my condition is not. I've just had my car broken into and the police station was closed when I went to report it."

"That's life in the peaceful provinces for you, Tim. It seems a minor transgression compared with Stamford's description. I gather you attend to the bumping off of respectable old ladies and art archivists now. Quite apart from stealing paintings instead of buying them for the Fund. What does Sue think?"

"Very funny. Thanks to you I'm on some sort of suspect list."

"Thanks to me you're not banged up in chokey. Stamford was thinking of detaining you but I did tell him that although of a mendacious disposition you're more of a danger to yourself than the public at large. Front row men are always tripping over their own feet."

"Charming. The way you rozzers blithely jug the innocent citizen these days is a national scandal. Remind me not to ask you for a reference, will you?"

"Innocent is not an adjective I'd apply to you. Thanks for expressing your appreciation however. Is that all? I have to talk to an anti-terrorist plainclothes armed response squad in five minutes and they tend to be punctual."

"Have you? Well tell them to try not to shoot anyone elderly, will you? Down here in Highton they take that sort of thing personally."

"I'll bear it in mind. You may want their help one day, though."

"Me? Never."

"Don't be too sure. Anyway, if you're in Highton it must be time for your carpet slippers and cocoa now, Tim. Got a nice cosy book to read in your armchair before you turn in?"

"Magazines actually, Nobby. Magazines."

* * *

The smaller pile of magazines from Mr Goodston's solicitor friend in Isleworth was stacked beside me. I started to go through their rather tatty pages recording events of long ago but somehow very familiar, as though school history lessons and the bombardment of the past on TV had imprinted these happenings as part of my own period. The presentation, though, was rather different.

I remembered that in the pages of an 1869 issue of the *Graphic* I once saw an illustration of a woodcut, *Homeless and Hungry* by Luke Fildes. The huddled people reminded me of the painting *Applicants for Admission to a Casual Ward* made famous by the same artist for its depiction of the terrible state of London's poor. Those writing about Whitechapel and Jack the Ripper sometimes use it as an illustration of the dreadful conditions in which his victims lived.

There seemed little order in the random pile beside me. The Afghan War was big news throughout and I realised that several copies were from 1880 like the one I'd looked at when loading up at Mr Goodston's. Spellings like Candahar and Gandamuk caught my attention. The Tay Bridge disaster got a lot of coverage too, with full page grainy black and white scenes by artists like Dadd. An Italian asphalt worker attacked the Italian Church in Hatton Garden, firing a revolver and damaging things but not people. There were sketches of the Queens Bench Prison. The St Gothard Tunnel was at last completed; another sharp black and white drawing showed diggers shaking hands through a hole in the rock face.

New novels by people called Mr Jephson and Holme Lee were advertised along with dear old Collis Brown's medicines. A Grosvenor Gallery exhibition was reviewed. Mr WN Nicholson's portrait, as the new MP for Newark, caught my eye. That was the future Sir William Nicholson's father; twenty-eight years later the son did a quick book cover sketch for *Imperial Brown of Brixton*. You can pick up connections everywhere if you want to confuse yourself.

It was the Irish stuff that tore the heartstrings. The magazines gave it enough coverage to make sure no one missed it. Evictions and distress came across in every issue. An 1882 copy illustrated Parnell's friends ploughing his land while he was in jail. An evicted family were shown on a rainy track with all their possessions in a cart; their old horse had fallen dead between the shafts. Here was an Irish fisherman's cabin in starving Connemara; there were prisoners in a police cell. No one could say they didn't know. The *Illustrated London News* said that that climate in Western Ireland was detestable, but no worse than Mull or Skye. Harry Furniss provided sketches of dismal life in Galway.

Then there were opium dens and convicts in Siberia. A coffee tavern called The Plimsoll Arms was opened at the entrance to St Katherine's Dock. A man called Maclean tried to shoot the Queen. He was the fourth to have a go, apparently. For some reason, convicts in Siberia were news; more of them followed.

Clarkson Stanfield, our very own fireplace painter, had a big page reproduction of his painting of a passage boat on the Scheldt. Luke Fildes illustrated scenes from some lady's novel. Someone with initials WHO showed sketches of gypsy life at Hackney Wick, Mitcham Common and Notting Hill. The magazine said that honest men and women, though of slovenly and irregular habit, might exist among this odd fragment of our motley population.

There didn't seem to be anything really significant or valuable to my eye. Nothing worth stealing or fighting for.

It was between pages depicting a coal mine disaster, the Leycett Colliery somewhere round Newcastle-under-Lyne, with an anxious crowd shown waiting for news of the sixty or seventy lives lost, that I found a letter placed carefully unfolded but smoothed flat by years of compression. The writing on the dull sheet was small and quite neat, in faded ink, with few loops.

Dear Henry,

I am sorry not to have replied to you but I have been away to the far end of Drenthe on a barge. The rainy weather persists and may continue for a while. It increases my melancholy – I need to work and the difficulties are great. Colliers here are suffering like yours, too.

It was good to hear from you; Theo forwarded your letter from Paris. The days at Isleworth seem so remote, even further away than Lambeth. My English I have not practised for a long time so excuse my lack of expression. The longing for religion amongst the people of large cities is great and they crowd to hear evangelists like you. I envy you the creation of the kingdom of God on earth and I hope you too have the feeling like I had of coming out from underground into the daylight of the pulpit.

Yet I must scrape to get the right colours and without a studio. When I walked along the Thames to Richmond after preaching the chestnut leaves were yellow against the blue sky. Here the long canals are like miles and miles of Van Goyens and would not catch the pleasure of Tissot or Millais, who I once met in the street.

Under this was an ink sketch of a bare landscape with a long canal bank and hatched fields with furrows and piles of something like small corn stukes dotted along them. The writing continued in a scrawl along the side of the sketch.

The light here is better than London but still not satisfactory. One's energy is absorbed and feelings of craziness or despair come and go together. I have had many conversations with Jews who are not like the nonconformist pigs I have written about before…

I put the letter down. A feeling I can't describe was overcoming all other feelings. It was that creepy feeling you get when you stumble on something you think may be shattering but you aren't quite sure. The feeling that says to you that this could be something unrepeatably important, something that you'll look back on in years to come and sigh for because it will never happen again. Life does not deal out many events like this.

But then you're terrified that you may be wrong.

I put that magazine down and went through the others with hands that shook and fingers that stumbled like thumbs, trying to prise open the old pages as carefully as I could. There were about two dozen letters pressed between the leaves of various magazines, most of them issues dating from 1880 onwards. The letters were from between 1882, when the writer seems to have been in The Hague and 1884, from a place called Neunen. Many of them had ink sketches to illustrate them. There was one of a bird's nest I liked and a gloomy one of poor people seated at a farm table. Then I found one of a night scene in which, beyond trees, the moon was let into a dark-hatched sky in which little daisy-like shapes, each a centre circle with radiating outward lines like spokes spotted through the ink-lined celestial squiggles. They were stars.

Starry, starry night.

All the letters were signed with the simple Christian name of the same man.

Vincent.

Chapter Twenty-Two

"Isleworth." Sue took a deep draught from her gin and tonic. "Isleworth. I should have known. I always think of Ramsgate. And before that Brixton, where he fell in love with the landlady's daughter, Ursula Loyer."

I made an unwise correction. I was still full of excitement. "They say now that it was Lambeth, actually, Sue. When Van Gogh stayed with them the Loyers lived in Hackford Road. Just off the Brixton Road, to be fair."

She frowned. Sue is the resident expert. She doesn't like to be corrected by ex rugby playing husbands. "Be that as it may, when he came back from Paris in 1876 – he was fired from the Goupil Gallery – he went to Ramsgate, where he taught in a boys' school, got paid nothing and the bed had bugs. The school moved to Isleworth but still no pay. So he changed to a Methodist school and preached on Sundays. That must be where he met this Henry Conway, evidently another lay preacher."

"Seems like it."

Her eyes were as bright as diamonds. "My God, Tim, what an important find."

I had brought the magazines and their precious contents home to our flat in Onslow Gardens before taking them to the Bank vaults in the morning. Telling Sue everything, and showing her, has priority with that sort of thing. When she first saw the letters she nearly had kittens. We sat together on the big settee, going through and through them with infinite care; gloves should be worn for that sort of examination.

"Well." I was still getting to grips with things, some of them having nothing to do with the letters in front of us. "If that aspect of the past is more important than his paintings, I suppose it is an important find. They are only letters and drawings but anything by Vincent Van Gogh, especially early stuff, seems to be hot property right now."

"In more senses than one."

"True."

She held one of the sheets in her hand as though it were made of gossamer. "No one has logged this Henry Conway that they are written to before. I mean, there are whole books of Van Gogh's letters, especially to his brother Theo but not this man. There was an English chap called Gladwell who befriended him in Paris but that ended when Vincent came back here. There are those sketches of chapels at Petersham and Turnham Green he sent to Theo. Lots of books show those. But this is the reverse; sketches made in Holland and sent back here. That time has always been considered as his dark days in Neunen. The starry sky – God, just look at it – predates Arles by four years. There are those who'd pay a fortune for these letters. Any of the big museum-galleries, especially Amsterdam."

"Some of those, as you call them, might do worse than pay a fortune to get hold of them."

"Indeed. But how would they know about them?"

"Ah. I wondered if you could enquire a bit more about that break-in at Amsterdam for me, Sue. As one in the trade, so to speak. It might cast light on the subject."

"I can try. But someone else must have got to know about these letters just about the time Mr Goodston's late widow-client – who presumably was a descendant of Conway's – died and her estate was disposed of by the solicitor. My God. Never sell all the contents of an attic until you've gone through everything. Even Mr Goodston didn't bother to look inside."

"Why should he?" I was feeling sorry for Mr Goodston and his telling remark that in my hands the magazines would be a good investment. "They were a job lot. And he'd got another job lot with Hope Anderson's things. A plethora of the *Illustrated London News* and the *Graphic*. The bloke who roughed him up probably contributed to Mr Goodston's neglect of them, too. It distracted him. He was pleased to sell them to me, to get them and their unpleasant aura out of his shop. Hope Anderson's copies are presumably being frenziedly searched right now by those two pug-uglies for precisely what we have, by pure chance, retained here."

"Amazing."

"What I don't understand is how the letters came to be inside the magazines. And how anyone would guess that."

She gestured at a book she'd been consulting. "In the early 1880s Van Gogh had a Brussels friend called Anton von Rappard. Rappard subscribed to that sort of magazine and showed him the illustrations by Fildes and Herkomer and presumably Tissot, whose work Van Gogh had seen at the Royal Academy when he was in London. Vincent bought magazines singly and in bound volumes. Old ones would have come cheaply to him. Some of the letters refer to the illustrations he wanted Conway to look at. Vincent Van Gogh had a phase of wanting to become a graphic artist. You must have read that he was keen on the urban poverty aspects rather than Tissot's socially well-dressed but supposedly vulgar society. Fildes was much nearer the mark; an urban version of Millet's rural poverty. Vincent made scrapbooks of all that stuff. The coal mine things were particularly his interest. Perhaps he sent Henry Conway the magazines and referred to doing so somewhere else. In letters to Theo, maybe. That might be where the information came from. It would require a lot of delving." She paused thoughtfully. "There could have been an archivist at work."

I put an image of Binnie Grant to the back of my mind. I'm not an archivist really, she'd said; I'm an art historian. Dennis Cash said he had no feel for the world of art curatorship; Larry Granger, often in Dieppe, wasn't an archivist either.

My thoughts came back to the present. "Van Gogh was stony broke. Sending letters was one thing; sending magazines would cost more."

Sue shook her head. "Not much in those days. His parents

were funding him to study in The Hague. If he hadn't caused such trouble by setting up with Sien Hoornik he might have got more money out of them. A diseased pregnant prostitute who'd had a daughter already wasn't exactly acceptable; his father thought of having him certified insane then and there. It was only when he was literally clapped-out that his father paid for him to have a rest in Drenthe." She looked carefully at the handwriting in front of her. "He doesn't mention much of this to Henry Conway, who would presumably have been horrified. These letters need careful analysis by an expert."

I thought of Binnie Grant again and frowned. Was that – no, that was to do with Sickert and Camden Town. This surely was something else. There was something else, too, that I had to get off my chest to Sue.

"What's up?"

"The irony is that I was going to buy the magazines myself. For us and our art library. I thought that Mr Goodston would underprice them if I told him they were for me, so I said they were for the Art Fund. He'd already given me Reggie Turner's book and I didn't want him to give the magazines away dirt cheap. So I said they were for the Fund and paid for them with an Art Fund cheque. That's why they belong to the Art Fund, not me."

She smiled. "You could refund the Art Fund's money and keep quiet."

I knew she wasn't serious. "I couldn't do that. I'd never live with myself. There's a saying in Chaucer: *mordre wol out*. The crime will always be detected. Besides, as a director of an art fund I couldn't deal in the same goods for myself on the side. That's dishonest. Reference books and magazines are one thing; gems like this are another."

"I hope Jeremy appreciates the ethics of his Art Fund director. I know I do. Dear Tim: we're not starving and I wouldn't like to own letters like these. They would bring criminals and they're a record of a man sliding into madness. I have my superstitions too, you know. You'll have your moment of glory when they're authenticated and Jeremy struts about in pride. In the meantime thank heaven they'll be safe in the Bank vault. When are you going to tell Jeremy about them? About what's in the magazines, I mean? They do belong to the Art Fund, after all, and he and Geoffrey are your fellow directors."

"Jeremy has been being particularly offensive about my misfortunes down at Highton. So I shall tell him at the right moment. When I know a lot more about several things. He might just scrabble through the vault himself first. I don't think he will, though; it's not the way we play the game. One of Jeremy's favourite quotations is 'curiosity killed the cat'. Pride and established procedure will make him wait for me to enlighten him. At the right time I'll suggest some sort of recompense to Mr Goodston. An *ex gratia* payment, perhaps, since the Bank is more fond of that expression than vulgar donations. I know we don't have to give Mr Goodston anything but I'll feel better if we do."

"It's a kind thought."

"I owe him for this and past assistance. Without the copy of *Imperial Brown of Brixton* I might not have become properly alerted to the dark side of George Harland's collection. Although Frank Stevens guessed at it without really knowing anything concrete. Binnie Grant was onto it, I'm sure."

"And she's dead. So go carefully."

"I wonder what she found. And why Larry Granger or Dennis Cash didn't tell me about the folder with the missing Sickert illustrated in it. Dennis has denied knowing anything about it; I haven't tackled Larry Granger on the subject yet."

"He might wonder why you haven't mentioned your acquisition of a Reggie Turner first edition. He collects them, you said."

"Yes. Dennis Cash told me at dinner the first time. Larry Granger rather glossed over it."

"Like you."

"Innate caution, Sue. Innate caution. Never tell everybody everything."

"Including me?"

"Of course not. I tell you everything."

"Liar!"

"What would I hide? My life is an open book to you. I only dissimulate with others."

"Is that what you call it? It sounds as though it covers a multitude of sins. I am well aware of your nature. So is Jeremy. You are clandestine with both of us."

"Sue!"

"You are. Which makes life much more interesting. Exciting, even. There is nothing worse than a life without excitement. Provided it doesn't affect William. So do take these" – she looked regretfully at the Van Gogh letters – "to your City vaults, away from trouble. Which reminds me; there's a new couple just moved into the flat upstairs. A bit loud on the distaff side, if they're married. She's a tycoon in the City too, goes out at about the same time as you normally do, but he seems to be a house husband."

"Wise fellow. Clever of him."

"Nonsense. You'd hate that. I think you might like to meet them although she's pretty strident; you would feel pretty bad if you depended on my income and I got like she seems to be."

"How very true." I looked at her empty glass. "What about my replenishing that before I go out and get us another curry?"

"You are ineradicably vulgar, Tim. I do not accept that this can become a habit." She then smiled knowingly. "But I think you deserve one this time."

Chapter Twenty-Three

"Portarlington Investments." Geoffrey Price put a heavy file down on the top of the polished mahogany table. Then he sat ponderously on one of the mahogany repro Chippendale chairs beside it. His striped suit crinkled at the elbows. "Portarlington Investments."

"Yes, yes, Geoffrey. You've already said it once." Jeremy White was all pinstriped, charcoal and white-cuffed impatience. "And we know why we're here."

Geoffrey put on his spectacles and gave Jeremy an old-fashioned look over the top of the frame. Geoffrey is an Accountant with a capital A and likes to bring a certain gravitas to his pronouncements. He is all too aware that people can take what he says for gospel and this bothers him. Far from being hewn in stone, accountancy pronouncements are as transitory as the dew on the petal of a rose. A balance sheet is a mere snapshot of a situation at a fleeting moment. A profit and loss account is as much a relict of yesterday as an old maid at a spinning wheel. Geoffrey may be the scorer but he knows that the game moves on far too quickly for comfort. Accounts are merely another form of history.

"I have done as you asked and made a much more detailed analysis of their portfolio and performance than would normally be the case."

"Good. And?"

"In normal circumstances the analysis would not be required to go into quite such depth as to matters of detailed downside exchange risk, withholding tax liability and other matters relating to the proportion of investment portfolio relating to exposure to say, ecological and ethical investment fund managers who can put a spoke in the works."

"Splendid. And?"

"There is, of course, a fiduciary aspect which, if taking into account the Inland Revenue's stated policy of examining

European investments in the light of the latest Brussels amend-
ments to –"

"Geoffrey! For Christ's sake will you stop woffling! Just tell
us what state Portarlington is in!"

"Really, Jeremy, at such short notice, all I can say is –"

"Short notice? Short notice?" Jeremy bridled. "We've had
Portarlington in our sights since –"

He broke off, seeing Geoffrey glance over his glasses at me in
warning and me scowling and tightening my lips.

" – since Tim went down to Highton," he finished lamely.

"Ha! A likely story."

"There is no need for truculence from you, Tim." Jeremy's
eyes flashed their whites at me sidelong. "Geoffrey? For heaven's
sake will you stop prevaricating and answer my simple question
in simple terms or not?"

"Certainly, Jeremy." Geoffrey took off his glasses. "In my
view Portarlington is as sound as a bell."

"What?"

"Given that investment generally since the 11th of September
2001 has been a dismal scene, Portarlington has shown remarkable resilience and realignment."

"It has?"

"It has. The performance has been commendable. There is an
admirable spread, a good cash reserve and prudent use of
resources."

"Get that use of the word prudent, Jeremy," I intervened.
"Used to be Gordon Brown's favourite."

Geoffrey shook his head gravely. "Not now, alas, Tim. The
economy here is in dire straits. Socialism has taken over from
common sense. But Portarlington is a well-managed fund. My
analysis leads me to no other conclusion."

"There you are! There you are! What have I said from the
beginning?" Jeremy was all over the place as usual. "I knew it was
a good prospect!"

"What about Bill Riley himself?"

Geoffrey picked up his glasses once again. "The majority shareholding and his position generally are very good. He benefits from enormous bonuses which the shareholders do not grudge him in view of his expertise. No challenges exist to his chairmanship. He is a very wealthy man. There is no hint of financial crisis in his situation."

"There you are! There you are!" A gesture flashed white cuff and gold link in my direction. "Could you, just for once, try to be a little less grudging and resentful? Try to ingratiate yourself just a little? Men like Riley are often difficult initially but they are merely putting one through one's paces. They have to put up with myriad dunning approaches, poor fellows."

I ignored Jeremy's outburst. "No hint of any scandal, Geoffrey?"

"Tim! Really!" Jeremy's blond hair rose in a shocked float above his brow. "We do not stoop to muck-raking in this Bank."

"None. I've chatted to a few contacts." Geoffrey shook his head. "He's a tough cookie but he appears to be devoted to his family. His main indulgence is golf."

"I gathered that. He plays all over Sussex, goes through France down to Spain and plays extensively there."

"*Ye-es*." Geoffrey drew the word out. "Not so extensively in Spain."

"No?"

"No. He is the joint owner of a very exclusive golf club down near Alicante. Inland somewhere. Its membership is highly select, I gather. European businessmen of like wealth and inclination."

"Hoity-toity."

"Tim!" My employer was off again. "You can't object to men like Riley wanting exclusivity. They don't want every sales manager from Frankfurt or Docklands dunning them on the green. There has to be somewhere one can get away. I entirely approve."

Jeremy is a yachtsman and keeps a fine ketch down on the

Hamble. Better than any golf course for isolation if needed.

"Strange. Dennis Cash seemed to think that all was not quite well with his affairs. He doesn't seem to have subbed the Highton Art Gallery much."

"Why should he?" Another flash of cuff swept across my view. "He gives his time generously as a trustee. The lamentable arts authorities should be looking after such places. Our taxes are being squandered by arts officials. I entirely agree with Larry Granger on that one. Geoffrey, you have done your work admirably."

"Thank you, Jeremy."

"Hmm." There was still something nagging at me. "Riley looks fireproof. Just golf, you say, Geoffrey? I know he collects quite a few paintings, too. I've seen his Sickert of Dieppe."

"Rich men tend to, don't they? He has one or two friends who are collectors, too, Tim. They play golf together. In Spain, mainly."

"There you are! There it all is! All perfectly open and above board." Jeremy waved a random arm, causing another gold cuff-link-flash to glint in an arc. "Golf and the arts; seldom could a man be so innocently employed. If you ask me this fellow Cash is deliberately trying to divert attention from himself and his own guilt. Casting vague aspersions on Riley; it's disgraceful."

"Maybe Riley has been preoccupied by something else."

"I should say so. With this government doing its utmost to ruin business conditions there's much for a man like Riley to be preoccupied about."

"Looks like it's between Dennis Cash and me, then."

Blond eyebrows shot up. "What? What is?"

"When I left Highton, Jeremy, the betting for an arrest was apparently two to one on Dennis, three to one on me and four to one on Larry Granger. With the painting snaffled by our Art Fund. Riley isn't in the running. It has been confirmed that he was with his wife at the crucial time."

"Good God! This is not a matter for jest!"

"Quite good money is being laid by the old folk, Gilbert Macintosh says."

"Who the blazes is Gilbert Macintosh?"

"Old rugger blue. Met him in the pub. Played full back for Scotland in –"

"Oh no! Not rugby! Please! You haven't been wasting your time yarning and quaffing flagons of beer with some old soak of an ex-rugby blue instead of getting on, have you?"

"Local knowledge, Jeremy. Reconnaissance is essential to strategy; Wellington made a point of it."

"Never mind what Wellington said."

"If you say not, Jeremy."

"Just try to get back and retrieve something out of the appalling situation you have created."

"Me?"

"Try to avoid being arrested. Try to keep the Bank's reputation clean. Look after Larry Granger, to whom we are indebted. See if you can find a solution to their funding problems. Without asking for money from us. And butter up Riley. Try to impress. Stay out of the pub. Do not become associated with Cash."

"Is that all?"

"Go! For God's sake, go! And no more red herrings about Riley. Cash is the man you need to watch."

"If you say so, Jeremy."

"I do say so! I do!"

"In that case, I'm off." I bowed at our accountant. "Many thanks, Geoffrey."

"My pleasure, Tim."

I got to the door before Jeremy's voice halted me.

"Oh, Tim?" It was deliberately casual.

"Yes, Jeremy?"

"I gather that you deposited some documents in the vault for safe keeping this morning."

"I did, Jeremy."

"Anything I should know about?"

"Nothing too vital, no."

"But important enough to go into the vault?"

"Yes, Jeremy."

"The moment you arrived?"

"Yes, Jeremy."

"God give me patience! This is like getting blood out of a stone. It must be to do with the Art Fund, I know it must. You're always at your most furtive when skulking about on Fund affairs. What have you deposited in the vault?"

"Some old magazines, Jeremy."

He gaped. "Old magazines? What old magazines?"

"Some nineteenth century copies of the *Graphic* and the *Illustrated London News* which, almost inadvertently, I bought for the Art Fund. Reference material."

"Inadvertently? In the vault? *The vault*? Why? For pity's sake, why?"

"They may have extraordinary value. They are almost certainly the target of criminal elements. They need protecting."

Geoffrey Price congealed into a pinstriped statue. Jeremy's face was a picture. Jaw open, blond hair over one eye, silk tie puffed over his charcoal jacket, he gaped at me in ill-concealed horror. I took pity on him.

"Be patient, Jeremy. Do not, under any circumstances, disturb those magazines. All will be revealed. As soon as I have made certain enquiries."

He swallowed. His voice was barely audible. "Enquiries? What kind of enquiries?"

"Into criminal elements who broke into my car to try and steal them."

"Dear God. Don't leave it too long. Please don't leave it too long," he whispered. "Will you?"

"I won't," I promised.

And left.

Chapter Twenty-Four

"My goodness." Charles Massenaux swung his long pinstriped legs down off the scratched oak desktop in front of him and sat up to gape at me in mock surprise. A Staffordshire pottery figure he held in one hand was put down on a precarious corner of the cluttered surface. "We are indeed honoured. One of our company directors no less, even if only of non-executive standing with a watching brief from White's Bank, come to visit us. And to visit us in the sturdy form of Mr Tim Simpson, Art Fund Director of that ilk, What have we done to incur this unexpected but signal honour? Is this not a dawn but a late morning raid? Is our efficiency to be assessed? Are we to be retrenched, downsized, rationalised, or some such euphemism for getting the chop?"

"Hello, Charles." I pulled out the small hard chair in front of his desk and sat down on it. "As one company director to another, how's trade?"

He pulled a face. "You get the financial reports and the management accounts like everyone else on the board. What do you think?"

"Diabolical."

"Succinctly expressed. Windows would be being jumped out of were it not for the fact that the bloody windows won't open for want of maintenance. The trade press, bless them, keep spotting the odd swallow but summer recedes further and further into the drizzle. Have you come to tell me I'm being posted to Hammersmith? Or Notting Hill? Or some such outpost in the hostile swamps of Outer London to which the night soil carts still rumble?"

I smiled. Charles is a smooth cove, a director of Christerby's International Fine Art Auctioneers no less, in which the Bank has a stake. He is always dapper in chalk stripe worsted suit, flash tie and white collar on the neck of a Bengal striped shirt. His shoes are much shinier black brogues than mine but he has a distressing habit of wearing wincingly pink or startlingly scarlet socks depending on the colour of his tie. The very dearest West End barber carefully maintains his wavy brown hair, which he tamps down with a thoughtful stroking gesture from time to time. Amongst the porters whose brown coated forms passed his partitioned office from time to time, staggering under Queen Anne furniture or aloofly bearing treasures whose owners would shiver at their casual carriage, he is known as Flash Chas. Never to his face of course.

His reference to Hammersmith and Notting Hill was an oblique cut at the movement of much of the fine art and auction trade out of the West End. Charles has always been a resolutely Bond Street man. Put him anywhere else and he is distressed. He will travel all over the country in pursuit of auctionable quarry and to appear glibly on the TV programmes of which he is an ornament as well as expert but his base is Bond Street. Charles has the manner and the elan of the Aston Martin salesman who knows that really topnotch clientele will not go to Grimsby or Hull for its fish; only a restaurant in the West End or Harrods will do.

"As far as I know, you are safe in Bond Street for the moment, Charles. The deep brown swamps are holding their fire until the they see the red of your ledger."

He was still sceptical. "I am as Saddam was to Baghdad for so long, you mean? The forces are merely heading in my direction; they have not yet opened fire? How long have I got before I need my private bunker?"

"I know of no forces heading in your direction. It is true that trade is very dismal at present but news of further retrenchment has not come to my ears. You must not get paranoid about the centrifugal forces which have closed so many Bond Street emporia in the last year or two."

"Must I not? It's hard to retain one's cool, dear Tim."

"There have been over one hundred thousand job losses in the City but I am retaining my cool. It is in cool mood that I have come to question you about Van Gogh."

His eyebrows went up. "Van Gogh? Don't hesitate; sell at once. Go and live somewhere warm, where wine is a reasonable price."

"Shocking! Defeatism of that sort is what is causing the Stock Market to spiral downwards."

"My dear Tim. You may recall an Australian entrepreneur called Alan Bond. His Van Gogh was funded at spectacular numbers of millions and used as collateral. You may also recall how the Japanese once flocked to buy the Dutchman's work. Times are not auspicious even if he is one of the highest scorers. A Van Gogh in my possession would be changed into good clinking coinage, so scarce these days."

"Which means that it must be a bad time to sell."

"Your implied reproof is heard. Van Gogh, true, is still a highly valuable star. For a good Van Gogh you can talk of double-digit millions. But I was being theoretical." He gave me a severe look. "You do not have a Van Gogh. The Art Fund, I mean, does not have a Van Gogh. Nor is it the policy of your excellent Fund to buy works that are foreign. That are not British. Even if you had the many millions required, which you haven't. Have you?"

"Never mind what cash we have. We have art works by foreigners with British connections or subjects. Monet of the Pool of London. Rodin of Gwen John. Winslow Homer of Cullercoats."

His face creased into a concentrated frown. "Van Gogh? Britain?"

"Van Gogh. England."

He brought his shiny shoes down off the desk with a swift muscular leg movement and slammed them to the floor. "My God! Brixton? Ramsgate? Isleworth?"

"Well done, Charles. You have the locations off by heart."

He sat bolt upright, staring at me with the same concentrated frown. "I don't believe this. You are thinking of buying something of Van Gogh's from that period? It must be sketches or letters."

"Both."

"They'll cost you a fortune. If White's Art Fund shows any

interest, they'll cost you your skin."

"No they won't. I did not say I was buying. I've already got them. Or at least the Art Fund has."

He gaped at me. A long silence followed, during which I looked at him steadily. Eventually I couldn't resist a grin. He put his face in his hands and let out what used to be called a hollow groan.

"Oh, no! Please, no!"

"Let me tell you how I came by them."

I gave him a fairly succinct précis about the magazines, keeping the violence down to the minimum.

He took his face out of his hands. "It's not fair," he moaned.

"I know. I could have owned them."

"You're sure? You're absolutely sure?"

"Sue has OK'd them."

"Then they're OK. But it's still not fair."

"When was life ever fair?"

"I suppose you've just come to rub my face in this, have you? Timmy's little triumph?"

"No, Charles. If the Fund ever comes to sell the letters on the open market, I swear you shall have the selling of them. We do realise assets from time to time, as you know. Like football clubs we take a view as to when we think a star's peak has been passed. Or receive an offer that can not be refused. Or new investment looks to have greater potential."

"A consolation prize."

"Better than no prize at all. What I have come to ask is: who buys the early work of Van Gogh?"

"The Amsterdam museum of course. Apart from the Museum of Modern Art in New York, that is, amongst others."

"Amsterdam has just lost two of them. Stolen to order, it seems. They were not necessarily the most valuable in the collection but they were early ones. Why would anyone do that?"

He frowned. "Presumably because they already have the later work."

"Is there anyone obvious?"

"Tim! Are you asking me to finger wealthy and respectable clients as possible thieves or recipients of stolen goods?"

"Yes. Possibly. No. Just who might be interested."

"Well that's a clear, forthright answer." He thought for a moment. "The sort of clients who go for Van Gogh in Europe and America are wealthy corporates and a few, very few, inheritors. They couldn't put stolen ones on show, though. I mean for many of those guys having a Van Gogh is like having a trophy wife: you flash the desirable object, as *deshabillée* as decency will allow, under the jealous and admiring nose of every rival dog on the block. You invite your banker to be impressed, providing he isn't called Tim Simpson."

"No good to look at them, then."

"No." He made the classic Massenaux gesture, tamping his wavy hair down with a long sweep of the hand. "There are, how shall I put it, one or two more discreet collectors who might enjoy private ownership of something like that. One or two who have bought from us through intermediaries, insisting on nil publicity."

"Who?"

"I take it you're not going to go charging after them with all the usual subtlety of a rugger ruck in full turmoil?"

"Me? Of course not. Scout's honour."

"You were never a scout. There's Ubaghs in Holland. That's Henk Ubaghs, the publishing tycoon. He's an alpha male where the Van Gogh pack is concerned. There's Henri Bertrand in France; a chemical industrialist who loves cool yellows; you should see his wife. Trench Werner in Texas, oil. Garston Holloway the film magnate. Can't think of any others. Oh, Devilliers Berengracht, a Swiss yodeller; music business, actually. All Van Gogh buffs. Don't go thinking they're mad criminal acquisitors though."

"Thanks."

"If you do ever decide to punt the letters to one of them –"

"It will be through you, Charles."

"Thank you guv, thank you, thank you." He adopted a mock Cockney. "Any 'elp yours truly can give is only hat our usual modest rates. Noblesse obligations, narmeen?"

"You'll never make a living that way. Your Cockney stinks. Stick to being a smooth bugger. The day job, in other words."

"Bastard."

"Thank you, Charles."

"When can I see these letters? And sketches?"

"Soon. Not yet."

"Jeremy must be like a dog with two whatsits."

"Jeremy doesn't know about them."

He gaped. "What? Why not?"

"As in the theatre, timing is everything. Jeremy has been obnoxious. He can wait. Keep mum until I tell you."

"What a bastard you are. Of course I will."

"Cheerio, Charles."

"Love to Sue, Tim. Why she stays with you I simply can't – no, please don't throw that piece of expensive pottery. It belongs to a very dear old lady who has entrusted me with it as one might one's life savings. It is genuine Ralph Wood. In perfect condition."

I put it down. Ralph Wood was immaterial but the possessions of old ladies were a bit precious to me just then.

Chapter Twenty-Five

The gallery office was still piled with a jumble of box files, heaps of papers, ranks of more files on shelves, some bubble wrap, a roll of brown paper and empty cartons. The central table, desk and other bits of furniture had every surface occupied by the evidence of accounts and administration. Over it all the light from the big window, its diamond-scissored grill drawn back, fell in a rather cold spring pallor but the room was warm.

I hesitated in the doorway.

Behind the desk, her fingers on a keyboard in front of a glowing monitor screen, Felicia Apps regarded me steadily over the top of a pair of reading glasses.

"I had to brace myself too," she said, factually. "But unless I get out this letter to the Friends in the next few days, it will be chaos. Life has to go on."

The door behind which the body of Binnie Grant had lain dead was wide open. Behind me the rather sombre walls of the inner gallery displayed their scenes of street, meadow and seaside. Flowers stood forever stuck in vases. Plates of lurid fruit lay frozen on pleated tablecloths. The splattered abstract still startled by its random scatter of smashed colour.

In the outer gallery, the shop as I thought of it, a subdued Dennis Cash in subfusc clothing presided at the counter, gravely talking to a group from Essex. Life, even if diminished, was indeed going on.

"It does have resonances for the moment," I agreed with Felicia Apps as I stepped cautiously over the threshold into the office. "But I suppose they will die away slowly as time passes by."

"The funeral is next Wednesday. They've allowed it at last."

I thought briefly of Detective Inspector Stamford, then put the thought away.

"Tell me," I asked, "did you know Madge Taylor?"

She stopped the typing she had restarted. "Oh yes, I knew

Madge. She was much closer to Veronica, but I knew her."

"Was she like Veronica?"

"Not really. Much more sympathetic. She was thick with Jane Harland. It rather irked Veronica."

"I have a letter to Madge Taylor from Jane Harland. Jane Harland was upset about something."

Her eyes widened. "How did you come by that?"

There wasn't exactly a challenge but it was implied; in Felicia Apps's world one did not "come by" other people's letters.

"It was in a book I bought in London. A book that had belonged to Hope Anderson. She must have forgotten it when she sold her library to a book dealer I know rather well. I assume Madge Taylor passed it on to her at some time long gone."

Felicia Apps's face clouded. "Poor Hope. She fell too, you know."

"I know."

"She left here a long time ago. When she married. They lived abroad a lot. Well, her husband was in the diplomatic, quite a catch. Fluent in Spanish and Portuguese and so on. They never came back to Highton but she always kept in touch with Madge. Veronica was rather miffed about that, too. Veronica wanted to be at the centre of things, you see."

"I rather gathered that."

"Fancy you getting a letter of Jane Harland's to Madge inside a book of Hope's. In London of all places. It's extraordinary. You have got in amongst our tight little Highton scene very quickly, haven't you?"

"Not really."

"Gilbert said you would."

That surprised me. "Did he? I wonder why?"

"I think he's a bit of a fan of yours."

"I'm very flattered. It was pure chance. The letter thanks Madge for being so sympathetic. There were clearly some worries about George. The letter is dated 1938. There's something about some images that Jane didn't like and George said he'd destroyed. I have a feeling, just a hunch, that he didn't."

She'd abandoned her keyboard completely and was staring straight at me. "How perceptive Gilbert is," she murmured.

"Sorry?"

"Nothing." She looked away into the recesses of the room next door, round at the window and then back at me. "It'll have to be said sometime," she murmured half to herself.

"What will?"

"You are under some sort of bond of confidentiality, are you?"

"Of course. In consultancy of this kind it is imperative."

"I thought so. Now you've said so, I'm sure it's true."

"There were some images, I believe, and I believe Veronica found them. Or copies of them."

She took her glasses off. "George was such a bastard," she said, in the same factual manner as before. "My husband said he should have had compulsory cold baths and regular thrashing. But my husband was in the Navy, you know. A Dartmouth man."

"I remember that."

"It was *The Yellow Book* that did it, apparently. At least, Jane made that the excuse. She was always finding reasons to excuse George. He was convinced that Henry Harland, the editor of *The Yellow Book*, must be some sort of distant relation. But Aubrey Beardsley was really the trouble. I mean, Henry Harland was an American and his wife was mostly French. George didn't care about that; he was a bit of a snob and the American Henry was related to a Sir Robert Harland, a baronet in Suffolk. George fancied himself as a possible baronet. Madge Taylor said it was nonsense; the Harland name is quite ordinary and there are a lot of them around Middlesbrough or somewhere like that."

"Aubrey Beardsley? Trouble?"

"Oh yes, George collected *The Yellow Book* and then all of those awful decadent pornographic drawings of Beardsley's. It's what started him off."

"Off?"

She rubbed her eyes. "Yes. Off. He went on to collect all sorts of lurid things. Sickert and those whores on bedsteads fascinated him. He used to pop up to Camden Town to visit the sites and probably do worse. He sought Sickert out when he had a studio in Kemp Town. They corresponded quite a lot. I imagine there must be letters in the archive. Jack the Ripper was a common interest, amongst other things George followed up. He drew himself, too."

"He drew himself?"

"I don't mean he drew self portraits, although there is one upstairs, but he used to go over to France regularly and take a studio in Dieppe. Like Sickert did before him. He rented some sordid back room or another. Then he'd draw and paint tarts in the nude and God knows what else. Frank Stevens calls it George's dark side. It was a regular thing until the war got in the way. As my husband said, Hitler must have stopped George's coughing in church."

"You knew George?"

"Oh no, George had died by the time we retired here. Jane was old and lived on quite a few years before she went and left this place to the town. The gallery is her legacy, not George's. Although that's not really fair. George had a marvellous eye for a painting when he wasn't otherwise occupied. We owe our Camden Town paintings to him. Even that Doman Turner." She gestured at the blank space on the wall above her where the sketch had hung. "I believe George bought that – I mean the drawing that's been stolen – from the artist some time in the twenties. Met him in St Valery. It's tragic that it's gone. George had some wonderful buys in Dieppe, too. Drawings and things. He had an eye, which most people haven't. So we must be grateful to him for that. His life wasn't entirely dissipated; the legacy hangs here."

"*Ars longa, vita brevis.*"

"Indeed. There were implications that he had a mistress in Dieppe until the war broke out. A fishwife like Sickert's, with red hair. Madame Villain, wasn't she? Sickert's one, I mean. I read

Mary Churchill's book – Mary Soames of course – about Clemmie finding her very daunting when she went to see him in Dieppe. All that thing about hockey sticks. It's all well before my time, though, and a long way from yours. Anyway, Hope Anderson used to get all this gossip from Madge, you see, and loved it, revelled in it, but Madge kept it away from Veronica. Veronica worshipped Jane and the gallery; Madge didn't want to spoil things for her. Amazing, really; for such a busybody Veronica had a strange sort of religious innocence."

"But then one day quite recently Hope Anderson came back to visit Highton like an old elephant nearing its end and, over a rather indiscreet lunch, thinking it all didn't matter any more, told Veronica all about George. From what Madge had told her."

"She must have. A good lunch is a bad confidante, my husband used to say. A glass of wine too many, I suppose, down at The Bistro. Veronica was distraught, absolutely distraught that evening at Binnie's talk." Felicia Apps shook her head in demonstrative wonder. "I couldn't think what was wrong with her. I saw her talking to Binnie after the talk. Intensely. Then Dennis told me about the folder she took away the next day. I put two and two together. Maybe someone else did, too."

"Binnie probably knew something already. From the archive. Her researches, I mean."

"Maybe. But she hadn't really got stuck in to everything here." Felicia Apps gestured at the heaps around her. "And she'd been away before her talk."

"Oh? Do you know where?"

"The Continent somewhere. She caught the Euroshuttle thing, the Tunnel train to Brussels for the first time. It was quite an adventure for her. Anyway I don't think she knew about the folder until – well –"

"Until maybe that night you saw her walking away from Veronica's front door? The night of her death?"

"Shhh! I said I could never swear for certain because of the bad light. Even though I think it was Binnie. Please, whatever you do, don't mention that. You and Gilbert promised, you absolutely promised."

I held up a calming hand. "Your secret is safe. But the folder – it's never come to light?"

"No. Larry and Binnie searched all over. Then this awful murder, right here. It's as though George has passed on an awful legacy as well as a good one. I think the police are going on the premise that she disturbed a burglar who was stealing the Sickert and the sketch. One of those thefts to order that you read about. What do you think it would be worth? The Sickert, I mean?"

"Before the Patricia Cornwell thing a good Sickert in the Camden Town Murder series would go for anything between forty and a hundred thousand pounds. I don't know, now."

"Good gracious. Although one hears of such bigger figures in the art world."

"One has to keep a perspective, I agree. Someone has just sold a hidden cache of William Blake's watercolours for nearly five million." I thought about the Van Gogh letters and moved quickly on to divert that thought. "Have you heard that you can pay twenty or thirty thousand for a small original sketch of Winnie the Pooh? There was one on the Road Show the other day."

"That's ridiculous." She smiled. "But I'd much rather have Winnie the Pooh than the Sickert."

"Really?"

"I'd be happy to leave Winnie the Pooh to my grandchildren."

"There speaks the great divide between youth and age in art. I'd go for the Sickert."

She picked up her glasses and let her lips move into a reproachful smile. "I'm shocked at you. I hope you'll take the lesson of George to heart."

"Lesson?"

"The effect of art on history."

"What effect?"

"If he hadn't started with Aubrey Beardsley and *The Yellow Book*, none of this would have happened."

She looked back at her keyboard. I opened my mouth to reciprocate by speaking of Reggie Turner and *Imperial Brown* but then thought better of it.

Why complicate things?

Chapter Twenty-Six

"Sherry?" Larry Granger took a quick glance at a small lantern clock on the mantelpiece of what seemed to be his study as he spoke. The hands gave the time as just past twelve.

"Sun's over the yardarm," said Bill Riley, with a broad smile.

"Thank you."

Larry Granger went to a sideboard on which stood a tantalus. "Dry? Medium dry?"

"Medium dry, thanks."

"Good man." Riley's voice expressed approval. He stood four square to the fireplace, clad in sports coat and thick brown corduroys. "Can't understand why people drink that stuff they say is very dry sherry. Fino, indeed: two nips of thin acid and you've got a headache."

"JP Donleavy, isn't it?" Larry Granger wielded a decanter over what looked like some very small cut glasses. "*The Beastly Beatitudes of Balthazar B*. One of his extravagant novels. The Anglo-Irish general in Dublin expresses exactly the same opinion in that book."

"Does he? Well I'm no Anglo-Irish general and I've never read JP Donleavy. But I do know my sherry from careful researches in the right place. Got a cask or two in Spain. One of my favourite painters, Munnings, used to keep casks of old sherry that people said were as strong as spirits. He knew his sherry all right. And so, evidently, does Tim."

I tried to balance up Granger's side to this blunt dissertation, since I could see he was pouring himself a fino. "There's an Irish element to your family, I believe, Larry?"

"My mother's side, Tim." He handed me a thimbleful of mid-amber coloured sherry, magnificently contained in bright cut glass. "They came from Dublin, too."

"Hence your literary leanings? Apart from Wilde, Maugham and Duff Cooper?"

He smiled. "Most certainly." There was a gesture at the book-shelves lining the room. "*Si monumentum requiris, circumspice.* If you seek for a monument, look around. Many of my books were left to me by my mother. I have been an avid reader all my life. Not only of Wilde, Maugham and Duff Cooper, although I still go back to them regularly."

"Dennis Cash mentioned Reggie Turner." I kept my voice casual.

"Ah. Your memory is excellent. Yes, it's a strange aberration, that. At least, to outsiders. Reggie Turner was an example of very dated wit, a wit that depended on rather Victorian punning. A bit Gilbertian, although Gilbert would not have agreed."

I took a sip of the sherry, which was very good but I still had an image of Damon Hill on Jeremy Clarkson's TV programme, taking a sip from a schooner and saying "Shouldn't you have a bad cough before you drink this stuff?" Sherry has become an old fashioned drink, a college habit bringing dons and diplomats to mind.

"Books," I said. "A weakness of mine, too. Men are seldom so innocently employed as when amongst books."

Granger gave me a sharp glance. "Maybe. Books as objects are innocent but their contents can inspire revolution."

"Or crime."

"Or crime, I agree. In that sense, in their contents lies the unexpected."

"You can say that again."

"But we have not brought you back down here for biblio-graphical discussion. Have you been in to the gallery?"

"I have. And things seem to be returning to normal. Felicia Apps seems to have got back to producing the Friends' newsletter again."

"Thank heaven. Bill and I have been dreadfully harassed about recent events. We are responsible, as trustees, for security. It was all too easy for someone to wait for the right moment and gain entry. Binnie's access to the office provided the opportunity. That dread-ful woman Cornwell, with all the hype and exposure of her nonsense about Sickert and Jack the Ripper, stimulated the demand. Clearly, someone planned the matter; Binnie's evening entry, all alone while Dennis was away, was the moment to seize."

I frowned. "You think it was a snatch to order that went wrong?"

"Of course. What other explanation is there?"

"The police seem suspicious of Dennis."

His face set. "I realise that. It is ridiculous too. I have given him our assurances of support."

"He did tell me how grateful he is to you."

"It's all absurd. I have been interviewed by Stamford yet again about Dennis's stewardship of the gallery. I know we don't pay much because we can't in our financial state, but the idea that Dennis has colluded in the theft is disgraceful. The suggestion that he absented himself deliberately so as to give the thief or thieves a clear run is nonsense."

"How would they have got in?"

"Presumably with keys and instructions from Dennis, which is clearly crazy. Such an inside job would be detected at once. But when Binnie turned up after our entertainment at Bill's it was a bonus. They must have been watching the place. They followed her in and gained access without any trouble. Presumably things went wrong when she tried to impede them and they hit her, fatally. Dennis is quite adamant that the gallery was locked when he came home after his visit to Newhaven but the police say the thief or thieves must have left without locking the door and Dennis locked it when he got back. To throw suspicion on others."

"There are such inconsistencies in all this that I can hardly start to deal with them. If Dennis gave them access it would point a finger straight at him, as you say."

"I agree. That's why the Binnie visit was a bonus, according to the police. You remember she told us she would be coming back that evening when I passed on Bill's invitation to all of us. She said she wanted to return and use the photocopier for some archive work. So the police say Dennis knew she'd be back and could have warned the thieves to be ready."

"You told the police that Dennis knew she'd return?"

He gave me a clear, unblinking stare. "I'm afraid I did. There was of course, no option. I was obliged to recount every event in detail. I had no idea in recounting the sequences of the day you arrived that I might cast suspicion on Dennis. But it was my obligation to tell the police everything that had transpired. As I suppose you did, too. I'm referring to facts, not speculation. That is confidential, of course."

"Of course."

I shut out another image of the inquisitional Stamford from my mind. To be fair to Larry Granger he had been doing no more than his duty but I wished he hadn't. It seemed to me that he had rather enjoyed doing it.

"So you see the way the police mind works," he said.

"Not really. How do they explain Binnie's house being ransacked? What was the purpose of that? Why didn't the thieves take anything else? The Spencer Gore would have been well worth it."

Bill Riley cleared his throat. "Look, I'm sure the police will reach the right conclusion in the end, Tim. Dennis will be OK. Life has to go on, as you say. It may seem callous but Binnie was dedicated to the gallery so I'm sure she'd approve of things getting back to normal as quickly as possible." He gave his sherry glass to Granger for a refill. "Now about your brief: have you come to any conclusions yet?"

"Only that without a substantial injection of capital or the guarantee of some twenty-five thousand a year of revenue funding the game will soon be up. In about seven or eight years to be precise."

"You mean you haven't looked at what fund raising activities can be undertaken?"

"The gallery is public space, open to the public free of charge. Twenty-five thousand a year to sustain an active cultural facility for this area is peanuts. The facilities and benefits to the public are remarkable. The local authorities should stump up. Of course you can go down the long hard route of fund raising but who is going to do it? I believe commendable efforts have been made voluntarily, by Larry and others, but so far without success. Fund raising is a full time job without any guarantee of joy. If you hire a fund raiser you have to pay salary and expenses for what may not be successful and simply accelerate your demise. It's a Catch 22 situation."

"It certainly is." Larry Granger's voice was sharp again. "I can hardly speak coherently when I start to think about all the hundreds of deadbeat layabouts drawing salaries to promote official, politically correct so-called art, which isn't art at all, when the salary of any one of them would keep a proper gallery like ours in the black. It's typical of the whole country. Hospitals close and there's a shortage of doctors but not one administrator gets fired." He took a swig from his glass of very pale fluid. "I've done the rounds of all the local jobsworths and not one of them has got a penny to spare for the gallery. They all talk big all the time but they're useless. It's a talking shop. Nothing gets done. Don't waste your valuable time on them. In any civilised country they'd all be taken out and shot."

"I will have to talk to them, though."

"They'll give you the usual gobbledegook. They think they know all about art when in fact they're trying to amuse children and the unemployed. Gimmicks and outings for geriatrics, condescended to by so-called arts graduates who ought to be doing something useful like clearing up litter when they're not drinking or smoking pot. Bread and circuses; that's what they think art is about. Dirty beds and flashing lights in empty rooms. Something to take the public's mind off the state of the country."

Bill Riley grinned at me and gave me a faint wink. "Larry is developing into a real old firebrand."

"I'm sure it's been very frustrating."

What has happened, I was wondering, to that ex-FO *homme du monde*? Where now was the urbane, detached man I first met and liked despite a sense of caution? Surely his diplomatic years trained him to take the long view?

"Maybe." Riley was still brisk. "But we have to deal with the situation as it is, not as we would want it. No one is going to fire all those arts spongers running all those circuses so we have to see what else we can do. So far, Tim, you haven't been very constructive about solutions. Are you saying you're bunkered?"

I shook my head. "I haven't finished yet. I will of course talk to the right people in the right places and see what they say. See if there's any likelihood of help. There are funds for public galleries."

"They'll want reciprocal funding." Granger was abrupt. "We haven't got any. We are a charity not a business. We can't run a disco or set up a beer cellar like some have. A charity needs charity. One of them had the nerve to ask me if I had arranged to produce a business plan for the gallery. I gave him short shrift. My dear man, I told him, we are a public gallery, not a business. We do not have a five-year plan involving the opening up of branches all over the country, then swallowing up the Tate. That is what a business does. We are a small town gallery. A public gallery. A charity serving the public: they do not seem to understand the meaning of the word."

Charity: I let my eyes rest on Riley until he spoke. "Larry and I made a decision," he said, looking straight back at me. "I and Portarlington will help the gallery once the gallery is properly funded by the arts authorities, the local council or whoever should be responsible. It's a matter of principle. The responsibility for public art lies with public bodies. Once they accept that, we're willing to help. But not before."

"Chicken and egg?"

"Chicken and egg."

"Look," I said, "I've not got any cards up my sleeve. My brief requires me to investigate the question of funding thoroughly. I will look round the obvious places and talk to some private contacts. If you get sponsorship, whether public or private, it will end your control. The only way to remain independent is for someone to give you cash without reservations. That's like a Victorian ending to a melodrama, not for real life. It might happen; you might win the Lottery. You can't plan for that. So brace yourselves; if I find a solution it is likely to come with strings attached."

"We can look at the strings when we see the solution." Riley was still sturdily watching me. "We've set up this feasibility study to get some new input."

"You'll get it."

Twenty-five thousand a year, I thought privately, is probably less than you spend on motor cars or holidays or golf. I agree there's no reason why you should be a philanthropist, though.

"Good." He almost glared at me. "When can we expect your suggestions?"

"Soon," I said. "Very soon."

"I rather prefer definitions of time to come in recognised units like months, weeks, days or hours."

I took a deep breath. "Two more weeks is within the timetable specified on the study proposal document you accepted. Two weeks it will be."

That made him nod. "Fair enough. I'm off down to Spain for a golfing break next week, so during the week after we can fix up a time?"

"We're a little nervous, Tim." Larry Granger's voice was more soothing than Riley's. "You must excuse us if we seem to press you."

"I quite understand. All these missing folders and things seem to have got everyone upset."

"Missing folders?"

"Yes," I said, looking him squarely in the eye. "The folder Veronica took, amongst others. Others that Binnie seemed to be going through."

"We were a bit bemused by Veronica's actions. I have confided my thoughts about Binnie to you, in confidence of course. Bill here knows them, too. What has happened to the folder she almost certainly obtained is a mystery. It contains, I am sure, the secret of her fate."

"And the others?"

"Others?"

"Binnie was going through a quantity the day I met her." An image of the Camden Town Murder illustration in *La Nouvelle Perspective Artistique* with its redolence of Gitanes or Gauloises was hard to suppress. "Are all those accounted for?"

"As far as we know. Dennis has never been much of an administrator but there is no reason to suppose that anything else is missing."

"Oh, good." I put down my glass. "Well, as Bill says, there's no time to lose. I must be getting on."

"Another sherry?"

"No thanks. It was very good but I have to make progress. Two weeks is little enough to get the future reorganised."

"We have great faith in you."

"Too kind." I paused. "Tell me: when you were in South America, how long did you coincide with Anderson?"

He blinked. "Anderson?"

"Yes. Hope Anderson's husband. He was an FO man and served in South America too, didn't he? I'm sure you must have met him. Did you coincide? Buenos Aires?"

There was a shake of the head, making the white hair wave. His expression had gone cold. Then he nodded very slightly. "Anderson, yes, of course. Briefly. We coincided very briefly. In Santiago, it was."

"Ah. Small world. You mentioned Hope Anderson when we were talking before and I hadn't appreciated you had known her in another context."

I walked to the door but his voice came after me, sharpened as before.

"It was a very slight acquaintance. Why do you ask?"

"Just curious. Thanks again for the sherry. It was excellent. "

I nodded at Riley, managed a smile, and left.

Chapter Twenty-Seven

At the bar of The Dolphin I picked up my pint of bitter and let a good quantity of its slightly burnt cool goodness swill the taste of sherry from my mouth. Then I had another swig of it. The sherry had been good quality but the company in which I drank it pissed me off.

Someone was having me on. Seriously misleading me. Perhaps I was muttering to myself.

"Problems?"

The voice cut through my scowling thoughts. Beside me Gilbert Macintosh smiled gently as his clear blue eyes took me in.

"You look as though you think Atlas had an easy time of it. Can I top up your glass while you prop up the world?"

"I rather think it's my turn."

"Not a bit of it. Another half?"

"Another half will be fine."

He gave orders, the beer arrived and I asked for a ploughman's lunch to blot up some of the liquid. He did the same. We sat down in a corner with a view over the flat water meadows leading down to Newhaven.

"Idyllic spot," he said, following my gaze.

"It is."

"You wouldn't think that it was once in the front line of national defence. Rape, pillage and counterattack were all in a day's work."

"I know. A lot of the men along these Channel ports lived off piracy. Before they took to smuggling."

He chuckled. "How peaceful it all is, now."

"Until I arrived."

"Och, dinna blame yourself. It was all piling up long before you arrived, I'm sure."

"Kind of you."

"You've just come from Larry Granger's?"

"You've been following me?"

"It's a small town. I guessed from the direction you came. A sophisticated man, our Larry."

"Yes."

"He was married once, you know."

"What?" I gaped at him, startled. "I was told he'd never – I mean –"

Macintosh smiled cannily. "Not generally known, no. Not like him, is it? Not a ladies man, you might say. Happened before he was posted to South America. Very secret. Didn't work, of course. But then Oscar Wilde and Somerset Maugham, his great role models, were hetero to start with, weren't they? Wives came before the fall, you might say, although I suppose that's not politically correct now, is it?"

"How do you know this?"

He put a finger along the side of his nose. "Friend of mine was at college with him. Dead now. When Granger's marriage ended it was a nasty, expensive break-up. Secret ones often are. Certainly were in those days. Maybe still is. Bad mistake, but we can all make them. Long time ago, though."

"Good grief. Does he know you know?"

"Certainly not. We don't mix. Not my type. Doesn't play golf at all, does he?"

"But Bill Riley does. Have you played with him?"

He shook his head. "Can't say as I have. Very wealthy company, he keeps. Big City men and international entrepreneurs." Then he paused. "No, I tell a lie. I made up a foursome once. Cooden, it must have been. Riley was quite genial enough. A tough cookie, though; ribbed his partner a lot. Dutchman, he was. The other was a City guy. He and I had a good day and won. Riley wasn't best pleased. Likes to win, you see."

"Do you ever play in Spain?"

"I have been to one or two courses there. Not really my scene." He smiled apologetically. "I'm still Scots at heart. I love links courses. The stiff breeze and the boom of the waves nearby."

"Over the seagulls and into the dunes?"

He grinned. "You must have played."

"Not really my game. No patience. Riley owns a course in Spain. Ever heard of it?"

"I've heard of it. Never met a member though."

"Not even the Dutchman at Cooden?"

"Don't think so. Is it important?"

"Not really. Do you remember his name? The Dutchman, I mean."

He shook his head. "I'm too old to remember chance names. Might have been Hank. Or Henk. Lot of those though, aren't there?"

"Yes."

Our ploughman's lunches arrived and he unwrapped his knife and fork slowly, putting the fork to one side as he contemplated a large pickled onion. "Look Tim, it probably isn't the time but could I talk to you when you're free for a moment? About something else entirely?"

"Of course. I'm sorry Gilbert; I'm terrible company today. What can I do for you?"

"There's no hurry. It's just about the family investment company. I'd really like to talk to you about it. There's a terrible mess going on. My late wife was – oh look, there's Felicia. She's coming over here. I say, is anything the matter?"

Felicia looked dreadful. There was a wild look in her eye and her ample bosom was heaving quickly, very badly, out of breath.

"Oh Gilbert, oh, I'm sorry Tim – but –"

"Here, sit down." He was much better at dealing with flustered older biddies than me. "What ails you dear lady?"

She sat down, scattering a cloth bag on the table. "I've had to close the gallery. The police – they –"

"The police? What about them?"

"They've arrested Dennis. They took him away. It was awful.

Horrible. All those words. I mean cautioning him and everything."

"Dear heavens. Here, let me get you a gin."

"Oh thanks Gilbert, you're an angel. It's such a shock."

He got up and moved quickly across to the bar. Felicia Apps
stared at me, white of face, without speaking.

I got a grip on my thoughts. "Dennis? They arrested Dennis?
On what possible grounds?"

She glanced round and dropped her voice. "I shouldn't have
but I heard them talking to him before they did it. They said –
oh, it's awful –"

"What?"

"He has no alibi for that night. They've talked to nearly
everyone who was at the pub in Newhaven where he said he was
at a blues session and they all say he wasn't there. The landlord
in particular knows Dennis and says he never turned up."

"Good God. What did Dennis say?"

"He didn't. He just stood there staring at them. He looked
very pale. Then they asked him – I really can't get myself to
believe it –"

"What?"

"They said how could he explain such a large sum of money
in his bank account."

"Dennis? Money?"

She looked up in gratitude as Gilbert Macintosh put a glass in
front of her. "Yes. Money. A lot. Sent from abroad somewhere."

"Oh, God."

"He said he couldn't explain it. So they said all those awful
warning words then they took him away."

Chapter Twenty-Eight

Mr Goodston took off his glasses, rubbed the bridge of his nose, put the glasses back on again and sighed so very deeply that I thought his corrugated convex waistcoat might collapse, leaving him a mere shell.

"What a conflict of emotions you create," he murmured.

I sat opposite him in silent sympathy for a moment, letting conflicting emotions of my own chase across my mind. My thoughts were of Dennis Cash, for instance, and my odd conversation with Kathy Marsden, who knew all about Sickert and Dieppe and had one of her paintings in his flat. Then there was my attempt to visit the police station once I'd left The Dolphin pub in Highton, where Gilbert Macintosh was doing a grand job of consoling Felicia Apps over the shock of the police visit to the gallery. At the station, the lugubrious PC Wallace had not actually told me to piss off and mind my own business but his carefully officious wording, conveyed across the counter between us, had an abundantly clear if subtle message: piss off and mind your own business.

So I clambered into my car, left Highton's crisp afternoon sunlight and headed for London. It seemed to me that with Dennis Cash out of action, the gallery closed and its most important trustee aggressively awaiting some sort of miracle funding suggestions from me, I might as well get another unpleasant task out of my hair. If you're going to have a bad day you might as well have a really bad day.

I went to Praed Street and told Mr Goodston about the Van Gogh letters.

"I am very sorry to be the bearer of this news, Mr Goodston," I responded, after a pause. "But as I say, when all is done and dusted I shall make sure that at least some small douceur, a compensatory element of some kind, will come your way. It seems only fair, in view of the circumstances."

"You are remarkable, my dear Mr Simpson. Your ethics do you credit. Although I am in purgatory, I hope that your Bank is aware of its good fortune in retaining your stewardship."

"I'm sure it is."

"If it had not been for your timely intervention, those villains would have got the magazines anyway. That, however, is small consolation. This is an object lesson to me. I should have gone through those magazines with proper, professional attention. But Isleworth? How would anyone seeing Isleworth today suspect that in its dingy recesses such treasure might lie hidden?"

"Oh steady on, Mr Goodston. Parts of suburban Isleworth are as excellent as the curate's egg. It may embrace the West Middlesex Drainage Works but along the river it overlooks the Old Deer Park of Richmond's, scene of many a famous rugger match. Whilst close by to the south lies Twickenham, which I do not have to mention is the most famous venue in the rugby world."

"No you don't, even though there are those who would dispute your claim." He took off his half-moons and rubbed the bridge of his nose with elaborate thoroughness, as though alleviating the itch would dispel his chagrin. "I never thought, in all the many errors I have made in a long life as an antiquarian bookseller, that Isleworth would be the cause of yet another piece of heartrending incompetence on my part."

"Don't take it too hard, Mr Goodston."

He sighed again mournfully. "Not long ago I turned down a batch of books in which it was later discovered there was a good first edition of Kingsley Amis's *Lucky Jim*, inscribed by the author to a fellow lecturer in Wales. And before that, a year or two back, I let a mint copy of John Le Carré's first novel, *Call For The Dead*, slip through my nerveless fingers. I was as mortified as the occasion on which, overwhelmed by piles of paperbacks, I inadvertently overlooked a first of Iris Murdoch's *Under The Net*. But this is even worse. I am getting old. Very, very old."

"Not many errors in a lifetime of eagle-eyed acquisition, Mr

Goodston. Do not be so hard on yourself. You have modestly omitted many brilliant finds. As for age, most younger men would have pitched the magazines out for a pittance. My own case is just as lamentable. I was going to buy them myself but instead I thought the Art Fund's library needed supplementing."

He shook his head dolefully. "In that case we are both mortified." He replaced his glasses with care. "Would a glass of Celebration Cream sherry be out of place as a small restorative?"

"I think it might be very appropriate, Mr Goodston."

As I say, I had stopped on my way back home to discharge what I felt was an unpleasant duty on my part whilst preoccupation with the arrest of Dennis Cash was harassing me. I wanted to clear my mind of extraneous, nagging obligations so that I could think rationally about the Highton Art Gallery. I am fond of Mr Goodston and I didn't want him to find out about the Van Gogh letters from some other source, at some other remove.

He slid open the deep lowest drawer of his pedestal desk and produced a bottle and two capacious, shiny cut wineglasses. I have often tried to calculate how large an order a customer has to place before Mr Goodston brings out the old sherry but it seems to vary. On my first occasion it was between four and five hundred pounds but I have known it not to emerge for larger orders since then. My guess is that it has something to do with the margin of profit.

He poured out the sherry expertly, spilling not a drop and filling the glasses to the brim. We held them up in a silent toast to each other and then took a soothing draught.

"Absent friends."

"Absent friends."

He wiped the neck of the bottle with a snow-white cloth. The sherry, much sweeter than Larry Granger's, seemed to restore his saddened spirits. "Singular, how quickly you discovered this find. The letters might have remained undisturbed inside the pages for some length of time."

"Indeed. If those thugs hadn't chased after the magazines so avidly I might have whiffled through quickly rather than making a careful search. It is now clear that they were after the magazines in particular when they raided you. They must have ransacked your account books and found the record of my purchase. Then they took a gamble that I'd keep them around or near me for a while to look through them. Pure chance that they got the wrong ones – Mrs Hope Anderson's."

"Villainous. I am relieved that I shall no longer be the centre of their attentions. My evil genies have departed and left me with the remorse such genies inevitably bring. But I am concerned lest you experience further conflict."

"The magazines are safe in the vaults at the Bank."

"Thank heavens." He rolled a little more sherry smoothly round his mouth and cautiously topped up our glasses. "Talking of Mrs Anderson reminds me that I was about to call you. It is fortuitous that you came to apprise me of your melancholy news about the Van Gogh material. Strange events beset us."

"Oh?"

"Indeed. The Reggie Turner book – *Imperial Brown of Brixton* – you have read it?"

"I have. To be honest, I found myself skipping bits of it."

"I am not surprised. But there were no more insertions in it beyond the private letter you mentioned? No Van Goghs, for example?"

"No. I fear that Van Goghs are unlikely to turn up elsewhere in your repertoire, Mr Goodston."

"I am relieved to hear it. As it happens, I was going to contact you about a strange matter concerning Reggie Turner. Or at least related to Turner."

"Oh really?"

"Indeed. A client of mine connected with the theatre, very much an aficionado of Oscar Wilde's, collects both books and photographs relating to the celebrated playwright. I have been instrumental in obtaining some items for him which, I may modestly claim, are quite unusual. In his collection he has some remarkable early images dating from Wilde's time and before. It includes, or rather included, some photographic shots of Reggie Turner and some of his letters. Not to mention rare sketches by Max Beerbohm. There was a photograph of Reggie Turner in Dieppe in 1900, at a café table with Walter Sickert and Henry Harland."

"Harland?"

"Yes, Henry Harland, editor of *The Yellow Book*. He too was a rather unsuccessful novelist, you know; an American related to Suffolk Harlands of some small title. The influence of Henry James was evident in his work although the material more romantic. I seem to recollect a series of titles like *Two Women or One?* and *Mademoiselle Miss*. He didn't have much success until *The Cardinal's Snuff Box*, which came after *The Yellow Book* was over. Somewhere there is a sketch of him by Aubrey Beardsley – he was Beardsley's editor, after all."

"Really? A Beardsley of Henry Harland? George Harland of Highton would have given his eye teeth for that."

"Doubtless. Anyway, in the collection there was a photograph of Sickert, Harland, Reggie Turner, William Nicholson and Max, all at Dieppe, which my thespian client treasured. With it was a sketch made of all of them by Max Beerbohm, except himself of course. They were sitting together at table on the pavement. Quite a collector's item."

"It certainly sounds like it."

"Oh and there was a child included as well – Ben Nicholson it was – he'd be about six years old at the time."

"Wow. I would really like to have owned a copy of that even if I couldn't have the original."

Mr Goodston shook his head sadly and drew in another draught of sherry, rather like a carthorse at a trough. "The whole lot has been stolen. My client is devastated. Inconsolable. Like you would have, he treasured the images. It was not long after the photograph was taken that Turner, who had returned to London, was called to Paris where he and Robert Ross attended Wilde's painful death. In Turner's correspondence there were numerous quotes from those events. Wilde had a terrible dream in which he said he had been supping with the dead. Turner, quick as ever, said "my dear Oscar, you were probably the life and soul of the party" which induced hysterical laughter from the dying man. Dying beyond his means, and all that. The following year Turner published his first novel, *Cynthia's Damages*. His family newspaper, the *Daily Telegraph*, gave it a puff for him. My thespian client liked it particularly, since the story is based loosely on that of the actress Cissy Loftus, a musical hall star of the nineties."

"It sounds like quite a collection."

"It had taken years to accumulate."

"But surely if the police do their stuff this very specialised material is unsaleable? It would be identified immediately. It is so unique."

"Like the stolen Van Goghs from Amsterdam that you mentioned, yes. One can only be staggered that there are people rich enough and unscrupulous enough to retain such things out of sight entirely for themselves. Only the most trusted confidante could share their secret. Otherwise what solitary, onanistic pleasure they must derive from their possessions."

"Bunch of wankers, you mean. That's true."

"I have always thought that one of the main satisfactions of the acquisitive urge must be the moment of pride when others admire the possessions. It seems so defeating to keep them out of sight."

Just like Charles Massenaux, I thought, and his trophy-wife comparison; why own the thing if you can't flaunt it to the jealousy of your peers?

"But it happens all the time. Remember the Wellington Goya?"

"I do, but I think in many cases that the reward was the motive. Or rather the ransom from some insurance company. Look at those two Turners recently. I mean the famous painter, not poor Reggie. They came back to light and to their rightful places on the walls of the Tate in front of Sir Nicholas Serota. Many things however have gone never to be returned. They must lie in clandestine darkness, poor articles, awaiting the touch of a switch to lighten their suffering. Like a Dumas prisoner languishing in an oubliette in the Chateau D'If. It is akin to keeping some poor dog chained up alone and only visiting it once in a while to replenish its bowl."

I raised my eyebrows. Perhaps the sherry was inducing a melancholy drift in Mr Goodston's train of thought.

He did not notice my expression as he refilled our glasses. "Artefacts, art and books are pack animals like dogs, you know, my very dear sir. Or plants. They need company. Isolate them in darkness and they wither. One of the joys of my profession is to rescue books from obscurity and place them where light and appreciation will nourish them." He glanced around his own gloomy premises, as though suddenly aware of a contradiction. "My volumes here know that I merely hold them in trust for a while. When I come down in the morning to spend the day with them they are revealed and accompanied. The lucky ones go out to appreciative owners. The others merely wait for me to place them. I would be desolate if I thought I were sending them to a covetous egotist's dungeon."

"It seems unlikely, Mr Goodston, that your clientele falls into that category."

"One never knows about collectors. Fortunately I believe not; my clients tend to be enthusiasts like yourself. Yet it prompts one to think, does it not? How could a man, or woman, who stole art works which are rightly public property, or snatched from private sources, enjoy them without the company of other people?"

"I can only assume there is a flaw of character which makes such solitary enjoyment possible, Mr Goodston. We are all of us secretive in some way or another, are we not?"

"Oh, we are, but only partly my dear sir. The vast majority are bursting to share their secrets. It is only those who are psychologically flawed, pathological cases like serial killers who want to keep their privy confidences. Most humans want to strut their triumphs to someone else." He paused to think for a moment. "Mind you, the man or woman who could solve the problem of how to share a stolen treasure without danger might have the key to great riches."

"Very difficult to achieve, Mr Goodston. One would have to threaten terrible consequences to the sharer if he or she broke the confidence. The only way would be a secret society like say the masons. Or the Rosecrucians. The stuff of *Foucault's Pendulum* by Umberto Eco?"

"Ah, that is a strange and fascinating book. But you may have put on your finger on the answer."

"I may?"

"Why not? Secret societies still surely exist. Not publicly of course, nor are they called secret societies."

I wasn't following his slightly oblique pattern of thought.

"What, then?"

He gave me a completely uncritical, confidential look over his sherry glass.

"An exclusive club, perhaps?"

Chapter Twenty-Nine

Thanks to Mr Goodston, that night I slept very badly. There was a sequence of nightmares, starting off with one in which a predatory figure with an eagle's head and a naked human female body moved towards me through trees in a menacing stalk. Half-awake, half-asleep, I reassured myself that this apparition was pure Kathy Marsden imagery and that I was having a nightmare but I didn't feel convinced. My semiconsciousness didn't stop me from being afraid of the figure, which had an obvious but horrible attraction. It kept moving towards me every time I dozed off again. I was confused.

I was sweating too.

The Wyndham Lewis reference to Sickert's family in Dieppe, which Kathy had quoted, was plaguing me. Lewis took Sickert's advice about a dose of gonorrhoea he had incurred in 1914, disastrously. Due to Sickert's counsel to treat the disease like a common cold Lewis neglected the infection and septicaemia set in, with dreadful subsequent effects on his health. The accounts of Lewis's corrective and expensive hospital operations in the Twenties and Thirties make grisly reading. Yet Sickert was remarkably inconsistent. According to Rebecca Daniels he had been deeply worried in the 1880s about what he thought was a dose he'd got himself and conferred with Sir William Eden, who told him not to worry; it was gout.

How do you mistake gout for the clap for heaven's sake? How do you get the clap if you're supposed to be impotent, Patricia Cornwell's cause of Sickert becoming Jack the Ripper?

Was it all just boasting or didn't he know?

The nightmare was worsening.

"Where's Dennis?" I asked Larry Granger, who I suddenly found sitting at a café table with me under a shady blind somewhere in the hot square of a Mediterranean city.

He smiled. He had been talking about Lawrence Durrell's

humorous stories in *Esprit de Corps*, particularly the mythical
Foreign Office man Antrobus. The one he liked best was *Case
History*, in which an ambassador called Polk-Mowbray sacks a
junior because in some memo or another the underling erro-
neously attributes a Latin quotation by Tacitus to Suetonius. In
those days Americanisms like "set-up" were expunged from
Foreign Office memoranda with thick correcting pencils. The FO
was still addicted to latinisms and the benefits of a classical education. It was agreeable to chat to Larry Granger in this urbane
fashion, swapping quotes and slightly showing off the way I had
that first night in Highton. I felt more relaxed about him.

"Look at us now," he had been saying. "Just look at us. It's
utterly appalling. Look at Iraq. What would Duff Cooper have
said about our craven role there? How can you compare Tony
Blair with Lord Salisbury? Not even Anthony Eden. He would-
n't kow-tow to the Yanks. Although I suppose Suez..."

His voice tailed off.

I tried to revive the previous talk but the bird-head figure,
with disturbing bare arms and breasts, had come into view again.
"I seem to recall that the stickler Polk-Mowbray meets his
Nemesis in an American drum-majorette, whose charms corrupt
him into the most exaggerated American behaviour."

"Ah, Nemesis," Granger nodded emphatically. "Always a
female figure, according to Antrobus. Never a he. Which is clas-
sically correct, of course. Durrell wouldn't miss a trick like that.
Nemesis, defined as retribution or the anger of God, was a
female deity, the daughter of Night. Binnie Grant? I don't know
where Dennis has got to. Why do you ask?"

"No reason. Just a figure in the woods reminded me of him."

"Woods? Dennis is supposed to be in Newhaven."

Across the sunlit square came a suited man holding a bag of
golf clubs but it wasn't Bill Riley. It resembled Gilbert Macintosh
in some way but not quite right. In it, I suddenly thought, they're
all in it. It's not one, it's a conspiracy. I've got to look all round me.

Nemesis was a female figure?

Binnie Grant?

Then I saw that Larry Granger had a bottle of Coca-Cola in front of him. There was a drinking straw in it.

"A Coca-Cola! Great Heavens, Larry" I was about to quote from Durrell, "surely you are jesting?"

But I never got time. Noises woke me.

"Tim! Tim! You're all over the place."

Sue was shaking me.

"You're having a nightmare. God! You're hot!"

I opened my eyes. A glimmer of light from the street outside produced a calm gloom. Solidity came back into focus. My head ached. "Sorry, Sue."

"What's wrong?"

"I was having a dream. Dreams. Woods and a café somewhere hot. Not Highton but about it. In the nightmare they were all in it. All of them."

She turned away slightly, warm and female, no nightmare of any kind.

"What time is it?"

I peered at the alarm clock. "Four thirty. Would you like some tea?"

"No, thanks. Try to go back to sleep. You can deal with Highton in the morning. You're obviously working yourself up to a crisis."

I sat up. "I need some tea. I'll check William while I'm at it."

"You don't need to."

"But I want to." This was true. For some reason, I suddenly needed a sight of William.

"For heaven's sake don't wake him." She turned further away.

"I won't."

I slid out of bed, went to the kitchenette and switched on the kettle. Then I went through on bare feet to look at my son.

He lay absolutely quiet, with just a faint burr of breath-sound coming from him. Small, not so much fragile as soft, with body and limbs relaxed like rubber, he was on one side with a hand in front of his face on the pillow. I stared down at him for just a brief few seconds before tiptoeing quietly out again. My mother-in-law and her sister came to mind for a fleeting second and I smiled to myself as I went back into the kitchenette.

He was safe.

Tomorrow it would be my turn to bung some mash at a wall.

Chapter Thirty

My nightmares and Mr Goodston's evil genies returned the next morning as I left for work. I should have known. I should have taken precautions, should have thought ahead, sent Sue and William away for safety, should have done all the things that afterwards are so obvious. Things that not doing make you look like a thoughtless, heartless, self-centred incompetent bastard. All right, made me look like a thoughtless, heartless, self-centred incompetent bastard.

I underestimated them. Maybe it was the atmosphere of Highton. Maybe it was because old ladies had fallen but it seemed that only one woman had really been killed, murdered, far away in that quaint medieval town. I hadn't been affected enough. Maybe I was lulled by the academic considerations, the louche but fascinating biographical connections and images, the civilised steady pace of the cobbled streets of flint and timbered houses from former days, or quiet canvases silent on spotlit walls. This had been about files and papers and sketches and books; the stuff of study, not extinction.

I should have remembered that serious art, like serious poetry, is always about sex and death.

I did one thing right: I phoned Nobby Roberts, at home, to get him before he left for work. He wasn't pleased.

"Tim? Oh no, don't tell me: Inspector Stamford has arrested you?"

"No."

"How strange. I would have thought you needed locking up."

"Nobby –"

"Another old lady has fallen over dead due to your influence?"

"Nobby, listen."

"Tim, this had better be good. I'm due, now, at an all-services terrorist prevention committee meeting that boasts no less than a full general on it. A very punctuality-centred, anally-fixated, bad-tempered full general."

"For Christ's sake, Nobby! I need to talk to you. Face to face. This is very important."

"Not now, I'm leaving. Can't Stamford deal with it?"

"Oh, of course, I never thought of that. You thick bastard. Do you want me to pass you a real, high-scorer's ball or not?"

His tone changed. "All right, all right, don't get all stroppy. I'll see you."

"When? Can we meet for breakfast tomorrow?"

"Sorry, no can do."

"When, then? Today? Nobby, this is urgent. I mean urgent, you know? Not urgent like in let's have a committee meeting with a stupid general on it."

"Tim, I'll have to call you."

"Call me, then. Soon."

"OK, I promise I will."

"Today, Nobby. You hear me? Today."

"I hear you. I will call you today."

"I'll be at the Bank. Otherwise it's my mobile."

"Gotcha, Tim."

I put the phone down. One of Nobby's chief characteristics is that he does do what he promises to do.

The door to William's bedroom opened and Sue came out of it, carrying him still in his pyjamas.

"Who was that you were phoning?" she demanded.

"Nobby."

"Things must be hotting up. When are you meeting him?"

"I don't know, but soon."

"I certainly hope so. I'd like a decent night's sleep."

"It will all be over soon, I promise." I went across to embrace William and kissed her gently on the cheek as I spoke to him. "Eat your breakfast, my boy. Get big and strong. Do as Mummy tells you. I'll try to come home early if I can."

He grinned and rubbed an eye with the back of his hand as

Sue took him across to the breakfast table in the window over-looking Onslow Gardens. Time for me to go; I kissed her farewell and ruffled William's hair. His cereal was waiting and a boiled egg cooling down for him.

No leeks.

I closed the front door of the flat carefully as I left and went across the landing to the wide staircase, thinking about Mr Goodston's telling question more and more as I resolved to see Nobby then get back to Highton and collar Detective Inspector Stamford as soon as possible. It never occurred to me as I strolled down to the high-ceiling hallway that my little family and I were in danger. I forgot that there were people in this to whom possessions were so important that life meant very little.

As I opened the front door of the building, still half-preoccu-pied, a man shoved straight into me, stopping my exit. Behind him was another man: the sharp-nosed, thick-necked codger from Mr Goodston's attack, shielding the view from the street and the gardens. Blocked from proceeding, I tensed for action until I looked down. The front man held a pistol close to my chest.

He poked me with the gun as he spoke softly.

"Back upstairs."

He was a different proposition from the other man in the shop pair. This was no soft-stomached bouncer from a bad night-club. He was hard, lean and muscular, with shaven head and clear blue eyes. Jeans and a leather jacket gave him a Continental appearance. He looked like a foreign ex-mercenary, a renegade from some specialist unit, keen to make a kill.

"I said upstairs!"

The accent was heavy, almost guttural. Dutch, a voice said to me, he's Dutch.

"Come on!" His words cut into my hesitation. I turned and he poked the gun into my back.

"Up we go: nice and steady. Let yourself in nice and quiet. No funny business. We get just what we want and you, your missus and the kid will be OK. Otherwise it's not nice."

My throat constricted, almost making me vomit. The sleepy Sue and William were going to be terrified, paralysed with fear if they were put at the mercy of this menacing, human machine.

I walked up the stairs to the first half-landing, turned the corner then onwards to the full first floor landing. We stopped outside my front door. The gun was still in my back. Both men were right behind me. If I wanted to keep Sue and William out of this, now was the only time.

Rooted to the spot, I braced myself.

"Don't even think about it." The thick, knowing voice was low and level. "Not a chance."

I took my keys out of my pocket, slowly, and held them in my hand. This was a professional; what had I done to deserve him?

Inside, in front of one of the long French windows overlooking the gardens, Sue would be talking to William as he ate cereal and egg for breakfast at the same table I had left so recently. A domestic, warm scene, sun falling on mother and child smiling together; fingers of toast cut as soldiers to be dipped in yolk.

"Get in." The voice was still low, level and controlled. "Open up, no surprises."

I promised her. I promised that whatever happened, William would not be threatened. In the past Sue had been involved, menaced, exposed to danger. She didn't hold any of those incidents against me. But William; the safe William I had looked down on to allay my fears last night...

I promised. She was serious; she said she'd never forgive me. I'd never forgive myself.

"I'm not going to wait." The gun was pushed harder into my back. The voice was edgier. "Open it!"

This was crunch point. I was the lion at the entrance to his lair, the elephant flapping his warning ears irritably at the camera-toting tourist, the rhino moving pig-eyed, spike up, across in front of the rhino calf. This was my lair, my hole in the ground. Life or death, this was the where the line got drawn. I started to turn.

"Don't turn round!" The voice was low but full of tension.

But I did. Suddenly I felt a tremendous calm, like people who have been in air accidents speak of, the calm before the plane hits the deck. Impact was due at any second and there was nothing else I could do. My mind said this isn't happening really but at the same time it was still working, cold and clear. This man relies on fear to succeed. You have to overcome it.

I turned round slowly, despite the gun, despite the eyes widening angry white at me.

"Didn't you hear me? You deaf?"

He wasn't that tall for a Dutchman; so many of them seem to go about seven feet up. He was about my height, not heavier, probably much fitter. But much more important, not heavier.

"What do you want?"

"The magazines. With the letters. You've got ten seconds: open up!"

"What letters?"

"*Van Gogh.*" The pronunciation was Dutch. "You know damn well what I'm talking about. I said open up."

I looked down at the hand holding the gun right at my chest. It was gloved. Both his hands had gloves on.

I knew then; I knew that this was final. This was a scene from which I wasn't meant to walk away. Once they'd got the letters it would be the end for me. I'd got too close, far too close, to his employers. When it happened, if Sue and William were present, it would be the end for them, too. Those were a killer's gloves, intended to leave no record. Not just a thief's; a killer's. I looked at the man behind him, sharp-nose from Mr Goodston's and the break-in at my car.

He was wearing gloves, too. This was it. Old ladies and soft-suited art historians meant nothing; why should I? Or my wife and child?

"You shoot me, you'll get no letters." I sounded quite calm.

His face was impassive. "We get the letters and we go. It's simple. Up to you. Open up!"

I grinned at him. I must have looked like a skull. He was relying on fear to get inside my lair. We were close, close enough to smell each other. "The letters are all in the Bank safe. Did you really think I'd keep them here?"

He pulled his face into a responding grin. There was no mirth in it.

"We'll check that ourselves. Open up now, or I'll shoot."

People who are going to kill you don't say I'm going to kill you or explain why they are going to do it. They kill you. The only reason I wasn't dead was those letters. Once they were sure they had them, I'd be gone.

"I've told you. We'd have to go to the Bank if you want the letters. I have a particular security number and there's a particular procedure at the vault. They can't be released otherwise."

"I said open up! If they're not here, we'll hold on to your lady and the kid while you get them. You bring the letters, they'll be OK. Nothing will happen to them. If not, it'll all get very nasty. You hear me?"

That would be it. Like a bank manager's family held hostage, Sue and William would be forced to wait while I went to the Bank, got the letters, and came back. What would it do to them? What might happen to them? What would happen to us all anyway once they got what they wanted?

My ears caught a vague sound above us. Any minute now the couple who lived on the next floor would be going out to work, or at least the raucous City lady would if Sue was right. A door would open, there'd be voices, movement.

He thumbed a catch back on the pistol and stuck it under my nose. "Five seconds. Open up or I kill you and go in anyway and search for ourselves. Know what I think we'll do once we're in and you're not there? Pretty lady, isn't she?"

That did it. They wouldn't want a noise on the landing. I threw my keys down on the floor beside me.

"Open up yourself."

His jaw opened very slightly. Then he jerked his head at sharp-nose, keeping the gun in my face. The other man moved out from behind him and bent down to pick up the keys.

"You'll regret this." The menace in the voice was terrible. "Really you will. I won't forgive this."

As he said it, a door opened upstairs and there was a loud female laugh. For just a split second, a flickering of his eye took a quick, alarmed glance up the stairway.

That was it.

I grabbed the wrist of the gloved hand, holding the gun with my left, and brought my knee up as I rammed into him. Sharp-nose, caught bending beside us, staggered under the impact of the push. The Dutchman brought his gun arm back as hard as he could but I'd got the wrist clamped as we tottered, locked together, towards the edge of the stairs. There was a loud bang as he pulled the trigger and a chunk of ornamental plaster fell from the ceiling.

I heard a startled female exclamation from upstairs.

He was a powerful bugger, I'll say that for him. The face close to mine didn't alter much; he knew he still had the advantage. He managed to stop my push to the edge of the stairs by swivelling himself against the banister rail. Then it was a straight arm grapple for the gun, except that sharp-nose had recovered his balance and grabbed me from behind. His arms went round me as he closed tight.

I jerked my head back sharply in a reverse head butt, hard into the face he positioned so unwisely behind, using all the neck muscles still thick from my early years of front row impacts, shoves and locks. There was a smack, squashy and unmistakable, of the sharp nose gristle getting smashed, a spray of blood spattering my hair at the back, a swift unbelieving intake of agonised breath, slobber of mouth and saliva. His arms dropped off me as he clamped hands to his face.

One to one, now.

The Dutchman was tough, fit and lean. He brought his left arm over to clamp his right, then started, slowly and inexorably, to bring the gun round towards my face. Only leverage would see me through the maul with him. Timing and leverage; it was an up-ender or nothing. I kept tight hold of the gun wrist to push it away to the left as far as possible and stooped down, bending my knees quickly, to scoop his legs together in a tight right-arm embrace. It wasn't what he expected.

I lifted him clean off the floor.

Using all the strength I had, I straightened up as high as possible, still clamping his legs together in my arm and, letting go of the gun wrist, grabbing the banister rail for leverage.

I'll never forget the look in his face, turning from triumph as he swivelled the gun round to get a shot at my head and changing to horror as the banister rail slid under his back. I brought his feet high up in the air just like up-ending an opposing forward over a heap of bodies in a rugby ruck.

He tried to grab me or the rail with his left hand and fired the gun in his right again, the shot hitting the wall high up behind me. He missed his grab.

Then he was over and I let go.

He didn't scream at first; he made a sort of grunt of surprise as he dropped, almost like a moan, but otherwise there was a pregnant pause, a short second of hurtling silence. Then came a hideous vocal sound, cut off sharply as he hit the lower stairs almost at the bottom step: head, shoulder, then body. There was a thumping bundle of carcase, head and limbs in a scattered thud of dull impact that was surprisingly brief.

The gun skittered across the parqueted hallway floor.

He lay absolutely still for a moment then rolled over the last step under gravity, piling up in a broken heap on the bottom stair.

There came a series of terrified female screams from the land-ing above me. Sharp-nose took his hands off his face and screamed as well, as best he could with a smashed nose streaming with blood but I had him then, punching his guts and grabbing him to shove him to the top of the stairs.

Our flat door flew open and Sue stood there, face electrified.

"Call the police!" I shouted at her. "Quick! And lock the door!"

She disappeared inside. The door slammed. I shoved sharp-nose down the first flight of stairs, hard, so that he tumbled headlong down to the half-landing, still crying out with terror and thumps of pain. I stepped on him as I jumped downstairs two at a time, over the Dutchman and into the hallway to grab the gun.

I wanted to kill him with it but I needn't have bothered.

He wasn't moving.

His head was cranked over at a funny angle, like someone try-ing to look upwards and backwards at something out of sight you know they can't possibly get to see that way. And never will.

Like Veronica Chalmers, maybe.

Chapter Thirty-One

From across the Highton Police Station interview room table Detective Inspector Stamford stared at me incredulously, as though what I had said was so preposterous that the mere pronunciation of the words was enough to certify me as insane.

Next to him, Nobby Roberts, Detective Chief Inspector of that ilk, rubbed the back of his sandy-haired head and permitted himself a slight smile. Nobby is a serious fellow but, having played superb rugby as a wing threequarter, is not without a sense of humour. Wing threequarters have to have a sense of humour. Viewing the game from their distant then sprintingly violent perspective requires a detachment that would destroy them without it.

"Let me get this straight. You are saying," Stamford ground out, "that I should approach the Spanish authorities? That I should ask them to obtain a warrant to search this private, exclusive golf club whose members are, to put it mildly, influential people, because there is reason to believe that within it lies a hoard of stolen art work?"

"Precisely. I should try the basement. There should almost certainly be a basement, an air conditioned one apparently for something like wine storage, to which access is extremely limited. In it, members can view these art works which are stolen to order."

"So the members are all complicit in the thefts and are thus parties, accessories, to theft or conspiracy in some way?"

"Those of them that have access to the said clandestine gallery, yes. The detail of that will be for you to discover. You will need to be very quick."

Stamford leant forward. "Have you any idea, any idea at all, of the complications involved in presenting such a case to the Spanish authorities?"

"Not a clue."

"Have you any evidence, solid, concrete evidence, to support your claim?"

"Ah. Let me start at the beginning. The Highton gallery has been plundered, not only of a valuable Sickert painting and a rare sketch by Doman Turner, but also of a collection of drawings, including some by Sickert, some by George Harland, of interior scenes of a squalid and possibly even pornographic nature. During the course of their discovery and theft at least two women have been murdered and possibly a third called Hope Anderson."

"Is that all?"

"You have arrested the wrong man on suspicion of part of the theft and the murder of Dr Binnie Grant. Dennis Cash had nothing to do with either crime and the money sent to his account will have come via some clandestine route arranged by a financial connection of Bill Riley's. Larry Granger will have provided the details of the account. As chairman of the gallery, he was responsible for paying Dennis Cash's salary. It is a set-up. Dennis is not the culprit."

"You conveniently gloss over his lies about where he was on the night in question. He certainly wasn't in Newhaven."

"I think you have the answer to that. Was he with Kathy Marsden?"

Stamford scowled. "If you knew that you have withheld evidence!"

"I didn't know for certain. I'm only guessing. Neither came to Bill Riley's drinks party that night. They were having an affair, weren't they? I saw one of her paintings in his flat."

His scowl stayed in place. "Miss Marsden has made a statement to the effect that she was with Cash that night, yes. Whether it is the truth or an attempt to aid and abet Cash remains to be established. He has made false statements to us that alone deserve prosecution. She could be the accessory to very serious crime."

"I think Dennis is a gentleman. Is Kathy Marsden married?"

"No, but there is a partner with whom her relations have deteriorated, according to their story. Cash claims that he didn't want to make matters worse but the partnership has in fact ended, according to Miss Marsden."

"Well there you are then. You need to get after Riley and Granger pronto."

"What?" Stamford was not pleased. I couldn't blame him: when you've fixed on a theory that seems to fit the facts it's infuriating to have someone come up with another theory that fits them just as well. "Are you aware of how serious these allegations are?"

I leant forward to fix him with an eye. "At some time during his South American sojourn in the diplomatic service, Larry Granger met a colleague called Anderson. Anderson's wife Hope came from Highton and was a niece of the foundress of the gallery, Jane Harland."

"This is the one that fell in Ladbroke Grove?"

"The very same. I'm glad you've grasped all the details. Hope, I suspect, was a bit of a gossip. She implied to Larry Granger that despite the impeccable exterior aspect of the gallery, Jane's husband George was a bit of a problem. He had a taste for the sordid side of art and was not only a Camden Town School and Sickert fan but collected the less salubrious side of that school's work. Quite apart from nipping over to Dieppe and up to Mornington Crescent to do a bit of practical himself. He was a reasonably good traditional painter, after all. After he died Jane set up the gallery but his secret collection was not part of the official bequest. I suspect Jane tried to destroy it but it was hidden by George, almost certainly in Dieppe somewhere."

"This is all speculation."

"No it isn't. Hope Anderson, who had retired to Ladbroke Grove on the death of her husband, came back for a last visit to Highton. She may not have intended it to be the last visit but it was. During that visit, on a lunch with Veronica Chalmers, she rashly confided the news about George's secret collection to Veronica and where details of it and its location might be found. Veronica was horrified. She went to the gallery office next morning armed with some knowledge or another drawn from Hope Anderson and dug out a folder with copies of the squalid scenes in it. Possibly even some original sketches as well. More importantly, she found confirmation of where the collection was located. She took this evidence home and phoned Binnie Grant to tell her she intended to destroy this material in order to preserve the reputation of the gallery. Binnie came over to see it and pushed her downstairs, keeping the folder secret."

"How do you know all this?"

"Larry Granger told me that Veronica had second thoughts and phoned to tell him all about the folder just before Binnie arrived. He told me he believed that Binnie pushed Veronica downstairs because the archive was so important to her. He said she never told him about the incident."

"Why didn't you report this?"

"I think Larry lied to me. Besides, it would have been very second-hand. He didn't tell you about it, did he?"

"No."

"I don't believe Veronica phoned him. I don't think Veronica was friendly with him. Nor would she risk him knowing about the folder, especially not if she intended to destroy it. I think he heard it all from Binnie after the event. Whether there was a struggle for the folder and Veronica fell or whether it was deliberate murder we'll never know. There is a limit to the speculation I can give you. One way or another Veronica Chalmers met her Nemesis that evening. Felicia Apps thinks she saw Binnie Grant leave her house."

He sat quiet for a moment. Then he asked the right question: "Why would Dr Grant confide in Granger if she was culpable?"

"Their relationship was not just one of fellow trustees, Inspector. Riley and Granger were employing Binnie Grant as a researcher. After this news they got her going through the archive quickly to see if she could confirm the whereabouts of George's cache. Larry Granger would do the field research in Dieppe. A town with which he was very familiar. Binnie had discovered an unknown correspondent of Vincent Van Gogh's in Isleworth for them. You know what has happened about that and how it led to the events of yesterday, which Nobby here has confirmed."

He glanced sideways at Nobby, like a collie that finds a bull terrier on its patch and hopes it'll leave the sheep alone. "That is an entirely separate matter."

"It is an allied matter, Inspector. They followed it up in their own way. Now there was a superb new opportunity. Binnie Grant and Larry Granger possessed the whereabouts of the cache of Sickert and other material, pretty squalid in some way. Patricia Cornwell had been making waves with her Ripper theory. Take this cache and it could be kept from public view forever, not being missed. Except that Hope Anderson knew about it. She was the last surviving link with the Harlands who did. So she had a fall, too."

"Who are you claiming did that?"

"No idea. I wouldn't have known about it at all if I hadn't bought *Imperial Brown of Brixton* from Mr Goodston."

"Binnie Grant – who killed her, then, if Dennis Cash didn't?"

"Granger or Riley. Or both. They both had access and opportunity. Riley has an alibi from his wife. Granger has none."

"Why kill her? If what you say is true, she was the goose that was laying their golden eggs."

"She knew everything about the secret gallery in Spain, where Riley and European collectors like his golfing partner Henk Ubaghs are salting away art stolen to order. Ubaghs is probably the one rabid to get the early Van Gogh material. First the Amsterdam paintings then my letters. They could all enjoy their private views together."

"Then why kill her?"

"Maybe Binnie Grant wanted more money. Maybe she really wanted something even worse. Something that frightened them."

"What?"

"Fame. She'd found a lot for them. To come up with the Van Gogh and the Sickert stuff she'd found would make the reputation of any art historian forever, especially after the Cornwell publicity. After years of obscure teaching in grinding technical colleges it would make any sixty-year-old's retirement years glow golden with something more than money: fame. I unwittingly hinted at it when we first met. She could have gone on a different lecture round entirely. It was that or much more money. There could be no end to it; they had to shut her up. They ransacked her place afterwards to make sure there were no references to her work for them left in it for anyone to find. Why would Dennis Cash do that, if theft was all he was about?"

"You mean you believe the tired old dictum about when thieves fall out –"

"I do. I was surprised by Binnie's depth of knowledge about Jack the Ripper that evening at Bill Riley's. I have an idea she wanted to come out with a theory of her own, with much new material from George Harland's secret cache of Sickert drawings. The publicity would be terrific for her. They couldn't let her do that."

There was a silence. Stamford stroked his jaw. "The source of Cash's lump sum of money seems to be untraceable," he muttered eventually.

"You have to be a financier to do that. Riley probably does it every day of the week."

Stamford was having trouble abandoning everything he'd built up. "A secret gallery? A rogues' gallery? In a golf club in Spain? It's fantastic."

"Riley is a recent addition to the trustees, thanks to Kathy Marsden. It all started for Larry Granger when he arrived on the scene. Both collectors, both somewhat alienated from johnny public. Granger may have a money problem accumulated from a failed marriage he's concealed for years. I think Riley was already a clandestine collector as well as a public one. He's never exactly been the man on the Clapham omnibus, has he? He let Granger in on the act in return for Granger acting as a bird dog for him. Using Binnie Grant, too. Life in Highton was really dull until Riley joined in. On the surface, anyway."

"It's all still speculation."

"To a certain extent. There are other indicators. Larry Granger mentioned a painting of Spencer Gore's to me, of a tennis match in Mornington Crescent. He said that there were two people watching the game. In the well-known public versions of the painting there is only one watcher. It is a stolen one, from a private collection, that has two seated people. I think Granger must have seen it in the clandestine golf club collection. I also think that they didn't steal the Highton painting of Spencer Gore's because they'd already got a better one: *Tennis in Mornington Crescent*, with all its associations, including Gore's father being the first Wimbledon Champion."

He looked at Nobby Roberts almost appealingly. "What do you think?"

Nobby didn't smile. His face had a look as rueful as Stamford's. "He's always been right before," he said.

"Just think," I urged Stamford. "What kudos you'll get. The publicity will be spectacular."

"So will the crap if it's wrong."

"What else have you got? Why did Dennis Cash do it? Who paid him? You've nothing to lose. Acting on information received you visit Spain. I believe you'll have to be quick. I think Granger is pissed off with not just Highton and the arts roundabout but this whole country. I think he's going to live abroad. A lot of people like him are voting with their feet just now. Spain and France are full of them."

Stamford wriggled for a moment. "It's a strange coincidence," he muttered, "I must say."

"What is?"

"I tried to talk to Granger about Cash yesterday. But he's gone on holiday."

"Not Dieppe again?"

"Spain."

"Bingo."

"I tried to talk to Riley, too. He's away playing golf."

"Don't tell me…"

"In Spain."

I leant forward again earnestly and repeated myself: "Be quick, Detective Inspector Stamford. Be very, very quick."

✳   ✳   ✳

We came out of Highton Police Station and Nobby looked at me accusingly.

"You'd better be right."

"You know I am. You're just hedging your bets. Keeping Dennis Cash in until Stamford does his successful Spanish tarantella."

"You're getting worse, though. How's Sue?"

"Sue has forgiven me. I think I actually got some golden credit for having defended my door so violently yesterday. She and William will be OK. I really owe you for all your help, Nobby. I might have been inside Chelsea nick making statements for years if it hadn't been for you. There's a good pub here and I'll buy you lunch. It's not every day I throw armed Dutchmen over the staircase."

"The Chelsea boys were impressed. They say he is on several wanted lists. I mean really impressed."

"So was I. But I'd rather not have been."

"The second guy you smashed up will go on saying he doesn't

know who hired him. On any occasion. I'm afraid he's too frightened to crack. But since the whole thing ties together I'll make sure Stamford follows it up in Spain quickly all right."

"Good." I paused and took in the quaint street on which we were standing. The flint and timber facades leant all over the place, like a Disney fantasy for children. You'd never suspect them of mayhem of any kind. "Ever heard of a chap called Macintosh? Gilbert Macintosh? In a rugger context, this is, now."

"I think I have. Scottish full back? Must be getting on a bit."

"Don't you believe it. He's waiting to buy us some beer. When I phoned him to say we were coming he said he'd always been a fan of yours and be sure to bring you along."

"Liar."

"He did. He said it's a pity you're lost to society but he can forget that you're a rozzer and talk rugby in mitigation."

"I bet he didn't."

"He's starved of good rugby talk down here, Nobby. It's a good pub and I'd be obliged if you'd butter the old boy up a bit. Not obviously, though; he's as sharp as a knife. I need to keep him on side."

"Why?"

"I'll tell you as we walk up these hallowed and misleading streets on our way up to The Dolphin. It's a story you'll really appreciate."

Chapter Thirty-Two

Outside the big sash windows of Jeremy White's office the traffic in Gracechurch Street murmured past in a ceaseless bustle, doubtless attempting to achieve things mendacious. Inside, across the hard shine of his mahogany table, Jeremy stared at me in stunned temporary silence. Beside him, Geoffrey Price sat like pinstriped charcoal stone, eyes resting on me in curious perplexity, as would a man at a zoo seeing a strange creature from distant lands for the first time. Frederick, Lord Harbledown, who had come from his own office out of deference to what was technically a meeting of the three directors of White's Art Fund, sat on the other side of Jeremy trying not to assume any sort of expression at all.

On the table in front of us lay black and white rectangular sheaves of old magazines, together with the letters, which were carefully contained in clear plastic folders.

After some moments, Jeremy cleared his throat. He sounded a little hoarse as he picked up one of the letters, very gingerly, and essayed a question.

"This was actually written by Van Gogh?"

"It was."

"From Holland?"

"From Holland. I believe that one is marked Neunen, actually."

"To this chap Conway, Henry Conway, in Isleworth?"

"The very same. They are all to Henry Conway, a man who befriended Van Gogh when they were both lay preachers. Methodist lay preachers I believe. They are, as it happens, evidence in the strictly legal sense and I have promised the police to make them available on demand. I have been allowed to bring them to this meeting today as a special concession."

He ignored the legal technicality. "So these drawings are all Van Gogh's?"

"Every one. Including the one with a starry sky, which predates his Arles one by four years and is, therefore, of massive interest to art historians."

Freddy Harbledown spoke at last. "Let me get this straight: you bought these off Mr Goodston for the price of a pile of old magazines?"

"I did. I would like to alleviate Mr Goodston's distress, by the way."

Geoffrey Price, still owlish, spoke carefully. "An *ex gratia* payment?"

"Precisely, Geoffrey. Much in the same way as we used make such payments to Larry Granger when he acted as a Foreign Office mole for us."

Jeremy frowned. "You are severe in your wording, Tim. Guidance of the kind he provided was not exactly commercial espionage."

"Not exactly, no."

"I sense we do not convince you." Freddy Harbledown was a bit terse.

"Let us say that one might detect the start of Larry Granger's taste for improbity from his unprincipled use of confidential information on the Bank's behalf when he was in South America. A duplicitous beginning, even if you can argue that the defect of character was inherent."

"I'll let that pass. I rather thought, from what you have told us, that it was a hatred of the way the country, and in particular its arts administration, is going that led him to do what he did."

"That might be understandable if it were the only motivation. Although murder and theft are hard to condone. There were much more personal and venal motivations, however. Unfortunately for him, he had already asked you, Freddy, for our help weeks before the Veronica Chalmers episode occurred. Things then had to be played like a poker game. What staggers me is the confidence he had during my work at the gallery whilst he was planning the sequestration of the Harland collection of

Sickert and other erotica for Riley and his pals. It indicates that he had developed a remarkable taste for duplicity. Perhaps it had indeed become like gambling; some sort of exhilarating vice to stave off boredom. The higher the risk the greater the thrill. I imagine that he will say that the deal was that in return Riley would make a substantial donation to the gallery's funds. In this he will claim to have been acting meritoriously on behalf of its trustees."

"Pah!" Jeremy's reactions can always be relied on. "Stealing its hidden assets in order to solicit something back from Riley. Who would pose as a public benefactor. Hardly a thing of merit. I hope that extradition takes place quickly."

"I don't know about Riley; money can do a lot. He's ruthless and I'd like to see him clobbered after what was tried on me. I imagine Larry Granger may try to flit to South America now that the storm has broken; extradition is more difficult from some of those countries than it is from the Far East. There is no doubt of his guilt. As well as money, he was rewarded by membership of an exclusive club in which he could enjoy art works never to be seen by the public, a public whose representatives he had come to detest."

"Quite a cache, it seems."

"The Spanish police and Stamford have found a remarkable collection, including the Highton Sickert, the Doman Turner sketch, the rare Camden Town Murder painting which Granger did locate in Dieppe and the two early Van Goghs amongst much else. A collection of Oscar Wilde memorabilia including Max Beerbohm sketches and photos of Reggie Turner with Sickert and William Nicholson with son Ben has also been recovered. Almost certainly it was stolen to order for Granger's pleasure. I hope he's taken plenty of opportunity to look at all this; he'll spend a long time not seeing it."

"It was risky of him to engage you for the gallery though, gambling game or no gambling game."

"He had to be seen to be doing something. Frank Stevens and Kathy Marsden were getting very concerned. He couldn't neglect the normal channels. By pandering to the bullshit brigade of arts funding with what he and Riley thought of as a useless feasibility study he confirmed his own prejudices about them – all talk and no action – and he thought we'd do the usual sort of review. His frustration and hatred of the way he sees the country going boiled over. He thought we'd tramp about talking to arts authorities and come up with windy platitudes about outreach, access, policy direction and expanding public roles or empowerment of audiences via consultative groups. Soggy management-speak all round about things like defining strategy criteria and so on. As they all do."

"He didn't know you, obviously."

"He must have known our real target would be Bill Riley and Portarlington. They colluded on that, I imagine. Granger didn't expect me to worry too much about the feasibility study. It was a long shot but we might even have found an outside sponsor. There was no reason for us to scratch through all those folders in the office; we needed the accounts and details of funding bodies, not the Harland history."

"The archive was this Grant woman's province?"

"She was a real asset. She'd learned about the Conway correspondence somehow from studying Van Gogh archives in Holland. When they found that a Conway relative was still living at the same address in Isleworth they thought they'd hit it rich. They rushed to the spot. As in the theatre, timing is everything. The old lady who was relict of the family had recently died and her solicitor sold her books and papers to Mr Goodston."

"And you bought them." Freddy Harbledown still seemed incredulous about the purchase.

"I bought them. For the Fund. Which now owns them. At first they thought they could just steal them back, sniffing round Mr Goodston's shop. But I'd taken them away. I became the target.

Actually, I had intended to buy them myself but I didn't. If I'd had them at home the outcome might have been very different. As it was, they were put in the vaults. Property of the Art Fund."

"I can not say strongly enough how this redounds to your credit."

"Thank you, Freddy. I owe the Fund and Jeremy a great deal; to make some return is a pleasure. The publicity fallout for the Fund should be tremendous."

"Tremendous!" Jeremy stared at the letters gleefully. "We shall have a field day!"

"Binnie Grant was upset about missing the Van Gogh material but they reassured her and sent their thugs out after it. I don't suppose she had any idea exactly how violent they were prepared to be. She thought they'd buy them and anyway she was busy researching. She even phoned Mr Goodston about the magazine called *La Nouvelle Perspective Artistique* to see if she could find an original with an acknowledgement to the Sickert's original owner. It would help with the painting's provenance."

"Let us hope she was at least partly innocent. One would like to credit her with some sense of outrage about violence."

"I'm not sure. Something in Highton perverted her. She was obsessive about research and the archive. I think Granger may be right about her pushing Veronica Chalmers downstairs at the threat of the file's destruction. We shall never know. I haven't seen the material of Sickert's in the secret collection of George Harland's – it's still in Spain – but it may add fat to Cornwell's fire. There's fun to be had over that."

Jeremy smiled. "Do you think it will support Patricia Cornwell's thesis?"

"I've no idea. People can be very coy about Sickert. The Musée de Rouen has about twenty Dieppe works of his donated by Jacques-Emile Blanche and they were very cagey, until quite recently, about giving them a public airing. Even in these libertarian times."

"So this Grant woman might have had a field day?"

"She might." I shook my head in wonder. "What a strange combination: Binnie Grant and Larry Granger, opposites in many attitudes; one all for elitism and the other all for cultural diversity and inclusivity, bottled together in Highton. Somehow she was persuaded to join in a clandestine, criminal party, like a lonely child being invited into a forbidden but admired playground group. As though all those years she'd spent being open and tediously politically correct deserved, finally, membership of a corrupt secret society. It's like a profound republican accepting a peerage at the end of his days."

Freddy Harbledown grinned for the first time. "I can think of quite a few of those."

I smiled back. "There was bound to be a clash with Granger eventually though. Devious man, spinning me his yarn of fake suspicions and imparting information to me whilst at the same time arranging to have the blame for Binnie's death fall on Dennis Cash. It's pretty certain Larry Granger killed her in a fit of rage over her demands, whether they were for money or for fame. I think he is a baulked man who finally exploded. The sad thing is that although I had an instinctive caution, I liked him at first. He has great style. It's a shame he fell into Riley's clutches. Frustration with getting nowhere for the gallery can easily be blamed for his turning to abetting a clandestine one. A sort of revenge on arts authorities stuck in the mud of bureaucratic conformity to current artistic and political correctness."

Jeremy picked up another letter very carefully, looked at it, put it down and then looked at Geoffrey Price. "What do you think?" he demanded.

"I'm speechless." Geoffrey promptly contradicted his statement. "The fall-out in the City when the news about Bill Riley hits the headlines will be massive. Portarlington will take a caning. I had no inkling, of course, when I did my analysis. In a way it did all seem too good to be true. The fund had done so well.

Riley is a fantastic manager of investment funds but what an immoral character on the sly. Deeply flawed. It will ricochet all over the Continent when the names of the other members get out. We are in for a rough ride."

"Dreadful. Everyone will be shocked." Jeremy turned to Freddy Harbledown. "I realise you must be deeply disappointed that we haven't made any progress towards a new investment fund client. Portarlington will never use us now." He held up a mollifying hand towards me as I opened my mouth. "Not your fault, Tim, I realise that, but our real objective has completely eluded us. The Art Fund has benefited massively but we haven't got in with an important investment organisation."

"Oh, I don't know," I said cheerfully. "I had a very encouraging talk with Gilbert Macintosh before I left Highton. He and Nobby Roberts got on very well. Backs chatting together and all that. Nobby did his stuff admirably."

"Gilbert Macintosh? Oh, your beery ex-rugby pub friend." Jeremy frowned disapprovingly. "I really do rather deplore that saloon bar culture, you know. Rugby heavies heaving pints of ale and that sort of thing. Such a distraction: I thought you'd left it behind."

"Gilbert is not a heavy. He was a full back. He is highly intelligent. A medic – technically I believe he's Dr Macintosh – but highly intelligent all the same. I'm pleased to say I have been able to persuade him to take on the chairmanship of the Highton Art Gallery's trustees. It seems he is pretty bored with life in Highton and I thought he would suit admirably. Scots prudence and common sense, that sort of thing. He'll replace Granger splendidly. Felicia Apps was very chuffed."

"Very thoughtful of you."

"He agreed on two conditions. The first was that I consented to be a trustee, too."

"What?"

"They're missing three, after all, and I was able to verify that their Trust Deed will allow them eventually to sell the rather dubious Sickert material once it is returned to them. It falls outside the scope of their permanent collection as defined in the Deed. It will get terrific publicity if it is handled well, especially after the Patricia Cornwell brouhaha. Which means the funds can be replenished for a while. There's a longer-term problem still to address of course, but Macintosh and Dennis Cash will work well with the other two to solve it. With my modest help."

"You? You mean you agreed? Fagging down to Highton every quarter? Was that really necessary? There are many other claims on your time, Tim."

"In view of his other request, I thought it politic to accept."

"Other request?" Jeremy almost snorted. "Politic? What was his other request?"

"That I bring you to the next meeting of his family investment trust to pitch for handling their affairs, Jeremy."

"*What?*"

"It seems their current investment bankers have been pretty unsatisfactory. Since September the eleventh and all that, poor devils."

"Dear God!" A lock of blond hair fell over his face in agitation and he pushed it back sharply, causing a flash of gold cufflink to glisten. "You've committed me, as a result of this bucolic beeriness, to make a sales pitch to some dreadful family trust?"

"To the MacLintock Foundation, yes."

"Eh?"

"He married well, I must say. His late wife was a full-blown MacLintock. Gilbert is one of the Foundation's trustees. Has been for many years. He'd like a complete review and a new approach to the Foundation's investment policy. The current mob haven't done anything right recently."

Geoffrey Price actually dropped his expensive fountain pen. His face was a picture. "Jeremy, the MacLintock Foundation is, well Christ, it's –"

"I know what the MacLintock Foundation is, Geoffrey!" Jeremy almost shouted the words.

"It seems quite large. And international." I smiled sweetly. "It meets most of the strategy criteria for objectives I seem to recollect being hammered to us all at that last, awful weekend management workshop-cum-seminar we had to attend."

There was a silence. Freddy Harbledown stared at me. Geoffrey Price looked inflated but was starting to grin, like a batsman watching an easy boundary hop to its destination. Jeremy White ogled me until suddenly he got back his speech.

"Let me get this straight." He sounded throttled. "As a result of your convivial rugby-club chumminess in some appalling pub in Highton, we are getting the chance to... to..."

"Pick up the MacLintock account, yes. Actually, it should be a foregone conclusion. Gilbert has given me all the info we need. The other trustees are all too ready. The meeting's next month in Glasgow. Unless we make a complete cock of it, Jeremy, the thing should go through on the nod." I smiled sweetly again, real saccharine this time. "If I do the preparation and promise to limit the beer intake, can I rely on you to turn up? Purely as a figurehead of course?"

For a moment he couldn't answer. Then his face crumpled into a grin as he recovered his composure.

"You are an absolute bastard, Tim. Really you are."